GOLDEN HARVEST

Promised Land

GOLDEN HARVEST

Promised Land

Rosanna C. Sharps

Word Sower Publishing

Nelson Home in Merced Falls used with permission by the Tuolumne County Historical Society.

"Exploration and Settlement: 1820-1835" map courtesy of the University Libraries, The University of Texas at Austin.

Book cover and interior design by Michael Sharps.

Printed in the United States of America

First Published 2021

ISBN: Softcover   978-1-7364833-1-2
          Hardcover   978-1-7364833-2-9
          eBook   978-1-7364833-3-6

Word Sower Publishing
Columbia, California

www.wordsowerpublishing.com

I would like to extend my gratitude to
those who assisted in my efforts in
publishing the "Golden Harvest Trilogy."

To God, for His inspiration.
To my husband, Michael for his support.
To Margaret, for providing the historical resources for Snelling.
To the Trout family for their model participation.

Contents

Preface

In 1864, Jonathan and Mary Sower were given direction from God to move their family from the war-torn town, Perryville, Kentucky to their new land of promise, Snelling, California. However, the new territory is not without its 'giant' encounters, especially for their children who are coming of age. The difficulties came in the form of disappointing ambitions, uncontrollable temptations, hidden intentions, bad discernment, and a desire to follow a calling. They discover their life assimilating the *Holy Bibles* "Parable of the Sower."

The story occurs during the late 19th century, yet the trials are as timeless as the parable itself. Although the family is fictitious, their life situations are common. The reader will relate to the struggles and the victories they experience. In addition to the main characters are actual people, places, and circumstances that occurred in California's frontier towns such as Jamestown, Columbia, Chinese Camp, Coulterville, Mariposa, Rio Vista, and of course, Snelling.

The author based the storyline around the Bible's parables and incorporated them into some of America's historical events and characters, whose names are slightly changed. The story brings relevance to the reader by providing hope through faith in God as He produces a golden harvest of learning experiences from life's challenges.

Prologue

Manassas Junction Supply Depot, Virginia
August 26, 1862

Bap, bap, bap! Shots rang out in the night and startled Union soldier Jonathan Sower and three comrades from their sleep inside their canvas wedge tent. His eyes flew open, and he propped himself up on his gum blanket.

"We're under attack!" A voice cried from a distant campsite, one of many surrounding the massive Union supply depot. More blasts echoed, interspersed with shouts, screams, and the muffled sound of a thousand brogans pounding the dirt.

After scurrying for his musket and reloading, Jonathan peered out of his tent, looking for a place to fortify himself. Chaos rumbled through the camps a few yards away as half-dress soldiers fled, being gunned down or captured by the boys in gray.

"Quick, over there." Jonathan pointed with the tip of his gun. He and his comrades hustled and hid behind the nearby stacks of crated rations lined in rows. "Fire at will, men," he said as the rebels neared.

Gray uniforms reflecting the moonlight rushed in on his unit. Edging his musket around the corner of the rows, Jonathan aimed and fired. The others did the same. Bodies fell, but the barrage kept coming. The Rebs took captive hundreds of Union soldiers still wakening in their tents.

His back against the crates and heart pounding in his chest, Jonathan reloaded his musket and paused before taking aim. *Lord, help us.* He pushed his body and his gun from behind the row. The rebel bullet came swift and landed square in his right shoulder.

"Urgh!" Jonathan fell backward, landing hard on his head. *Darkness.*

After a few minutes, he regained consciousness. He tenderly rub the pain in his skull and crawl behind the rations to hide. With his left hand, he grappled the wound on his right shoulder. *No. I'm shot.* He pulled his hand away, opened his palm, and trembled at the crimson seeping to the ground. *Are you calling me home, Lord?* Jonathan's vision became cloudy from the pain and the sight of blood. Soon, he succumbed to the darkness.

"BITE DOWN ON THIS, SOLDIER." A loud voice rang in his ear. Jonathan cracked open his heavy eyelids, trying to focus on the blurry figures hovering over him.

"Where am I?" he asked.

"You're in a grim cluster, man. You're alive." The owner of the voice applied pressure on his left shoulder as another set of hands held his legs down on the table. "Be still now. This bullet needs to come out." The man shoved a small dowel of wood into his mouth.

"Urgh!" Jonathan reeled at the pain and bit down hard on the object between his teeth. The cold, steel blade plunged into his shoulder, digging around the shattered bone. The man dug out the Minnie ball lodge in his flesh as fast as the blade went in. But the pain. Darkness immersed him once again.

After six weeks in a makeshift hospital, Jonathan was honorably discharged and sent home to Perryville. Returning in a horse-drawn ambulance, he viewed his devastated town from the open end of the wagon. Buildings were torn or burned to ashes, and the streets were lifeless. *My Lord, what have we done?* His boyhood town in shambles; broken windows, bullet-ridden walls, and blood-stained streets.

The sight made his head throb, and his shoulder still ached with sharp pain. *No heavy liftin' for at least six months. Get plenty of rest. You're still on the mend.* His doctor's words rang clear in his mind.

His heart sank as the ambulance approached his farm. *The wheat fields… they're gone.* Only a sea of hospital tents and scattered Yankees gather on his property. He ought to feel honored because the Union Army chose his home for his country's defense, but anger boiled under his skin instead.

"Since when did my farm become a hospital? What's become of my wife and children? I've not received a post from her in over three months," he said to the medic sitting between him and a wounded soldier.

"Only recently. About two weeks ago. Early part of October, Major General Buell brought in several Union divisions to attack the Johnny Rebs under General Bragg's command. Bloody battle it was. There weren't enough grim clusters to handle all these men. We had no choice but to use the outlying farms for shelters and hospitals," he said, taking a drag on his rolled tobacco and exhaling. "Don't worry. Your wife and children are safe. More 'an likely, they are assistin' the soldiers. The General spared your livestock in exchange for the use of your farmhouse. Be thankful ya have a home to come home to. Some of us ain't so lucky."

"Ma, more ambulances just arrived. Where do ya want to place these soldiers? We're plum outta room," Sarah said, holding a ceramic bowl filled with bloodied bandages.

Mary finished washing the surgical tools, placed them on a tray, and brought them to the kitchen table where the Union surgeon was prepping another soldier. "I'll be right back, doctor. I need to find room for the next group of soldiers."

"Fine, ma'am. Do what you must," the doctor said. "Will you hand me that scalpel before you leave?"

"Indeed. Here ya are." Mary turned to her frowning daughter. *This is too much for an eleven-year-old to handle.* But what were they to do when the suffering that surrounded them far outweighed their emotional trauma? Her four children spent the last two weeks in her arms at bedtime, exhausted and trembling. Oh, how she wished her husband was home to comfort them. "Let's see what room is left, dear."

Treading at a slow pace, Mary and her daughter maneuvered around the wounded bodies in the hallway, living room, and the front porch. A bloody and bandaged soldier occupied every inch of space in their home.

Her sight shifted to the ambulances lined along the dirt path leading to the farmhouse. She could see her thirteen-year-old son Samuel assisting the wounded soldiers on stretchers. *Lord, when will this end.* She and Sarah walked over to him, trying to avoid staring at the tormented soldiers. Once there, their backs face the wagons.

"Son, they'll need to go in the barn. There is no other place to put them," Mary said.

"All right, Ma. I'll let the other privates know."

Sam wiped the sweat on his face with his gloved hand, smearing blood on his cheek. Mary took a hanky from her skirt pocket and rubbed it off.

"Thank ya, darlin'," she said, placing her hand on his broad shoulder. His physique was developing more into a sturdy farmer, like his father.

"Excuse me, ma'am. Would ya kindly help me to my room?" Jonathan tapped Mary on her shoulder from behind.

What in the world? Mary turned about ready to give the man a piece of her mind for making such an absurd request. "Look here, soldier…" Her eyes caught his, the only recognizable feature of her husband. A full-grown beard now covered his face. His slender body now a mere resemblance of the man who enlisted a year earlier. "Jonathan?"

"Yes, dear. It's me."

Mary's jaw drop. She froze as she studied him from head to toe.

"Pa?" Samuel said.

"Pa!" Sarah wrapped her arms around her father's waist.

Jonathan reached out and embraced his wife, who still stood in shock as tears began to roll down her cheeks.

"Oh, Jonny. You're alive. You're home!" She wept and returned his embrace.

Soon, eight-year-old Naomi and six-year-old David came rambling down the porch and into their father's arms. "Pa! Pa!" they cried, and the entire family embraced.

"Ouch." Jonathan yelp in pain. "Easy now—my shoulder. I was shot six weeks ago and also had a bad concussion. I'm not altogether there, quite yet. I think I need to lie down."

"Of course, dear. You're right. We've got a room reserved just for you," Mary said, followed by a warm smile. "Come on now, soldier. Put your arm over *my* shoulder, and I'll help ya upstairs."

Jonathan did as he was told and swagger to his room with his wife beside him.

"DARLIN', WON'T YA SIT BESIDE ME A LITTLE LONGER?" Jonathan held the gentle but calloused hands of his wife. His eyes rest on her blood-stained apron.

"Jon, ya know I would love to." Standing by his bedside, she kissed his forehead, pulled away, and tucked the sheets around him. "It won't be long before the day is over, and I will be back at your side again. Rest now. The sooner ya heal, the sooner ya will be able to help me and the children tend to your wounded comrades." She gathered the lunch tray at the foot of the bed. "The medics need as much assistance as they can get. Once these soldiers are back on their feet, we can get our lives and home back in order." A tear escaped the corner of her eye and ran down her cheek. She forced a smile, turn on her heels, and walked out of the bedroom.

Oh Lord, be merciful to my wife and children. I fear the repercussions of this war have scarred them. What will become of us and our home? It shall not be the same. The farmhouse will be forever sketched in our minds as a hospital, filled with the hauntin' anguish of my wounded comrades. Lord, have mercy on me. Please tell me what to do.

1

Divine Direction

Perryville, Kentucky
April 1864

"Ah! Doggone, ya Rebs." Union veteran Jonathan Sower squelched the pain in his right shoulder after he and his eldest son Samuel lifted the weighty wooden chest on board one of two Conestoga wagons. He was told by his doctor to avoid lifting heavy objects, but he had to get the work done.

"Pa, are ya all right?"

"Yah, yah. I'll be fine, Sam. Thank God this is the last of the cargo. There'll only be a few light things to pack tomorrow when we leave." He forced a shaky grin as he compared his son's strapping fifteen-year-old physique to his aching thirty-eight-year-old body.

"What do ya need me to do next?"

"Help your brother make sure the animals are bedded down for the night and secure the barn. I need to sit down for a minute. My shoulder is hurtin' somethin' fierce."

"Okay, Pa." Sam wiped his forehead with his sleeve and walked toward the barn.

Jonathan tread in pain toward the family gravesite a few yards from the farmhouse to say farewell to his departed parents. Afterward, he aimed to rest on the front porch steps before heading inside for the final evening meal in their farmhouse he sold two weeks earlier.

As he approached the gravesite, his father's dying wish replayed in his mind. *Son, as heir to my estate, I pass this property on to you. I pray you, Mary, and my grandchildren will enjoy the bounty from this land for many years to come. My hope is to keep it in our family as an inheritance for future generations.*

The rusted gate surrounding the family graveyard squeaked and clanked as Jonathan lifted its hinges. He paused and drew in the stale, humid air while staring at his parents' headstones. Still working out the soreness in his shoulder, he fell to his knees at his father's grave.

"Thank God all is not lost," Jonathan said to his departed father, all the while doing his best to restrain his sorrow. His guilt of selling the farm wrestled with the thought of his father's hopes and dreams. "I'm so sorry, Pa, but I can't hold on to the farm. Please understand. We must find a new home if we're to survive. With the money ya left me and what I got for the property, we can start again in California and create new memories. I believe this is God's will for us."

Upon lifting his gaze to view the devastated wheat fields, he envisioned himself as a young boy plowing with his father instructing him.

"I'm takin' our heirloom seeds, so our family legacy will live on just like you did when ya left Virginia, and Grandpa did, too, when he sailed from England."

The grieving farmer leaned over and laid his hand on the headstone as if to give his father a final embrace. "This move wouldn't be possible if not for you. We're all so very grateful for what ya gave to us. Thanks, Pa. It may be some time before we return to Perryville. If we don't make it back, then, Lord willin', we'll see each other again in Heaven. I'll always love and remember you and Ma."

He lifted himself from the ground, shut the gate behind him, and trudged over to the farmhouse. His shoulders lowered, and his muscles relaxed, confident he could move ahead after justifying himself to his father.

The old steps creaked beneath his feet. At the top plank, he sat trying not to make a sound, being careful not to draw his spouse and daughters' attention in the house. As he lay his sweat-stained slouch hat beside him, he tilted his head side-to-side and cracked his neck joints to relieve tension. He removed his tattered leather working gloves, ruffled his receding shaggy mane, and rubbed his temples.

The previous four months' moving preparations had availed him little time to rest and reflect. The days had flown by like dust devils in the fields, devouring anything in its path. Now that they finished loading the cargo, he purposed to steal a brief moment to reminisce.

He crossed his arms over his knees and scanned the farm, which had raised him to become the man he was today. *Farewell, my old friend. You've been very good to me and I will truly miss my growing years spent with my family cultivatin' these fields.* The solemn thoughts melted his heart like wax.

From his vantage point, Jonathan performed a visual check of the dilapidated estate one more time as dusk's long shadows stole the remaining light. A few yards away, vacant corrals and chicken coops stood lifeless except for the littered shards of hay, corn stubble, and down scattered about the dirt. He viewed the soil's uneven clods, which now marred the once majestic wheat fields. In his mind's eye he saw the sea of grim clusters and wounded Union soldiers on his property two years earlier in October of 1862, now remembered as the Battle of Perryville, Kentucky.

Thank the Lord. The Union Army spared some livestock in exchange for usin' the farmhouse as their temporary hospital. They could've left us with nothin' but the shirts on our backs like most other folks.

He mused at the silhouettes of his two sons at work inside the barn. They dashed from one stall to the next to prepare the nine oxen, two horses, cow, three chickens, and rooster to be relocated to the new western frontier.

"Urgh! Dagnabit." Stretching his arms above and behind him, the excruciating pain in his right shoulder demanded his attention again. As before, he applied pressure to ease the discomfort as the horrifying moment from the almost-fatal day flashed before his mind's eye.

When the ache subsided, he pulled his hand away to inspect the trembling extremity for blood. His heart raced, and his body formed beads of sweat. After determining there was no red seepage on his hands, he snapped back to reality only to be overcome by shaken nerves and nausea. He realized another flashback had occurred, so he inhaled a deep, long breath and began to experience some relief, knowing that that time had already passed and he was safe from harm.

Sorrow gripped him having to leave his boyhood home, which the ravages of war now haunted. Yet he was elated, knowing a better future lay in wait for him and his family in a region God had promised him four months ago during the Sunday service at church.

The pastor's message that day had come from Genesis 12:1. 'Now the LORD had said unto Abram, Get thee out of thy country, and from thy kindred, and from thy father's house, unto a land that I will shew thee.'

He recalled his wife's awestruck face when they both perceived in their hearts that God breathed those words for their sake.

Further confirmation came that day when a friend informed them about the homestead land available in California. Those desiring to relocate could join a wagon train bound for the West scheduled every month.

Jonathan's life might have drowned in sorrow if not for the Lord's saving hand, which had pulled him from the mire. God had answered his prayers by providing direction and financial help through selling the farm and its furnishings. It also released him from the promise he made to his father and his dying wish to pass on a legacy in Kentucky. Instead, he will continue the legacy in California.

AT THE SOUND OF HER HUSBAND'S VOICE, Mary put down the basket of boiled eggs she had prepared for the journey. She opened the kitchen curtains, peeked outside, and noticed Jonathan sitting on the front porch steps. He finished his work and soon he'd be ready for supper.

Conscious of her appearance, she smoothed down her unruly auburn strands and tucked them neatly into the braided bun behind her head. She pivoted on her feet and hurried to the living room door to call her daughters. They had spent the day upstairs tidying their rooms for the new owners.

"Girls, come down and set the table and warm up supper. Your pa has completed his chores. I'll go fetch him and your brothers."

Eerie, she thought as the imprints on the faded, custard-yellow walls caught her attention. Square and rectangular patches remained where their tintypes used to hang. She shuddered to think about her and the children tending to the scores of injured soldiers in this room two years earlier. Gut-wrenching screams, blood-drenched uniforms, amputated limbs. Too much for her to bear, let alone her young children.

"ALL RIGHT, MA. I'LL BE DOWN IN A MOMENT." At age thirteen, Sarah, the oldest sister, thumbed through the garments she had laid on top of her dresser, accounting everything she needed for the next day. Besides the clothing lay a small box filled with her simple jewelry and hair accessories. She held a looking glass to her face, used a hanky to wipe the dust from her cheeks, and simpered at her dimpled reflection, which became more like her mother's every day. After putting the mirror down, her hand braised the faded rose given to her by an admirer, Franklin. She picked up the brittle flower, held the fragile memento to her heart, and whispered a prayer.

"God, watch over Franklin and my friends. I'm gonna miss them terribly. I still don't understand why we must leave Perryville. Forgive me for bein' angry at my parents for makin' us move. God, I know I asked this many times. Please, can ya make it possible for us to stay? I beg ya."

Rat-a-tat-tat, click-clack, clunk. A myriad of items fell on the wood floor behind her. Sarah jumped and turned her head toward the noise so fast the curls of her tawny ponytail whipped her cheek.

"Darn it! Don't ya start laughin' at me, Sarah." Nine-year-old Naomi stood over the fallen crate, which she had knocked over by accident from atop her bed. Jacks, marbles, wooden spinning tops, sticks, bats, balls, and trundling hoops lay scattered on the floor.

Oh, my little sister. You're growin' faster than ya realize. You're Sower stock indeed. Better you workin' the farm than me. Sarah compared her sister's stocky frame to her budding ladylike figure. She recalled friends commenting on how Naomi was a handsome young lady and how she has her father's spittin' image.

"Is everythin' all right up there?" Mother called.

Grr. Naomi growled and hollered out the bedroom door. "Yes. In a minute, Ma!"

Sarah grimaced at her sister's braids coming loose from the bun in the back of her head and the deep furrow between her brows, much like her father's when he became upset.

Compassion filled Sarah's heart, so she stepped in to help, picked up some items, and placed them back in the crate. "Calm down, Naomi. Don't ya start gettin' angry. Try to focus on the fun you'll enjoy tomorrow on the trail."

"Oh, fine and dandy, Miss Prissy! You're all done with your packin'. I spent all day gatherin' those things."

"Well, if ya started a week ago when I told ya to, you wouldn't be scramblin' around like a chicken with its head cut off, would ya?"

"Girls, now!" Ma bellowed from the steps below.

Shuffling down the stairs and into the kitchen, Sarah and her sister gathered the tinware and arranged them on the rickety old table.

"All right, the macaroni pie is ready to be warmed in the skillet. The stove is already nice and hot. Ya think you gals can handle that?"

"Yes, Ma. Supper will be ready by the time you and the boys return." Sarah glanced around the room to survey the food items sitting on the counter, which her mother had prepared for the next few days of the journey.

"Okay. Holler if you need me."

Her mother's ash-color day dress swished and swayed as she moved around the room. She wrung her hands on her apron and scurried outside.

MARY SAW HER HUSBAND WIPE HIS EYES on his sleeves as her heels tapped on the wooden porch floors upon approaching him.

He turned his head upward, smiling at her, and patted the step beside him. "Come enjoy the sunset with me one final time, darlin'."

She grasped his hand, delighted to sit next to him.

"There's a golden glow about you, my love. Either it's the sunlight or you're in a pleasant way. You're as beautiful as the first day I met you. Farmin' life has not diminished your beauty one bit." The backside of his hand brushed her cheek and as she smiled.

The swelling around his eyes betrayed his attempt to hide his distraught demeanor. Mary had grown accustomed to his pain-shrouded smile.

"Oh my, I am the most blessed woman on this side of Heaven, havin' ya for my husband." She pushed some strands of hair away from his forehead, kissed his cheek, and felt his right shoulder tense as she leaned toward him. "Oh dear, you're in pain again, aren't you? Here, turn around." She rubbed his strained shoulder muscles and sensed his troubled spirit.

"Yep, I hope I didn't overdo myself. Thank you, my love. Your touch is what I needed."

After a few more strokes, he turned around and she tucked her arm under his. She rested her head on his shoulder and stared out into the field as he did.

Perryville's memories streamed through her mind like a moving picture. Her life as a child playing in wide-open plains. The heart-thumping moment she met Jonathan at her sixteenth birthday celebration. And giving birth to their children and raising them on the same soil his parents raised him.

"I understand how difficult this is for ya, Jon. Moving from our beloved farm is upsettin' to me, too."

"As much as I love our home, Mary, I can't seem to rid the bad memories from my mind. The war sure made a mess of the good times our family enjoyed here." Jonathan used swift movements to wipe away the tears on his cheeks.

"I pray we're making the right decision to relocate. Uprootin' the children is my main concern. All their friends are here, especially Sarah's. The young'uns are doin' so well in school, and the six-month journey will only set them back. I'll have to continue schoolin' them until we settle down."

Her mind drifted from her children's education to the notorious reputation of the Wild West. "I keep hearin' about all the struggles that others have experienced on the trail, such as Indians, outlaws, and, worst of all, starvation in the desert. I hope we brought enough provision." Her brows furrowed as she glanced at the two Conestoga wagons. "My greatest fear is that our children will fall prey to California's notorious perversions. I hear gold, gamblin', saloons, and brothels are more common than churches." She shuddered. "Darlin', Samuel and Sarah are at a vulnerable age. Those things are horrible temptations."

Prompted by her husband's labored breathing, she changed the subject to a more positive reinforcement, instead of her fears. "However, I do look forward to the sunny, mild weather that the West has to offer. It's the best for growin' crops. The thought I cling to is the direction God gave us to move to California. We must remember His promise. I really do have faith in what the Lord is plannin' for us." She squeezed his arm and gave him a smile of assurance.

"I'm also anxious for our new start, Mary. Thank the Lord for the many who paved the way out west. My heart tells me this is God's will for us, so we don't need to fear 'bout movin'. He'll protect us."

He cleared his throat, staring at the flat landscape contrasted by the dimming sky. "Imagine my love. Beyond the horizon is the land's end. We'll be on the other side of America touchin' the Pacific's shores. It'll be our land of milk and honey."

"I hope our promise land will be suitable for our children as much as it'll be for us and that they'll be able to prove worthy of their inheritance. The farm is a big responsibility."

Minutes passed until Samuel's and David's burnish silhouettes caught her attention. She grinned as the sparring brothers closed the barn doors while their two hound dogs, Boomer and Ann, followed close behind.

"Looks like the boys have finished their chores." Mary chortled when Sam nudged his unsuspecting brother's shoulder and turned to hustle away toward them. "I betcha Sam challenged David to a race."

"What makes ya say that?" Jonathan asked.

"Oh, I've seen him do it time and again, and I've scolded him for bein' so mean. But he tells me it's his duty to toughen up his little brother through constant competition. Besides, I think David enjoys the challenges and adventures his brother throws at him. It makes them all the more closer. My observation, of course."

"Well, if ya ask me, Sam's adventurous spirit may get him into trouble one day if he's not careful. I know he's eager to blaze the trail tomorrow and move westward to where all the action is happenin'." Jonathan half-grinned and shook his head.

"Ah. No fair!" The early evening breeze carried David's voice as he shifted his footing to balance himself. His fists clenched as he chased after his brother. The dust flurry behind his boots and his arms moved in rhythm with the speed of his legs.

The brothers approached, spewing boisterous laughter. They clamored up the porch steps breathing heavily and toppled at their parents' feet.

"We're all done, Pa, and the barn is secure," David spoke between gasps of air. He removed his low crown beehive hat and fanned himself to cool down. Sweat molded his russet mane's layers about his head and beaded on his cheek below his brown puppy dog eyes.

Mary gazed at her youngest child, whose maturity exceeded his eight-years.

"No need to worry. Everythin' will turn out fine tomorrow," David said, peering upward at them.

"Thank ya, sons, for takin' care of the animals." Jonathan leaned down to pat their shoulders. He winked at David and slipped him a half-smile.

"I'm starvin'. Is supper ready yet?" Samuel glance at his mother as he lay on the steps flat on his back, arms and legs spread out. The grin on his face gleamed, lightening the gloom.

Mary shook her head. "Ya rascal!" She playfully nudged the top of Samuel's head using the toe of her leather boots. "I can always count on your stomach to bring ya home on time."

Chuckling aloud, she stood and turned toward the house. "Yes, supper is ready. Wash up, and let's ask for God's blessin'. Afterward, y'all better get to bed for our early rise tomorrow."

She moved out of the way as the anxious father and his sons stumbled to their feet and ran into the kitchen, rinsed their hands in the basin, and dove onto the bench seats beside Sarah and Naomi at the table.

The family joined hands for their last meal in the farmhouse while

Jonathan said grace. "Heavenly Father, we appreciate your kindness and mercy upon our household and the direction to move us to the land You promise. Please accept our humble gratitude for Your provisions, guidance, and protection as we travel west to California. Bless this food we are about to receive. In Jesus' name, we pray. Amen."

THE MORNING SUN BEGAN TO PEEK OVER THE HORIZON, waking Mary from her slumber.

"Oh … I miss my bed already." The giddy mother rolled to her side and propped herself up. She stood and stretched her arms above her and walked down the hall between the bedrooms. "Rise and shine, everyone. This is the big movin' day."

Moans and groans transformed into excited squeals. Eager as children on their first day of school, they donned their traveling attire, devoured their breakfast, packed their bedding, and loaded themselves into the wagons. Even Sarah rushed out the door with an ear-to-ear smile on her face.

Mary gathered her family's pajamas and brought them to her husband, who sat at the kitchen table. "This is the last of our belongings, Jonny. These go into the chest amongst all the other clothes in your wagon."

Jonathan grabbed the pile and proceeded to the Conestoga he and David planned to drive as Mary stood by watching. He crawled about in the back, located the wood trunk, and attempted to reposition the heavy container to unlatch the lid. "What in the world did you pack in this box, dear? It's heavier than gold."

"Huh? What? Oh, our family's clothin', two sets for each, darlin'." Before she turned and scurried away to her wagon, she murmured in a low voice, "and just a few books."

Jonathan cocked his head and smirked. "And why am I not surprised at that?"

"Ma, I placed the food behind the seat. Let us know if ya want anythin', and we'll get it for you." Naomi scooted to the center of the bench close to her older sister to give her mother ample room to drive. Their Conestoga contained the cookware and non-perishable foods.

Father and son secured the wagons one more round. "All right, I think we're as ready as we'll ever be. Sam, double-check the oxen's bits and their hitches on your mother's wagon, while I do the same for mine."

"Everything is set to go, Pa. Let's hit the trail!" Sam mounted his steed and whistled for his hounds to follow.

Mary snapped her reins and followed her husband's heavy-laden wagon.

"Get one more look at the farm, y'all. This may be the last we'll see of her," Jonathan yelled.

A lump formed in Mary's throat as she watched her family steal one more glance at their once beloved home. However, she kept her sight toward the end of town where they were to meet up with the other fifty families headed west. She began singing the song, "Hard Times Come Again No More," and the family joined in filling the air with laughter and chatter about the adventures that lay ahead.

"'Tis the song, the sigh of the weary,
Hard Times, hard times, come again no more
Many days you have lingered around my cabin door;
Oh! Hard times come again no more."

2

Westward Journey

The experienced wagon train master, Major Fuller, kept the group safe, knowing which territories to avoid and the tactics needed to protect them from outlaws and Indians in the Great Northern Plains. Five months on the Central Overland Route and California Trail brought the large band of waggoneers through Fort Laramie, Wyoming downward to Fort Hall in Salt Lake City, Utah, where they replenished their supplies. In preparation for the first major hardship, the tough-as-nails leader called a meeting in front of his covered wagon with Jonathan, his family, and the other pioneers.

"Folks. Allow me to begin by sayin' you've done a fine job ... so far." The glow from the campfire magnified the deep sun-drenched lines on the trail master's face as he paced about the intense onlookers. "The past few months is nothing compared to what we are about to endure from here forward. In a couple of days, we will be entering the Forty Mile Desert. This stretch of barren wasteland is the nightmare which all of you have been dreadin'. I say this because we are going to travel by night to escape the heat of the day, which can reach upwards to one hundred twenty sweltering degrees. At night, the temperature should drop by about fifteen or so notches."

He paused for questions after gasps came from the crowd.

"All right. With that said, my suggestion to y'all is to increase your supplies, especially your water, because this fort is the last drinkable watering hole until we reach Carson City. That is a good seven to eight days away."

A man's voice vaulted from the masses. "Major, sir. Can we draw water from cactus or desert plants should we get desperate?"

"Don't press your luck. This trail has been well traveled by our predecessors. If you do find water, don't drink the rancid stuff, unless you want to burn your innards. The pain will be like pourin' salt on a slug."

More grumble and chatter filtered through the night air.

"Ration, ration, ration! Plan on four maybe five days at the most in the desert. Purchase what you need and get plenty of rest. We will be headed out tomorrow night at nine o'clock." The major glared at the wide-eyed civilians. "Well, would anyone like to say something?" He paused and scanned the group. "Then y'all are dismissed."

THE DESERT'S NIGHT TIME TEMPERATURE still raged in the high nineties to the low one hundreds. Mary peered up at the twinkling stars above her, hoping to see a change of color in the night sky as she held tight to the oxen's reins. It was the fourth day and only one barrel of water remained for their family and animals. The silhouetted sight of abandoned wagons, makeshift wood grave markers, and skeletal remains of animal carcasses framed in the pale, silver moonlight became more frequent along the hot desert trail.

Mary saw Sarah shudder as they passed by another ghost-like campground. Her daughter lifted her shoulders, embraced herself, shivered, and turned her head at each memorial. To the left of Sarah, Naomi slept while curled up on the bench seat. Mary sat to Sarah's right as she fixed her gaze in front of her, flick the reins, and crack the whip to keep the oxen moving.

"Ma?" Sarah mumbled.

"Turn around, dear. Focus straight ahead. We'll be stoppin' any moment once the sun rises." Only Mary understood the family's dire water situation, and she prayed their fate would not be as those along the roadside. She did not want to alarm the children by telling them the truth. Yet she also did not want to make any hopeless promises. So she changed the subject. "Why don't ya play me some songs on your mandolin to help keep me awake?"

"Good idea, Ma." Sarah reached behind the seat, grabbed her instrument, and began playing some soft melodies. Her velvet, soothing tones wafted through the warm night air. In the wagon in front of them, David brought out his instrument and strummed along as Jonathan drove and Samuel rode his horse between the family's two Conestogas. The weary group trudged on for another two hours until the sky shifted its color from midnight blue to a pallid gray.

"Campsite ahead!" came the call of the trail master.

The parched pioneers arranged their caravan in a circular formation, gathered their livestock in the center, and gave them their ration of water. As the men set-up the camp, the women prepared a simple meal before the sunlight flared over the horizon.

After consuming their breakfast and putting the children to bed, Mary handed a cup of coffee to Jonathan and sat next to him on a gum blanket under the shade of the canvas fly set between their wagons. Her voice was low, being careful not to awaken their sleeping children. She expressed her concerns. "Jonny, we are down to three-quarters of a barrel. At the rate we're goin', the water will be gone by this evenin'."

Sitting by a wagon wheel, shirt drenched in sweat, Jonathan extended his arm to caress his fretting wife's hand and slurred, "Darlin', cut my portion in half and give it to the children and the livestock. Major Fuller thinks we should arrive in Carson in about two more mornings from now." He reached for the red bandana in his back pocket to wipe the perspiration dripping from his head and neck. His face became as white as buttercream. His sentences were short, encouraging, and direct. "We'll get there, my love. Don't worry."

"Are you sure you wanna give up your portion? We won't survive without you. You need to keep up your strength, dear. Besides, I'm not so sure your servin' will be enough. The animals are not lookin' so well with the rations we're givin' them now."

"Of course, I am. You and the children must go on carryin' the family name if somethin' were to happen to me."

"Well, if you're surrenderin' your share, I suppose I can do the same. Don't argue with me, Jon." Mary peered down at her cup and back at Jonathan. "Well, let's pray the good Lord will help us."

"Yes indeed, dear." He sighed as fatigue claimed him, and he drifted to sleep.

"PA, WAKE UP. PA." Samuel jostled his father.

The late afternoon heat made sleeping unbearable, and Jonathan could hear the other children moaning and clamoring for their tin cups. Beads of sweat rolled from his forehead and into his hairline. "Yep, I'm awake. What's wrong, Sam?"

"We lost one of the oxen. She's flat out dead. I tried proddin' her. But nothin'."

Mary rubbed her eyes, sat up, and wiped her temples with her sleeve. "Was I havin' a dream, or did ya say one of our animals died?"

"Yes, Ma. One of the females."

"No need to panic. Her portion of water may get us through the second evenin'." Jonathan positioned himself on a crate, and the family gathered around him on the gum blanket. "Children, if we are to survive, then we must cut our remainin' water rations in half. The trail master assures us we should reach Carson by sunrise in two nights."

"Oh, Pa, I'm so thirsty," Naomi grumbled and touched her chapped, bleeding lips.

"Yes, I'm aware, dear. Be brave. Be strong." He winked at his young daughter, whose face became dull and pale. "We all must try. Go slow and use as little energy as possible. The ox's death may be a blessin' in disguise. Sam, it must be butchered before we head out again. The juice from the steaks should help quench some of our thirsts. I'll cook up enough for the next two days. You gals prepare the rest of the meat for jerky, all right? Let's wait till dusk when the sun is not beatin' down on us."

"Okay, Pa," the children said, frowning.

The weary and dehydrated family did their best to relax and stay cool under the shade of the Conestoga and canvas fly. Once the golden globe drop below the horizon, they began their chores in preparation to hit the dusty road again.

"WAGONS HO!" came the call of the trail master and the enervated band moved into the darkened desert, heat rising from the dry, sunbaked ground. The livestock snorted and groaned, yokes creaked, whips cracked, and wagon wheels churned.

"Water! I see water ahead!" A voice would penetrate the night air every mile or two. Enthusiastic whoops and laughter came from all the wagons. But deadening silence would soon follow when the water never appeared. The call soon became untrustworthy, much like Aesop's story of 'The Boy Who Cried, Wolf.'

Jonathan's heart sank to see David's languid eyes peering up at him as he leaned into his shoulder. "It was just a mirage, son."

"What is a mirage, Pa?"

"Hum." Jonathan paused. "It's kinda like the steam that comes from the water kettle when it's boilin', but you can't see the vapor. You can feel the heat and when you stare at it, it's like lookin' into a movin' pool of water." He flicked the reins. "Well, think of the desert sand as the hot kettle puttin' out waves of heat. It can look like a lake of water."

"So, how will we know real water from the fake one?"

"I think the trail master will let us know. He's traveled this land often enough to know what to look for. We just need to be patient." Jonathan placed his left arm around his young son and squeezed him. "Why don't you try to get some shut-eye? We should be there when you wake."

"All right, Pa."

SMALL STARS SEEMED TO FORM A LINE above the edge of a

dark band on the earth's horizon.

"Carson Lake and city ahead!" came the familiar, raspy voice.

The response was slow to come from the wagons. But one by one, a cackle or a whoop could be heard as the pioneers craned their necks for a glimpse. The dark band became wider and broader as they approached. The scent of wet grass and cattail willows enveloped the air.

"Wake up, David. We're here." The fatigue father nudged his young son as his eldest came alongside the wagon on his horse, Fire.

"How ya doin', Sam?" Jonathan leaned slightly forward to the right to make eye contact with the sleepy-eyed youth galloping close enough to make conversation.

"I came across lots, Pa, but I'm fine. I nearly fell off my horse a few times from the heat, and I could feel Fire's legs wobblin' beneath me." He adjusted himself in the saddle and pointed forward. "Scouts say we're to line our wagons up along the lake's edge."

"All right, son. Lead the way."

Sam kicked Fire's side with his boot's spurs, and he trudged ahead until he came to the campsite.

The reflection of the stars glistened on the motionless Carson Lake. The thirsty caravan of travelers and their animals lined the lake's banks, lapping until their bellies were full and their depleted barrels refilled. A few miles away, the dull glow of Carson City beckoned them like a lighthouse in a storm.

"Glory hallelujah. That is a sight for sore eyes! I can't wait to be around civilization again." Mary chortled paraphrasing Jonathan Swift's quote. She wrapped her arms around her husband's waist as they and their children stood to gaze at their next destination.

Jonathan embraced his family and recited Psalm 23. "The LORD is my shepherd; I shall not want. He maketh me to lie down in green pastures: he leadeth me beside the still waters. He restoreth my soul. He leadeth me in the paths of righteousness for his name's sake. Yea, though I walk through the valley of the shadow of death, I will fear no evil: for thou art with me; thy rod and thy staff they comfort me. Thou preparest a table before me in the presence of mine enemies: thou anointest my head with oil; my cup runneth over. Surely goodness and mercy shall follow me all the days of my life: and I will dwell in the house of the LORD forever."

CARSON CITY MERCANTILE STORES BUSTLED as pioneers from different trails converged on the crossroads town to replenish. Groups of wagon trains clustered together around its borders.

Mary sat next to her husband at the table under the fly, as she gathered the children around him to listen to his instruction.

"All right, y'all, we have a week to sift through our cargo again. Keep things that are absolutely necessary. We must lighten our load if we're goin' to survive the 7100-foot climb up the Sierra Mountains. I'll try to sell these items at the mercantile. Remember, we can replace them once we settle in our new home."

"None of you touch the cedar chest. I'll be the one to sort through it alone!" Mary warned the others, hoping to rescue some of the precious belongings she had collected.

Jonathan lowered his chin and displayed a disappointing grimace at his wife. "Now darlin' ... think of our lowly beast and the burden we are placin' on them to haul the cargo."

"Stop, Jon. Say no more. I reckoned with what I need to do." She waved her right hand toward her husband trying to shoo him away as she walked over to the weighty treasure chest on the ground and began emptying its contents. Disgruntled, she placed the clothing in a canvas bag and left her cherished books in the t4runk.

"Ha. What's this?" She said under her breath. Her fingers braised a hard, heavy object wrapped in the quilts she made. Her heart lept when she unwrapped it. *Ah, mother's china! How did I miss packin' this? I would've been lost without them durin' the holidays and when visitors came a-callin'. But who?* Someone regarded the antique finery and decided to bring it with them despite the added weight. Her intuition suggested her gallant husband did the stowing. *Oh, my darlin', you know me well. You are the sly one. All right, I'll play along with your little secret.* She did not want to ruin his scheme in front of the children. To reveal his good intentions would make him a hypocrite to the demands he now placed on their family.

"Jonathan, this I cannot part with. Please, darlin', allow me to keep my formal ware. You've kept your family's heirloom. This is the only remembrance of mine." Picking up a platter, she held it to her chest.

Her husband embraced her and peered into her eyes as she continued to hold the plate to her heart, "My dearest, yes, of course. The few extra pounds does not compare to your weight of remorse if you were to part from the only sentiment from your parents. I know how much the china means to you. I do promise this, dear, once we settle down, you may replace all the things you've thrown away. Heaven forbid, I am not one of those ogres in your fairy tale books." He kissed her forehead and her soft rosy lips.

Grinning from ear to ear, Mary leaned her head on Jonathan's chest. "Thank you very much, my love."

"My dear, even I carry excess baggage from my past. We have to learn how to sort our experiences and keep what is good if we are to move ahead in life. If we must take something with us, I suppose it should be an item which has a purpose, makes us happy, and has eternal value."

"Well, then if that's the case, Jonny … can I keep some of my books, too?" Mary snickered, hoping to receive a nod of approval from Jonathan.

3

The Sierras

After a week of rest in Carson City, the anxious family and the much leaner wagon train resumed on the trail, desiring to complete their expedition and call the new frontier their home. Samuel and Sarah rode the horses through the lower Carson River Valley while Naomi stayed with Mary in her Conestoga, and David with Jonathan. Sarah would join her mother and sister after they passed the broad and shallow waters.

"How much longer till we arrive, Ma?" Naomi peered out the wagon's front end.

"Well." Mary took a deep breath as she reviewed the map in her mind. "First, we need to climb past this valley. Then we will tackle the foothills called Carson Range." She exhaled like a hot kettle relieving itself of pressure. "But ... you see them tall, dark mountains over yonder?" She continued, pointing at the stretch of Sierras in the far distance. "That'll be our greatest challenge. We'll need to clamber over them. Once we're on the other side, we'll go south a ways until we arrive in the valley floor and find some flat farmland. So, I figure maybe we have another month," she said, snapping the reins.

The oxen wagged their tails as they snorted and huffed, pulling the lighter load. The family left all the barrels, but one behind because of the abundance of water coming from the mountains' snowmelt. Luscious grazing meadows dotted the landscape throughout the Carson River Trail.

"Come on, Fire!" Samuel jerked the reins to lift his horse's head up and away from eating the tall grass along the trailside. He strode near the oxen of his mother's wagon. "Keep a-movin'. There'll be plenty to eat, boy, when we stop for a break.

"River comin' up, Ma. I'm gonna move ahead to Pa's oxen. Then I'll come back and help you through the waters." He waved to his mother. "Giddyup, boy." He heeled his horse's side and scurried forward.

"He-ya, Belle." Sarah urged her horse on the other side of Mary's wagon and moved alongside the burdened beasts. "Gee, gee, ox," she yelled.

The wagons barreled over crags and rushing currents while four scouts used ropes, pry bars, and levers to assist the heavy laden transports through the rigourous waters. Maneuvering over the river's uneven and rocky ground, the oxen groan to pull their load and the wagon wheels creak. David and Naomi did their best to keep things secured in place as the items inside were tossed around.

After passing the river valley, the wagon train began the climb up the Carson Foothills. The long winding turns up the hillside progressed higher in elevation. Just when they thought they conquered the peak of a hill, another one met them at the bend. Finally, the caravan arrived at a clearing at the top of the foothill amongst the dense oak.

"Campsite ahead!" The trail master yelled down the line.

The band of travelers stopped for three days to rest their animals, regroup, and make repairs to their wagons before convening on to the most difficult section of the journey… the Sierra Mountain Range.

Mary approached her family, whose faces were aglow as they sat around the warm fire burning in the half-barrel grill. "Looks like the china survived all them bumps in the river." She placed a wooden-framed folding chair behind Naomi, who sat on a quilt and began undoing her daughter's braids and brushing her hair.

While cleaning his shotgun, Jonathan said, "I think that was the worst of it. The road ahead of us was cleared of most large boulders several years ago by the Mormon battalion. Doesn't mean we won't encounter some granite slabs, though. Let's pray our wagons hold up."

"I sure am glad we're on this route instead of Donner Pass north of here. What a horrifyin' event to be stranded in the mountains durin' the winter with nothin' to eat," Mary said, not realizing she was brushing harder.

"Ow, Mama," Naomi said.

"Sorry, dear."

"Heard they had to resort to cannibalism." Sam grimaced while sharpening his hunting knife.

"Shush now." Mary raised her eyebrows at Samuel, nodded toward David, who sat on a quilt reading his Bible and looked down at Naomi sitting in front of her. She did not want to have to explain what that meant to her young children. Sam shook his head to acknowledge his mother.

"Well, if all goes as planned, we'll get through the mountains before the snow comes. There'll be plenty of good huntin' in them hills." Jonathan stood and walked toward the Conestoga to put store his gun. "All right, I'm ready for some shut-eye."

"I'm right behind ya, dear," Mary said. "Sarah, is everythin' stowed away in the chuckwagon?"

The eldest daughter put her knitting down. "Yes, Ma. I'll double-check before I go to bed."

"David, place another log on the fire, all right?" Jonathan returned, removed his boots, and stretched out on his gum blanket and quilt.

"Yes, Pa," the young boy said as he closed the Bible and placed it by his pillow. He crawled to the pile of wood set nearby the grill and grabbed a couple of pieces. Using the poker, he moved the burning coals about and laid the logs on top. Soon the flames roared again and spat embers into the night air. "I'll say good night, too." He returned to his quilt, removed his boots, and tucked himself between the blankets as the others did the same.

"WAGONS HO!" The trail master hollered, slapping the hindquarters of the lead wagon's oxen as Duke, one of the four scouts, cracked the whip. The coach jolted forward.

The ascent began. The hillside landscape of rounded oak trees turned into mountains filled with groves of cone-shaped pines, redwood, and fir. Enormous, unmovable marble slabs remained on the steep trail. Hairpin turns allowed for one animal-drawn vehicle to pass at a time. Groups of men teamed together using levers and pry bars to assist the covered wagons over boulders while the women controlled the reins.

"All right, Mary. We're ready when you are." Jonathan called out to his wife, who drove his wagon while he, Samuel, and two scouts stood by the first set of wheels on each side.

"He-yah, he-yah! Come on, oxen, pull," Mary shrieked. The powerful beasts tugged and strained against their yellow birch yokes.

"Heave, men," Jonathan hollered as the men applied pressure to the lever under the front wheels to lift it over the huge boulder. The wheels creaked and groaned as it tumbled over.

"Whoa," she bellowed, pulling back on the reins. The oxen came to a stop, allowing the men to reposition the levers behind the back set of wheels. Again they repeated the same maneuver. Afterward, Mary moved the first wagon off to the side of the trail and walked down with the men to the second.

"All right, one more time, darlin'." Jonathan extended his hand to his spouse to help her onboard her Conestoga. "Accordin' to Major Fuller, this is the last of the turns and boulders to climb before we reach the top. If we make it past this, then it'll be smooth sailin' through the upper meadows and down the mountainside."

Seated on the bench, Mary readied herself as the men placed the levers under the front wheels. "He-yah, he-yah," she shouted, and the oxen moved forward and then stopped after the wooden cogs settled on the other side of the slab. The four repositioned themselves for the back wheels. "He-yah, he-yah," she called out again.

"Heave, men." As Jonathan and the three men bore down on the lever, the familiar pain in his right shoulder spiked. "Argh." He gave every ounce of energy he could all the while enduring the agony. The wheels careened over the huge rock when *crack!* Splinters spewed from five spokes of the back left cogwheel.

Mary pulled hard on the reins.

"Ah! No, no, no." Samuel cried out, stepping back and shielding his eyes with his arms from the splintered projectiles. "Pa, the wheel broke."

"Dag nab it." Holding his aching shoulder, Jonathan scurried to the other side and inspected the shattered spokes. His face grimaced. "Well, it looks like I can repair it. But this will set us behind a day from the rest of the group." He turned to the two scouts. "We're goin' to have to use the levers to pull the Conestoga off to the side so the others can pass through. I guess my family will camp here tonight and meet up with y'all tomorrow at the campsite."

The men applied the same maneuver to the back left wheel as the wagon hobbled over to the shoulder of the trail. Father and sons spent the remaining portion of the day pounding out the iron ring and replacing the broken wooden spokes as the ladies set up camp and prepared the meals.

"Whew. What a day." Jonathan wiped the sweat from his forehead onto his sleeve as he sat down for his supper. "How 'bout we all take a little swim in that small tricklin' waterfall over yonder after we eat?"

The children gasped.

"Can we really, Pa?" David asked.

"Yep. As long as we still have some sunlight," Jonathan answered.

"This'll be a good opportunity for me to catch up on some of our laundry," Mary said.

"Imagine, we'll have the pool all to ourselves." Sarah's eyes enlarged. "No one will see us in our undergarments." She smiled as her cheeks turned a rosy pink.

"Just don't scare any of the fish away." Sam cracked a silly grin.

"Ya creep." Sarah guffawed and threw her spoon at her obnoxious brother.

"Now, children." Naomi teased.

"All right, y'all. Let's finish up here and go for a swim," Mary said.

THE NEXT DAY, five miles up the road, they reached the summit and were greeted by Hope Valley, saturated with acres of green meadows and sparkling streams. The terrain leveled, although the altitude created some difficulty. The atmosphere thinned and made breathing strenuous for a while until their bodies acclimated.

Moved by the natural beauty, David whispered, "Lord, You are amazin'."

"Ah ... smell the fresh mountain air," Jonathan said, inhaling while driving the wagon.

As David sat next to his father, he followed his instructions and filled his lungs. He inhaled the pungent aroma which permeated the gentle breeze brushing his cheek. He rubbed his nose. The sweet bouquet of wildflowers, such as heather, red paintbrush, lupine, bluebells, primroses, wallflowers, and larkspurs, interspersed with the pine scent of the tall trees tickled his senses.

The majesty of the mountains and the pleasing floral array caused David's heart to leap with gladness. The wondrous moment inspired him to jump to the back of the wagon in search of his favorite book, the Bible. He returned to the bench seat and thumbed through the pages to Psalms 147:7-9, and he read out loud. "Sing unto the LORD with thanksgiving; sing praise upon the harp unto our God: who covereth the heaven with clouds, who prepareth rain for the earth, who maketh grass to grow upon the mountains. He giveth to the beast his food, and to the young ravens which cry."

"Now tell me, wasn't that long climb worth our efforts after seeing God's handiwork on top of this mountain?"

His father smiled at him as the young boy's heart filled with inspiration.

David loved the presence of the Holy Spirit of God as He moved inside of him every time he spoke of scripture. The rush of energy felt like the mighty waterfalls plunging to the pit of his belly, raging like a river pulsing through his veins, gushing up to the crown of his head like a freshwater spring, and pooling into his radiant smile and glistening eyes like a clear mountain creek.

"Pa, I sure am glad you listened to Him and obeyed His instruction. This really *is* God's country." David set the book down on the seat between them and continued to survey the colorful amber, crimson, and russet flora and fauna along the early autumn trail. Not far away, the river flowed, creating a soothing calmness. And the music of the sparkling water splashing against the rocks, the gentle rustling of leaves from the breeze, the soft clip-clopping sound of the oxen's hooves upon the red soil, and the creaking of the wagon wheels, played into an enchanting orchestration, which began to lull the youngster into a very relaxed state of drowsiness.

"I SEE THE CAMPSITE AHEAD!" Samuel called, breaking the rhythmic persuasion and tranquility when he spotted the familiar circle of wagons. He kicked Fire's side with his spurs, and the horse quickened alongside his father's wagon.

"Pa, what are those men doin' over there at the side of the river?" The teenager inquired as he noticed some men squatting as if washing dishes.

"I believe they are pannin' for gold," Jonathan replied as he slowed the oxen to join the circle. "Some pioneers say a sizable glistenin' yellow vein was exposed in some mine just north of here and on the American River near Placerville. This little town is where most of these waggoneers are headin' in search of gold. I betcha they're testin' the river for any chance of findin' some."

The mention of the precious metal piqued his curiosity. "Ya mean like the rings on your fingers?" he asked, trying to figure out why they would search for jewelry in this remote area.

"Yep. But the gold is still in its natural state, similar to a small rock, a grain of sand, or even flakes of snow, all mixed up with the mud or tucked in between rocks. Some collect the nuggets and take them to a town's assay office to have it weighed then formed into coins. Others sell it to jewelers to melt and fashion into jewelry. Yep, like my weddin' band and the ring Grandpa gave to me," Jonathan explained as they stopped to set up camp. The wagon train would stay here for five days to allow the oxen to rest and recuperate from any abrasions caused by the friction of the harnesses and yoke during the steep climb.

"That sounds like fun. I betcha a feller can become rich!"

"I reckon. But I hear its risky business. You better stick to farmin'. It's a lot more dependable," his father said as he parked, pulled the brakes, and jumped off to unhitch the oxen.

Samuel glanced at the stooped figures by the river as he rode over to assist his mother with her wagon. His mind swam with curiosity.

"Sam … Sam? Hello, son." His mother hollered at him as he trotted on his horse.

He snapped out of his gaze, jerked the reins, and harkened his attention toward the blaring voice. "Yep … yes, ma'am!"

"Can ya pull the oxen over a little to align our wagon better?"

"All right. Understood, Ma."

After he dismounted Fire, he grabbed the beasts by the straps of their bits, pulling them closer to his father's wagon. Forcing himself to concentrate on his chores, he corralled the livestock into the center of the circle and watered them.

His father approached. "Sam, here's your shotgun. Let's see what we can find in these here woods."

"Bears, mountain lions, wolves?" The anxious young man smirked.

"Ha! I don't know if your ma and sisters would appreciate that game too much. More like venison or wild turkey is what they're hopin' for." He handed Samuel his gun. "How 'bout we go scout out the crop of trees by the ridge over there?"

"Sure, Pa. If we don't shoot anything, I suppose we can always go catch some salmon or trout at the river." He hinted, hoping to be near the prospectors. He whistled for his hounds, and the four ventured off into the woods.

"NAOMI AND DAVID, PLEASE GATHER SOME WOOD or cow chips so I can start the fire," Mary said as she began her culinary duties.

"What'cha cookin' tonight, Ma?" Sarah asked.

"It depends on Pa and Samuel, and how well they'll do at huntin' today." She balanced herself while shuffling through the wagon, trying to locate her wooden cooking utensils and a cast iron pot. "Why don't ya help me by cuttin' up some taters and carrots, dear?"

The clanking sounds of pots and pans rang throughout the camp as the women clamored through their wagons in search of supplies to set up their grills. The young children piled the collected kindling, chips, and branches into the metal half-barrel, which stood above the ground on four iron legs. Once the coals became hot and steady, Mary placed a grill on top. On one side of the grill, she did the cooking, while on the other, the gallon kettle boiled for washing the dishes.

"Here you are, dear. No big game today. Just these," Jonathan said beaming with pride as he and Samuel returned to camp with two brown-feathered turkeys hanging from a stripped branch held between them on their shoulders. They threw the carcasses on the rickety wood tabletop set on wooden sawhorse legs.

"Great catch, boys. Well, at least we won't have to share with the other waggoneers." She began plucking off the feathers. "Ooo-wee. Grilled turkey tonight with the vegetables Sarah chopped up." Mary hummed as she toiled in her makeshift chuckwagon kitchen.

Wild game was the usual affair for the families. The leftovers, if any, were kept for the following day's lunch. Nothing went to waste on the trail.

The evening ended with a few rounds of old-time tunes, also known as hillbilly music, played by the Sower family. "Oh Susanna," "Beautiful Dreamer," "Shall We Gather at the River," and other melodies from the hills filtered through the night air. The pioneers stomped and clogged around their campfires until they exhausted themselves and went to bed for an early rise. In the morning, the redolence of fresh brewed coffee, biscuits, bacon, and eggs woke everyone from their restful slumber.

The caravan enjoyed this routine for the next few days while they await the trail master's wailing call to move on again. "Wagon ho!"

4

Mountain Towns

The wagon train stayed for two days to rest and resupply at the Sierra foothill town called Jackson. As Jonathan reloaded his wagon under the cool arbor shade, he mused at the pioneers and miners passing through the major crossroad. Some headed west toward Stockton, others north up to Placerville, or, like his family, south along the Gold Country Highway. Gigantic black oak trees surrounded the gold mining hub, where many enjoyed picnicking and drinking from the town's freshwater spring.

"Whew. Sure am happy we're finally past them mountains." Holding several plates in her arms, Mary began to serve lunch to the family, who sat at a table beneath the umbrella shade of a black oak tree. "I'm lovin' the weather in California. Plenty of sunshine and no humidity. If we did our homework right, then goin' south to San Joaquin Valley should bring us to the proper wheat-growin' climate. How much farther, Jon?" She inquired as she walked around the table, setting their lunches before them.

Hungry as a bear, Jonathan fixated on the meat sandwich at his fingertips. "If all goes well, maybe one more week." He paused and took a bite. Without thinking, he continued. "You're right, Mary. The mountains sure were pretty, but those grades near killed me tryin' to get the wagons up those steep climbs. The ol' war wound was aching somethin' terrible in my shoulder. But the tall pines and mountain air helped me get my mind off the pain. I'm glad we're done with *that* ordeal." His unwilled comment caused Mary to nearly drop the plate in her hands as she turned to face him.

"Oh, Lord!" She put the food down and shoved her fists on her hips. "Jonathan Sower, are you okay? You didn't mention any pain while we were up there."

Upon realizing his mistake, he put his sandwich down, swallowed, and returned her gaze. "I'm fine, my love. Don't you worry your mind none." He smiled ambiguously hoping to keep Mary from becoming anxious. He remembered how devastated she was two years ago when she nursed him back to health, and he knew she was aware the wound might never heal.

"Ya always say that *I'm fine* when ya really aren't." She walked over to him, placed her hand on his injured shoulder, and sternly stared him in his eyes. "Darlin', you need to let us know if the work gets to be too much for you. After all, farmin' is what we're raisin' our young'uns to do." Glancing over to the children whose attention now focused on her, she asked, "Isn't that right, kids?"

"Uh. Yes. Right. I guess so." Soft-spoken responses mumbled past the siblings' lips as they tried to take hold of their parent's conversation.

"*Right, children?*"

"Yes, ma'am!" The wide-eyed brood sat up straight in their chairs and firmly confirmed.

"Pa, you can count on me to help you out," Samuel responded with shoulders back and chin up.

A broad smile covered David's face. "Pa, Ma, I just remembered a perfect Bible verse for this moment. May I share it?"

"Of course, you may, son." Warmth flowed through Jonathan as he received his family's loving support. He placed his arms around his wife's waist as she stood next to him. He listened attentively to his spiritually gifted young son, who was brilliant at memorizing scripture he learned from Sunday school and from reading the Bible.

"Lo, children are an heritage of the LORD: and the fruit of the womb is his reward. As arrows are in the hand of a mighty man; so are children of the youth. Happy is the man that hath his quiver full of them. Psalm 127:3-5."

"David, you are an amazin' young man. Pa and I do believe that God plans a special callin' for you." After encouraging her youngest, Mary praised her eldest. "And Sam, we're so pleased you are steppin' up and takin' on your responsibilities as the main heir." She turned to him as he grinned, expressing relief and gratitude. "Now, this is what we want to hear. Isn't that so, Jon?"

"Indeed. I am humbled and a truly blessed man. Thanks, children." He turned his chin up toward his wife. "Thank you, my love."

She bent and kissed him on his cheek.

"All right, I'll do my best to let y' all know the next time I'm in pain. Please, take a seat, dear. Let's eat lunch."

FROM JACKSON, THEY HEADED SOUTH along the west side of the Sierra Foothills. The winding road connected all the small mining towns such as Angel's Camp, Jamestown, China Camp, and Coulterville—a seventy-five-mile stretch—a seven-day journey.

On the second day of traveling, they arrived at Jamestown. The mining town bustled with prospectors who rode in and headed straight for the bank, where they weighed their gold findings and traded it for certificates equal the value.

Intrigued by the enthusiastic miners, Samuel found himself tagging along with a scraggly, middle-aged man who walked into town, leading his equipment-laden mule by the reins.

"Hey, mister, is there actual gold in these mountains?" Samuel's eyes nearly popped out of his head from curiosity.

"Ya betcha, kid!" The prospector, dressed in a worn-out, mud-stained pair of wool trousers with suspenders and muddied, dark, linen shirt, beamed. After he stopped his mule, he reached into a dusty leather pack hanging on its side and pulled out a small canvas sack. He untied it and poured its glimmering yellow contents into the palm of his hand. Six golden stones lay shimmering in the sunlight.

"What does this look like to you? It took me all summer to find these gold nuggets." He allowed Samuel to touch the shiny stones.

Samuel's jaw dropped as his fingertips braised over the precious treasure. "Whoa … I've never seen gold before. Thank you for showin' this to me, mister!" The dumbfounded teenager yearned to hold the glistening minerals, but the older man put them away.

"Sure, son. Be careful now." The prospector wagged his index finger at Samuel. "Gold fever is very contagious." He grabbed the mule's reins, turned, and grinned, displaying his coffee-stained teeth, as he continued strutting to the bank.

"Sam, don't ya get no ideas in that head of yours." Mary cried out to her curious son, who gawked in the center of the street, mesmerized at the miners. "Son, help your Pa water the animals."

Samuel snapped out of his daze and turned his head toward his mother, who stood by the wagon holding empty baskets in her arms. "Huh? Oh, all right, Ma. Here I come!"

MEANWHILE, MOTHER AND DAUGHTERS moseyed over to the mercantile store to purchase supplies. The vast array of ethnic merchandise reflected the cultural differences from the stores back East.

"Oh, girls, look at the hand-painted clay pottery." Fascinated by the Mexican artwork, Mary ran her fingers across the sculptured design. "I'm goin' to buy some of these when we get settled."

"Mama, what are these star-shaped pots covered with colorful paper? They sure are pretty!" Naomi eyed the dazzling orbs hanging from a wood rack.

"I'm not sure, dear." Mary removed one of the unique objects to examine it.

"That's a Mexican piñata." The store owner snickered as he approached. His round belly bobbled under his apron as he laughed. His spectacles rested on the tip of his nose on his balding, shiny head. "It's a children's game played at birthday parties or during a New Year celebration."

He took the piñata from Mary's grasp. "You see this hole on top? Parents would place candy, fruit, and coins inside, and then it's sealed and hung on a rope from a branch of a tall tree, like a star in heaven." Lifting the brightly colored orb above his head with his right hand, the storekeeper pointed his left index finger toward the sky.

He lowered his arms to review the piñata's components. "For our Mexican folk, the pretty paper symbolizes Satan and his beauty. The paper-mâché points stand for the seven sins: greed, gluttony, sloth, pride, envy, wrath, and lust. The clay pot is the emblem of charity, and the treats inside are the just rewards of faith."

"Hum. How delightful. Please go on, sir," Mary remarked as she nodded.

"Yes indeed, madam. Take this here stick." The vendor placed the club in Naomi's hands like a baseball bat. "It is symbolic of virtue. The object of the game is to blindfold the child." He cleared his throat. "You know … blind faith." He chuckled. "Then spin them around a few times to disorientate them." Placing his hand on Naomi's shoulders, he spun her around thrice. "Afterward, the youngsters are given a chance to take a swing to break the dangling star. Once the stick bearer breaks the piñata and the goodies spill on the ground, the children are allowed to gather them."

"Oh, Mama, can we buy one? Please, please! This will be fun to play on my next birthday."

"Shush now, Naomi. You know we can't go buyin' a bunch of things yet." Mary took the stick from her youngest daughter and handed it back to the jolly gentleman. "That is an interestin' spiritual concept, sir. Thank you so much for educatin' us. We're only in town for a couple of nights, and then we're headed to the valley in the hope of findin' ourselves a new home. So, for now, we only have room in the wagon for provisions." Mary opened her reticule and pulled out a folded piece of paper and gave it to the clerk. "In fact, if ya don't mind, sir, this is my list I'll need fillin'."

"Oh, why of course, madam. I do understand. A lot of folks pass through these parts." He turned to Naomi. "Young lady, I do believe this won't be the last you see of this game. Many mercantile stores carry this type of item for our Mexican folk as well as for locals like you, who are open-minded about other cultural traditions. You certainly won't go wrong with this activity." Tapping her nose with his finger, he smiled and turned on his heels and began gathering the items on Mary's list.

Naomi tugged on her mother's sleeve. "Mama, what is virtue?"

"Well…" Mary tried to put the answer into simple words for her young daughter to understand. "It's when ya do good things, especially for those around you."

"So…" Naomi rubbed her chin. "The bat is the good things we do and we use it to break evil…the pretty paper star points, so that rewards can be shared with others…the candy!"

"Correct." Mary smiled.

"Geewillikin. I like that." She giggled.

"Shall we go find your sister?" They glanced around the store and walked over to where Sarah stood staring at the brightly printed bolts of calico fabric.

"Mama, I plum wore out the two dresses I brought with me on the journey. Do you suppose…?"

The mindful mother understood her drably dressed daughter's needs, so she completed her thought for her. "I can sew as many garments as you want, Sarah, once we are…"

"Settled!" Both daughters responded in unison with their mother.

After the men had finished watering the oxen and the ladies their shopping, they returned to their wagons outside of Jamestown, where they planned to stay two nights.

THE NEXT MORNING after pouring himself a cup of coffee, Samuel sat across his father at the table, grasping his hot beverage between his palms. "Hey, Pa. Any chance I can go to Woods Creek today? That's where I hear the prospectors go to do their gold pannin'. It's just a ten-minute walk outside of Jamestown." In Samuel's mind, he knew it would be too much to ask since the wagon train would be back on the trail the next morning. All he could think about was the gold in the old prospector's hand the day before. He just had to try panning.

"Sorry. Not this time, son. I'm goin' to need you to bring Fire and Belle to the blacksmith in town. It looks like they will need new shoes. The last time it was done was in Carson. Might as well have them refitted now since we are past the rugged mountain top."

"But…"

"No, son. We're so close to our promised land. I can feel it in my bones. Let's stay focused on gettin' down this mountain. Maybe another time. All right?"

Samuel knew he could not win this argument. He realized he inherited his mule headedness from his father. Nothing was goin' to stop him once he had a goal in mind. He breathed in deep to calm himself knowing the reshoeing would consume his day. "All right. I'll get the horses after I finish breakfast." Samuel plowed into his meal as his mind raced on how he might return to Jamestown.

"WAGON HO!" came the trail master's call at nine o'clock the next morning.

"Hee-yah! Let's go, ox." David yelled as his father cracked the whip.

The wagoneers seemed to be moving at a faster pace. Within four hours, they arrived in Coulterville and were veering downhill toward the west on John Muir Highway for twelve miles.

David sat next to his father on the wagon's bench seat, and his jaw dropped as California's immense lowlands came into view. It stretched almost the entire length of the Golden State, bordered by the Pacific Ocean on the horizon. An image came into his mind of the Old Testament story when God commanded Moses to send one man from each of Israel's twelve tribes to spy on the promised land. He felt confident, like Caleb after he returned from spying to give a good report to Moses. David recited Caleb's word in Numbers 13:30. "Let us go up at once, and possess it; for we are well able to overcome it."

"Thanks to the good Lord, for He goes before us and is with us. Yes, it *will* be ours!" His father's chin jutted forward, and his chest puffed up.

"Merced Falls Road is coming up, Pa. This is where we turn." David shielded his eyes from the sun's rays as he pointed to a post bearing a wooden sign at the next intersection. When they turned south, his family waved and yelled good-bye to the remaining waggoneers as they foraged westward.

Continuing south on Merced Falls Road for sixteen more miles, they approached an industrial town seated by the Merced River. "If I'm correct, that should be Merced Falls up ahead. Check the map, son."

David studied the wrinkled and tattered drawing. "You're right, Pa." When he turned his gaze toward the town, a familiar tall smokestack and three-story building, much like the mills in Kentucky, came into view. "Hey, Pa. Look yonder." He read aloud the name boldly painted on the side, "Nielson's Flour and Woolen Mill."

"Yep. I see it, son. I've got goosebumps all over me."

With gusto, David howled to his mother, who followed close behind in her wagon. "Yahoo! Flour mill ahead. We're close, very close," he said.

The flour mill indicated that the territory was vital for wheat farming. David perceived the mills as a marker from God.

THE ROAD MADE A SHARP RIGHT TURN, running parallel to the north side of the river. After seven miles, a simple wood sign greeted them. *Welcome to Snelling. Merced County Seat.* As they traveled toward the town, they passed untouched fields of golden open ranges and an occasional wheat farm. Jonathan's heart thumped so hard from the excitement that he thought his wife could hear it pounding beneath his shirt. He signaled to pull her wagon beside his.

"Mary, the land is mostly flat, and the river is a stone's throw away. It's perfect for growin' our crop."

"I agree, Jonathan. I agree. Hallelujah. Are we home?"

"I do believe we've arrived, so be sure to keep your eyes out for the parcel of land which suits us best."

5

Settling in Snelling

The last seven miles of open range along the rushing Merced River excited the entire family as they searched for possible sites to plant their wheat and build their farmhouse and barn. Naomi hollered, "Look, Mama and Papa, how 'bout over there?"

"Oh, whoopee! What about this place?" David pointed in another direction.

Small herds of cows and an occasional oak tree dotted the golden, undeveloped land as they passed through acre upon acre, which stretched north as far as their eyes could see. The acreage appeared ideal for growing crops because it lacked trees and boulders to be cleared.

Where am I goin' to build my home? The thought kept crossing Jonathan's mind. No particular plot stood out or reminded him of his boyhood abode.

Finally, at the intersection of Merced Falls Road and La Grange Road, the small town called Snelling came into view a half-mile away. An abundance of oak trees and shrubbery grew wild around the wood-structured buildings. Some rooftops peeked above the lush trees, exposing themselves to the sunshine.

Oh, my Lord. Now this plot of land feels like home. The river is to the left, a creek to the right, and the town is only a stone's throw away … an easy stroll for my family. It can't get more perfect than this. He envisioned his farmhouse and barn seated beside the creek. He yanked the reins to the right, and the oxen veered north on La Grange Road.

"Mary," Jonathan called to his wife in the other wagon. "Let's pull up under the crop of oaks by the creek over yonder."

"I'm following ya, Jonny." She cracked the whip.

Sarah and Naomi gasped at the variable landscape of their new homestead. The community was comprised mostly of flat land, a few gently rolling hills, a river, a stream, big shady trees, and, the most superb panorama of all, nearby stores!

"The first thing I'm gonna do is to go to the mercantile and buy me some calico for a new dress." Sarah tugged at the tears and patches on her faded day dress.

"They'll be plenty of time for that, girls, once we are settled," Jonathan said.

Jonathan and Mary pulled the Conestogas to the left of the road beneath the cover of the massive oaks as Samuel dismounted Fire and tied his horse to a branch of a tree. The children bolted off the wagons and ran to the sparkling creek, screaming and laughing. "This is it. It's perfect. We even have our own swimmin' hole!" The boys picked up some smooth, flat rocks and skipped them across the surface of the water. The girls playfully splashed each other.

As Jonathan held his wife's hand and strolled to the water's edge, he imagined his body glowing from the top of his slouch hat to the bottom of his dusty boots. He felt like Moses did in the Bible when he came down off the mountain after spending time with God.

"Children, come and sit in the shade, and let's listen to what your pa has to say." Mary waved. The family found a grassy knoll beneath the cool of the arbor, gathered around, and listened intently.

"Well, my beloved, I do hope our searchin' is over. From what we've seen, I do feel this place is our destination. Everythin' we need seems to be here." Jonathan crouched to grab a handful of earth. He squeezed the moist soil to examine how well it clumped. Then he took the ball of mud and rubbed it between his palms to measure the amount of rock, pebbles, or granules compounded in the mixture. The small chunk crumbled into fine dirt mixed with grains of sand as it fell to his feet. "Even the soil is perfect." Jonathan stared into his family's vibrant faces.

Naomi scratch at the mound beneath her. "We can grow taters, corn, green beans, and all kinds of things in this ground beside wheat."

"Let's not get our hopes too high. Tomorrow, your ma and I will go into town and inquire about this acreage. If the parcels are available, we'll purchase them and start layin' down our roots once the deed is in my hand. For now, we'll live in our wall tents, but I intend to construct a small cabin before the rains come. Once our wheat business gets off the ground next year, we can build us a proper farmhouse and barn. Are there any questions or concerns? Now would be the time to ask." Jonathan glanced around, waiting for hands to rise, but noticed only heads shaking and nodding.

"All right, if we're all in agreement, then let's set up camp. We'll pray for God's will for this property at supper time."

As the family did their chores, Jonathan made a mental note of the location on the south side of the creek where he hoped to establish the cabin, farmhouse, and barn. He visualized the 500 acres of wheat surrounding the humble dwelling. He breathed in the musty scent of the tall wild grass warmed by the sun, which covered the acreage. In his mind, he sent short yet repetitious prayers to God. *Lord, if it is Your will, please let this be our home.*

JONATHAN WORE A PAIR OF WOOLEN TROUSERS and frock coat, and his wife wore a floral printed day dress, hoping to impress their new neighbors. After breakfast and prayer with the children, the couple boarded one of the wagons and hastened into town.

Driving slowly on the main streets' dirt road called Lewis, the newcomers cringed, conscious that they were on parade. The citizens strolling the thoroughfare turned their heads to examine them and their unfamiliar Conestoga.

"Good day." Mary and Jonathan hoped the onlookers would accept them.

The friendly return of a nod or wave from those standing on the storefront's boardwalk indicated an open invitation to take part in their quaint town.

Neighborly warmth filled their hearts, so Mary and Jonathan relaxed their shoulders and took the time to pay attention to the community landmarks and business establishments.

"Jonny, there's the Snelling Ranch Post Office." Mary pointed to the left of the road as they rolled along.

As they approached the Fourth Street intersection, she recognized other buildings of interest. "Oh, and there's the county courthouse on the right, and across the way is Jacobi's Mercantile. The Snelling Hotel and Saloon are adjacent to the store, and next door to it at the corner of Third is the livery stable and meat market."

Addressing each location as Jonathan drove, she continued. "Across from them is the doctor's clinic … Doctor Cassidy." Pausing, she chuckled. "I'm sure we'll need his services with our growin' brood."

She stretched her neck to get a better view of the farthest southwest block where people with conical-shaped hats bustled together. "I do believe a Chinese camp is on the far end of town."

Eyes aglow, Mary turned to her husband. "We can glean our future farmhands from that bunch. Everythin' we need is here and all within four blocks, darlin'!"

Returning her gaze with a smile of approval, Jonathan said, "How 'bout we park this wagon and we walk over to the Mercantile to see if we can't get some direction from our new neighbors?".

AFTER DROPPING OFF THE OXEN and wagon at the livery, the enthusiastic couple strolled over to their first stop, Jacobi's Mercantile. Straightening her hat and dusting off her skirt, Mary checked her reticule once more for her grocery list and money. She anxiously clutched her husband's arm as he led her into the general store.

The proprietor, Mr. Simeon Jacobi, busied himself behind the counter as he assisted a vendor in delivering goods. The clerk, Darryl Niber, stacked jams and jellies on one of the shelves. With one glance at the newcomers, the owner excused himself to greet them cheerfully. His heavy German accent converted the letter *W* into *V*, so the couple listened carefully.

"Velcome folks. You must be new to this area. My name is Simeon, and the fellow over there is Darryl. Is there anything ve can help you vith today?"

A tall, middle-aged Jewish man from Germany, Simeon's sparse grayish-blond hair peeked from beneath his dark, tightly weaved Yamaka. He wore small, round spectacles, which hung on the tip of his nose as he peered through them to read and over them to stare his customers square in their eyes.

Because of the owner's cheerful and friendly greeting, the new patrons sighed as they glanced at each other.

Jonathan extended his hand to Simeon. "Yes, you've guessed right, sir. This is my wife, Mary. And I'm Jonathan Sower. We arrived yesterday from Kentucky with our four children with the hope of settling here in Snelling. We heard that grain farmin' is much needed in California."

Simeon removed his glasses, cleaned them on his shirt, and placed them back on his face. "Vhy yes, more settlers are moving into this state, and food production is a necessity. Vhat type of crop are you planning on growing?"

"Wheat is what my family has farmed for several generations. I've brought the seed with me, and all I need now is land, a home, an' some reliable farmhands."

At that moment, the lean, yet muscular, vendor of Norwegian descent, whom Simeon attended to earlier, overheard the discussion and found himself drawn into the circle.

"Hello, folks. I apologize for listenin' to your conversation. Allow me to introduce myself. Patrick Fay from Mount Ophir." He extended a firm hand to shake Jonathan's and tilted his worn-out broad-brimmed hat to Mary. "The wagon with the oxen just outside the store is mine. My line of work is haulin' grain to

Howard Nielson's flour mill in Merced Falls. I also know several China men who live in Snelling and are excellent farmers too. Can we be of service to ya folks?"

"Well, it appears the good Lord is guidin' us into the right place, at the right time, and to the right people." Jonathan smiled, trying to size up the bold character.

Patrick's black hair concealed a gray strand or two, which spilled out from beneath his hat. His beard of the same color was scraggly. Sweat trickled from his forehead to his brow, and the weathered wrinkles on his face denote his life of hard work. But his bright blue eyes twinkled, and his ear-to-ear grin displayed his coffee-stained teeth. He wore a long sleeve cotton shirt under his tattered overalls, which displayed a fine layer of white dust sprinkled over the front. Somehow Jonathan perceived he would be doing business with this man.

"Yes, in fact, Patrick here was deliverin' some bags of flour from the Nielson's mill." Darryl walked over to shake their hands and introduced himself. "There is plenty of land north of Snelling along the Merced River, which you can purchase. If you go to the clerk's desk at the county courthouse, she will show you a map of what is available."

"Well, gentlemen, that's mighty fine news to hear. That'll be our next visit, but after my dear wife has these provisions filled." Jonathan positioned his palm on Mary's waist and brought her forward.

Mary handed her list to Darryl, who pulled the items she needed and placed them on the counter for Simeon to tally. In the meantime, she found herself meandering toward some books on display in the store window.

"Aw, *Little Folk's Delight,* and also *Pictureland!* Can I start my new collection with these, Jonathan?" Mary rushed to the cash register.

"Of course, dear, as I promised."

Simeon added up the provisions. "The total comes to seven dollars and thirty cents, Mrs. Sower."

She opened her reticule, counted her money, and handed it to him.

"Oh, and by the vay, ve plan on building a schoolhouse in town. Maybe by next year this time, they say."

"I do thank you kindly for the information, Mr. Jacobi. We should be settled down by then. For now, I'm teachin' the children. What I look forward to is settlin' down and sleepin' in my own bed and cookin' food in my own kitchen." Mary extended her hand to bid him a good day.

Patrick scribbled his address on a piece of paper and noted the days he usually delivered. "This is where I live, but it's best to reach me here at Mr. Jacobi's store since I'm often gone haulin' throughout the area. I'll see what I can do to call on the China men to work for you too," Patrick said as he handed over the slip of paper.

"I am much obliged to ya, sir," Jonathan replied, quite pleased.

While Darryl loaded the provisions into their wagon at the livery, the couple moseyed over to the courthouse. Jonathan left Jacobi's with a sense of assurance that God wanted his family to be in Snelling.

MARGARET, THE COUNTY CLERK, an older woman with faded-red, graying hair tied back in a bun, assisted the public with methodical patience. She wore rectangular spectacles, which hugged close to her pale-blue eyes that contrasted with her dusty-blue, calico-patterned day dress.

On the wall hung a map of Snelling and the Merced County line. Jonathan removed his slouch hat as he and his wife approached Margaret's desk. He hoped she'd be patient to assist them as they sought information about the property on the corner of La Grange and Merced Falls Road.

"Excuse me, ma'am. I'd like to inquire about purchasin' some land here in Snelling," he said.

"You're in the right place, sir. I can help you," Margaret replied, sizing them up and bending her ear. "Is that a Kentucky accent I hear?"

"Indeed, it is. I'm Jonathan Sower, and this here is my wife, Mary. May I show you on your map where we are interested in makin' our new homestead?"

"Why certainly. That was the next thing I was going to ask you." Margaret chuckled.

Jonathan walked over to the topography and pointed to the location where they were camped. He further explained his intentions.

"Our farmhouse is to be built right here, and the barn over there, and this 500-acre section will be where I will grow wheat."

Margaret viewed the area and wrote down the parcel numbers and sizes until they arrived at 500 acres. With a cheerful disposition, she encouraged Jonathan and Mary.

"That is a grand endeavor, indeed! You can purchase those parcels at fifty cents an acre." She paused and stepped closer to the map to examine it more intently. "Hmm. There may be one slight problem."

The smiles on the couple's faces quickly dimmed.

"Problem? What might that be, ma'am?" He stepped back.

"It's the creek. Jackson Montana might already own it." The clerk's eyes saddened as her disappointment met the worried couple's gaze.

"And who is this feller? Can we purchase the property from him?" Jonathan asked with desperation in his voice.

"Well." She sighed. "He so happens to be the wealthiest cattleman in California. He owns practically all the watering holes in the San Joaquin Valley."

Margaret paused, and she shook her right index finger above her head. "But, hold on now. Let's find out for sure."

She scurried back to her desk. As she searched through her files, she mumbled on.

"Not too long ago, farmers protested against Mr. Montana's hoarding of the water supply. So, many of the counties limited his purchases and instituted a law prohibiting the damming of irrigation water. So it is very possible..." She didn't finish her sentence because she located the file and reviewed its contents. "Aha!"

"Yes, yes. Don't keep us in suspense. Please divulge your findings, ma'am." Jonathan gripped the edge of the clerk's desk as Mary stood beside him, biting her nails.

"The good Lord must be watchin' over the both of you." Margaret lay the open file down and turned it toward the anxious couple. "Look here." She pointed to the unclaimed form. "This parcel, along with the creek, is still available. It appears there were some attempts by others to purchase the land, but they were canceled for some reason. From what I gather, the town's mayor did not want Mr. Montana to overrun our community as he has in other counties. After all, that rich cattleman already has a street named after him in our town. What more can he ask for?" Margaret shook her head in dismay. "So the mayor did everything in his power to disallow the sale of the property to Mr. Montana. How he did this, I don't know, nor do I want to ask. Sometimes it's best to leave it that way, if you know what I mean." Her eyebrows rose as she peered at the Sowers over the top of her spectacles.

Relieved, Jonathan hugged his wife as the sprightly woman located the files for the 500 acres they requested.

"Well," Jonathan replied with high hopes. "We'd like to start with 160 acres available to us through the Homestead Act. I believe I will not be charged as long as I provide a note explainin' our intentions to develop the land. Is this correct, ma'am?"

"Yes, it is. You've been doing your homework, I see." Scribbling on her writing pad, Margaret giggled.

"We'll pay for the remainin' 340 acres. That should be a total of 500 acres." He did the math in his head.

"Well, let's start by having you folks take a seat, and I'll get the paperwork started and notarized."

Jonathan and Mary spent the remainder of the afternoon filling out forms.

"Now, Mr. and Mrs. Sower, all that needs to be done is to sign this deed and make your payment of $170, and the property is yours!" Margaret handed them the final documents.

Heart pounding, Jonathan pulled out his pocketbook and paid the clerk cash, part of the proceeds from the sale of his father's farm in Kentucky.

"Congratulations to you both. Let me shake the hands of our newest citizens of Snelling." The satisfied clerk extended them a firm handshake and the deed.

JONATHAN AND MARY RETURNED TO THE CAMP to share the good news with the children. Mary made a savory beef pot roast for the family to celebrate.

Sitting around the campfire, they held hands while Jonathan prayed. "Dear Heavenly Father, You're Almighty God and provider, and we are so grateful for Your love and travelin' mercies, and gettin' us to our promised land, Snelling. We thank You for protectin' and guidin' us every step of the way, and for Your provision in findin' this property as our new homestead. Lord, we ask for Your blessin' upon this meal. In Jesus' name, we pray. Amen."

And everyone responded in unison, "Amen."

"All right, all. Now we can start layin' down our roots," Jonathan exclaimed as he passed the pot roast.

6

Humble Beginnings

"Good mornin', Ah Yung." Jonathan extended a hand to the middle-aged Chinaman and tipped his hat to the ten comrades who stood in front of the wall tents erected for the workers at the new homestead, Sower Farms. He trusted Patrick Faye's recommendation for this able-bodied farmhand as a superintendent since he spoke English and had proved himself as a competent and reliable worker when he assisted Patrick in delivering cargo throughout the county.

"Allow me to introduce to you my wife, Mary and my children, Sam, Sarah, Naomi, and David." Jonathan faced his kin, who waited with patience.

Mary dismissed the brood to their daily chores, stood by her husband, and smiled at their new hired help. "We are pleased to meet you, Ah Yung. Our family has been lookin' forward to this day for a long time. We are so thankful to have you and your men workin' for us."

"The pleasure is ours, Mr. and Mrs. Sower. We are the ones grateful to you for choosing us to work on your land," Yung said in his broken English, shook the hand of his new employers, and bowed, as was customary in his culture. The men followed suit, bowing and tipping their conical-shaped bamboo hats.

"Well, gentlemen, please help yourself to as much water as you need. Bein' by the creek, the barrel will always be full. You must drink a lot of fluids in this autumn heat," Mary said. "Now, if y'all don't mind, I must carry on with my chores." She curtsied, her corded petticoat and skirt swirling as she moved, and returned to her makeshift outdoor kitchen.

"Mr. Faye informed me you desire build cabin, corral, and sheds for animals in two months' time. I bring with me ten men with good carpentry skills." Yung turned to the Chinese men dressed in indigo-dyed cotton trousers with matching loose-fitting shirts that resembled pajamas.

"You're correct. I do believe between the twelve of us; we can complete this work by the end of November. Are your men aware of the tasks involved?" Jonathan felt leery because he did not know much about this ethnic group other than what was rumored by other farmers. He recalled them referring to the Chinese as the Celestials, because of their spiritual beliefs, which may be the cause of their punctuality, willingness to learn, excellent craftsmanship, and good behavior.

"Yes, Mr. Sower. No problem. My men hard workers. We finish everything before rains come," Yung replied.

"Very well. Once the grounds are complete, then the next task will be to prepare the land for farmin'. I'll need to hire more men, but we can discuss that when the season gets closer. For now, let me show you and the men the plans." Jonathan walked over to the table under the fly and unfurled a scroll with the drawings of the property. "Please tell your men to gather 'round and you can interpret the instructions.

"As you can see, the cabin is near the creek, and this is what we're goin' to build first. This area next to it is where I plan to establish the farmhouse next year. The animals' shed and corral go right here by the main wayside road. Eventually, I would like to erect a barn next to the corral. That, too, will be next year's project."

"Ah, I understand." Yung nodded his head and turned to the men and translated the map into Mandarin.

Jonathan unrolled the next drawing. "This is the instruction for the cabin. It has one main room and two bedrooms. Do you and your men know how to build a log home?" His back straightened while he stared into the dark, narrow eyes and smooth, bronze face of the man before him.

After removing his bamboo hat under the shade, Yung revealed the top of his shaved head, and his long, black hair braided into a queue, which went down his back to his waist. The men did the same as they viewed the scroll.

Yung stood attentive. "Of course, Mr. Sower. We make roads and homes at Gum Sham, uh, Gold Mountain. You call … California." Grinning, he proudly reassured them. "Do not worry. You give us plans, and we make for you." He translated to the men who grin and mumbled. "Men say pine cabin very easy to build compared to bridges and railroads."

"All right, forgive my ignorance," Jonathan said. "Shall we begin then?"

"Yes, Mr. Sower."

"Let's start with the foundation. The men will need to remove some stone slabs at the bottom of the creek and arrange them flat in the perimeter prepared for the cabin. That'll probably take several days of work."

Yung translated the instructions.

"Once the men complete this task, the logs for the walls and roof will need to be measured, cut, and notched. Mr. Faye delivered the pine wood from the Sierras last week and stacked them where they are to build the cabin. I'll provide all the necessary equipment. Let me know if there are other tools you may need. Are there any questions?"

Yung translated again, and the men nodded.

"Please plan on workin' Monday through Friday from eight in the mornin' to five in the afternoon. You can take an hour lunch break and any time needed for water or goin' to the outhouse. Are we agreed upon twenty dollars a month for your men's wages and twenty-five dollars for you as my superintendent?"

"Ah, yes, Mr. Sower, we accept your offer." Yung shook his hand to seal the agreement.

"All right, then let us begin our work." Jonathan positioned small stones over the opened scrolls on the table and led the men to the creek, where they began excavating the slabs of rock for the cabin's foundation.

TWO MONTHS CAME AND WENT. Yung and the men finished the cabin, corral, and animal sheds as promised. Mary was busy washing dishes in the small two-bedroom home when she heard a knock. Elbows deep in soapy dishwater, she peered up, locked eyes with Sarah, who dried the plates next to her, and then Naomi, who cleaned the kitchen table after the lunchtime meal. "Who might that be? Pa and the boys wouldn't be knockin'."

Frightened by the recent article in the town's newspaper regarding outlaws and Mexican bandits who caused a ruckus in outlying areas, Mary took extra safety measures by mounting the shotguns within easy reach on the mantel.

The cautious mother dried her hands on her apron. "Come away from the door, Naomi."

"Yes, Mama." The second daughter put down the cleaning rag and walked to the washbasin beside her eldest sister.

Mary paused near the door. "Who is it?"

"A delivery for you, ma'am." The high-pitched male voice chortled from behind the door.

She grabbed the shotgun, propped it on her shoulder, and used the tip of the gun to lift the latch and crack the door enough for her to peer through. Mary's eyes enlarged when pine branches stared back at her. She kicked the door wide open. Boughs sprung out, pushing her back a step. "What?" she cried aloud.

"Happy Christmas!" A raspy voice cheered from behind the tree, which now stood in her doorway.

Upon recognizing the familiar voice, Mary uncocked the rifle and shook her head in dismay. "Patrick, is that you?"

A bearded face with glistening blue eyes and witty smile peeked around the boughs. "How'd ya guess?"

"You darn frightened me to death! We don't know anyone in these parts yet who would come callin' on us." Changing her tone,

Mary laughed, relieved to be acquainted with the unexpected visitor. "Do come in, Pat. Welcome to our humble home. And what are ya doin' with this adorable little tree?"

"Aw … just a little house warmin' gift for y'all."

Not a moment too soon, Jonathan, Samuel, and David came bursting through the door.

"Are you gals all right? What is goin' on in here?" Her worried husband was ready to grab hold of the intruder whose back faced him.

Patrick swung around. "Whoa. It's me, Jon. Happy Christmas. I thought I'd drop in and say hello. Heard from Yung that their work was done for now. I had to come by and see the finished product. Thought I'd bring a little housewarmin' gift too. Chopped it down myself after I dropped off a load of firewood. Fresh from the Sierras."

"Hey, Patrick, my friend. Happy Christmas to you too." Jonathan's countenance changed to a cheerful glow. "Here, let me take that." He placed the tree in the corner and returned to shake Patrick's hand. "Please take a seat by the fireplace and warm yourself."

Her husband pushed some of the wood dining chairs near the fire for the adults as the children sat on the hand-woven rug on the floor.

"Why, thank you. But only for a moment. I must hit the road so I can get home before dark. My wife will have supper waitin' for me."

"Can we offer you some tea?" Mary asked.

"Sure, it'll warm me up before I brave the elements again."

"Sarah, why don't you pour a cup for Mr. Faye?"

"Yes, Ma. Right away." Sarah reached into the cupboard for the chinaware and filled it with hot water from the kettle over some mint leaves in a strainer. "Here you are, Mr. Faye. Would ya like some cream or sugar?"

"No, darlin'. This'll do fine." Patrick held the delicate cup and saucer in his calloused hands.

Jonathan rested his elbows on his knees, cupped his hands together, and addressed Patrick. "I think I can speak on behalf of my family. We're ever so grateful for your help in gettin' us settled. Without your guidance and suggestions, I don't think we'd be sittin' cozy in front of this warm fire with a solid roof over our heads right now. The Celestials you recommended proved their worth a hundred times over. They did a mighty fine job, wouldn't you say?" He glanced around the room, a sense of contentment shone in his eyes.

"You're quite right. The home is charmin' indeed. The farm animals seem happy, as well, in their new corral." Patrick grinned.

"This is the best we could do with such little time before the rains. Please pardon the tight quarters. Hopefully, next year we will build a farmhouse more suitable for our large family." Jonathan's face turned rosy pink.

"This is a mansion compared to what we've been livin' in durin' the past eight months. I'm enjoyin' every moment in it," Mary said, pride swelling up in her heart. "How does Apostle Paul put it? 'I have learned, in whatsoever state I am, therewith to be content.'"

"You're correct, my love. I could be the richest man in the world, but I would be nothin' without you, my family, my friends, and my God." Jonathan's face glowed with warmth as he perused the loving people around him.

"No need to apologize. Everyone who moved to California has been in your shoes, startin' a new life. Your kinfolk are doin' better than most. Hardships do bring out the best in us. It helps us to realize what is important in life." Patrick grinned as he finished his tea. "Well, I must be gettin' on my way. Thank you so much for your hospitality. You know where to reach me if you need me." The gruff man set the cup on the table, embraced his new friends, and departed in his oxen-driven cargo wagon.

"WOW! THAT WAS A LOUD ONE, PA." Samuel put down his whittling knife and nativity wood piece he carved as he sat near the stone fireplace. Bright rays beamed through small cracks in the cabin walls whenever a lightning bolt flashed through the Christmas Eve night sky, followed by rolling claps of thunder.

Splat, splat, splat.

"The rain is comin' down heavy now," Jonathan said as he peered up at the ceiling from his chair near Samuel. He hoped no more leaks would occur. "I wonder if the rainstorm will pour as much as it did two years ago and flood the town. Mr. Jacobi said the banks of the Merced River overflowed by almost three feet. Many of the residents are still recoverin' from that horrible season."

Samuel's eyes grew wide. "Golly, I hope not."

Drip, drip, drip. The water seeped through some holes in the ceiling and into the containers below.

"Do ya need any more bowls, Jon?" Mary asked as Sarah, Naomi, and David continued decorating the sugar cookies and stringing popcorn at the kitchen table.

"No, dear. I think the roof is holding. At least I know where I'll need to do some patchin' when the sun comes out." Jonathan smirked as he finished punching holes in the tin can star he made for the treetop.

"I'm ready to put the cookies on the tree, Ma." Naomi snickered.

"I'm done too." David showed off his bell and star-shaped confections.

"How ya doin' with the popcorn garland, Sarah?" Mary paced around the table, enjoying her children's Christmas craftwork.

"What do you think? Is it long enough?" The eldest sister lifted the stringed fluffy white oil-popped kernals above her head.

"Looks good to me." His mother took one end of the festoon and stretched it out. "All right, let's go decorate the tree. It seems awful lonely in the corner. Come on, Sam. Why don't you help us out."

Mary and the children decorated the boughs as they sang "Deck the Halls," "Hark! The Herald Angels Sing", "Oh Come All Ye Faithful," "It Came Upon a Midnight Clear," and "Jingle Bells."

Holding the carved nativity with reverence, Samuel placed his handiwork beneath the tree, front and center. He began singing "Silent Night," and the others chimed in.

"We're done, Pa. All we need is your final piece." Naomi cheered.

"All right, I'm ready too." The joy-filled father fastened the tin star at the top of the tree and placed a small candle behind it. "Who wants to light it?"

"I do," David said.

"Well, who would be more appropriate to light the Star of David, but David himself?" Mary cried.

"Okay, young man, why don't ya stand on the chair and I will hand ya a long match." Jonathan stationed a chair beside the tree and David stood on top.

"Here you are. Be careful." Jonathan handed him a lit matchstick.

David leaned forward, reached toward the candle, and touched the wick with the flame.

"Oh ... ooo ... .ah." Gasps of exhilaration filled the room as light trickled through the patterned holes.

"The Christmas tree is beautiful, dear ones." Moisture formed in Mary's eyes. "We've certainly come a long way to follow the Lord's star to this place in California, our new beginnin'."

"We sure have, my love." Jonathan embraced his wife.

Mary wiped away her tears. "All right, children, let's tidy up and get to bed. Tomorrow is Christmas mornin'."

Squeals of laughter filled the air as the siblings cleaned the kitchen and headed to the bedroom, too excited to sleep. However, the rain slowed to a purr and lulled the children into blissful slumber.

Meanwhile, Jonathan and Mary gathered the gifts hidden under their mattress. They wrapped the presents with stealth and placed them under the tree. Afterward, they collapsed into bed for a restful night of shut-eye.

"HEE-HEE. WAKE-UP Y'ALL." Naomi threw off her quilt cover, clambered down her bunk ladder, put on her slippers, then nudged Sarah in the bed below and her brothers in the bunks across from them. "It's Christmas."

"Today is Jesus' birthday!" David's eyes flew open. He sat up and climbed off his bed and slipped on his woolen socks over his long underwear.

"Shhh," Naomi said, holding her index finger to her lips. "Keep your voice down so we don't wake Pa and Ma."

David nodded. "Let's go see what's under the tree. Are you goin' to join us, Sam and Sarah?" He whispered.

"Huh, what?" Samuel rubbed his eyes.

"Yes, of course." Sarah rolled out of bed and donned her slippers. "Get up, lazy. Don't ya want to see what you got for Christmas?" She threw her pillow at her eldest brother.

"Yep, I'm comin'." The sleepy-eyed youth yawned and stretched, not bothering to put on his socks.

The brothers and sisters tiptoed into the living room. The sight of the tree with the brown paper packages tied with red ribbons and bows hastened their steps and bolstered their laughter.

"Whoa!" David fell to his knees and pulled the gifts from underneath as he read the tags. "This one is yours, Sam. And this is for you, Sarah."

Soon the four found themselves sifting through the presents and distributing them to one another.

"A new dress and bonnet." Sarah gasped, placed the hat on her head, and held the garment up to her body.

"I got one too." Naomi did the same as her sister.

"Trousers and shoes." The boys whooped and hollered.

"Pale Rider boots. I've wanted a pair of these. This is what all the men are wearin' these days," Sam cheered.

The laughter and gaiety filtered into Jonathan and Mary's bedroom, and soon they too moseyed into the living room near their family.

"Happy Christmas, children!"

The siblings leaped into their parents' arms with fond embraces and glad tidings. "Thanks, Pa and Ma. We love our new clothes."

"Ma and Pa, I do believe there are some presents with your names on the tags under the tree." Naomi prodded.

The parents knelt and exchanged their gifts.

"Oh, Jonathan. A new gown and headdress. It is absolutely beautiful." Her mother put on the Victorian wide-brimmed touring hat decorated with claret-colored satin and plumage, black netting, and lace, and a single pale pink rose. She caressed the details of the matching tailored day dress, trimmed with black cording and white faux sleeves.

"All right, it's your turn, Jon. Open yours." Her mother urged.

Tearing the wrapping, her father mused. "Darlin', you shouldn't have. A Callahan frock coat with a double-breasted Baker City Vest, and Wickham trousers, too." With delight, he held up the suit.

"You're goin' to make a gentleman out of me yet." He guffawed.

"Well, now our family can look presentable when we go out on the town or when we finally find a church to attend." Her mother smiled as she twirled around with her new attire.

LATER THAT DAY, JONATHAN REMOVED THE ROASTED BIRD from the spike on the outdoor grill, placed it on the platter, and brought it indoors on the kitchen table. "Turkey is done," he said, pleased with his accomplishment.

"All right, children. Put down your games. Christmas supper is ready," his wife called.

"The food smells wonderful." Samuel breathed in the aroma of the cooked stuffed fowl, mashed potatoes, cornbread, and apple pie.

The family sat down and held hands as Jonathan prayed. "Father, we thank You for givin' Your Son, Jesus, as our gift for eternal life. There is no better treasure than this. We are also grateful for Your protection, guidance, and provision for our brand new life in Snelling. We do ask for Your blessin' upon our first upcomin' season of harvest and for the hands which will be set to the plow, Superintendent Yung and the Chinese farmhands. Please grant safety over Patrick Faye, who will help haul our wheat to the mill. May You bless this bountiful meal to nourish our bodies so we can be the ambassadors of Christ which You call us to be. In Jesus' name. Amen."

After Christmas dinner, they huddled by the stone fireplace and Jonathan read the nativity story out loud from Luke 2:1-20.

"And there were in the same country shepherds abiding in the field, keeping watch over their flock by night. And, lo, the angel of the Lord came upon them, and the glory of the Lord shone round about them: and they were sore afraid. And the angel said unto them, Fear not: for, behold, I bring you good tidings of great joy, which shall be to all people. For unto you is born this day in the city of David a Savior, which is Christ the Lord. And this shall be a sign unto you; Ye shall find the babe wrapped in swaddling clothes, lying in a manger.

And suddenly there was with the angel a multitude of the heavenly host praising God and saying, 'Glory to God in the highest, and on earth peace, goodwill toward men.'"

7

Cows in the Field

February 1865

"Patrick, I sure do appreciate you sellin' us two sets of oxen at such a good price. With the four teams, the farmhands should be able to plow the eight back-forties within two months." Jonathan discussed the property on a land map stretched open on the kitchen table while Mary, Samuel, Patrick, and Yung listened.

"I realize this is rather aggressive, plantin' 320 acres for the first season, but I must recoup my losses since we spent most of our time movin' and settlin' down last year. Currently, I haven't any income, and my lovely wife is beginnin' to fret." Jonathan winked at his sweet smiling spouse, who sat on the other end of the table, tightening the shawl around her shoulders.

"I'm much obliged, Jon. After all, you're bringin' me much haulin' business between your ranch and Merced Falls. We'll be keepin' the Yosemite Lumber Company and Nielson's Flour Mill busy this season, that's for sure," Patrick said.

"You're right, Pat. If all goes as planned, then I hope to build the barn in June before the harvest, and the farmhouse after the crops are reaped. It sure is handy havin' that industrial town only six miles away."

Jonathan shifted his gaze around the table. "The tall California pine sure makes for excellent cabin walls, and there is no shortage of it in the Sierras."

"However, first things first. Let's talk about the number of men we'll need to hire." He locked eyes with his superintendent. "Let's start with twelve farmworkers and ten carpenters. The farmhands will work in three groups of four: one to clear the land, the second to plow, and the third to broadcast the seed. Each team will complete one back-forty in five workin' days, with two acres a day per man for a total of ten acres per week. If each group maintains its daily quota, then they should be able to finish all eight back-forties in two months.

"I'd like the men assigned to clearin' to start next Monday. The plowin' workers will begin the second week, and the seedin' team the week after them. After they complete their tasks, they are to continue cultivatin' and weedin' the crop until harvest in July and August. Yung, can you arrange this for me?" Jonathan struck a lucifer on his boot sole and lit his clay pipe.

"Certainly, Mr. Sower. You will need twelve men to clear, plow, seed, and cultivate. Is this number correct, sir?" The superintendent repeated the orders.

"Yes, that's correct," Jonathan said as he wrote down the instruction. "Now for the irrigation ditches, barn, and farmhouse, I would like to use the carpenters who built my cabin and corral. It'll be almost a full year of labor for them as well."

"Ah, plus ten carpenters. I know many countrymen eager for work," Yung replied. "I will notify them and schedule four farmworkers to start every Monday for next three weeks until all twelve farming positions filled. The carpenters begin digging ditches next week."

"Very good. Now that the rain has let up, the soil should be soft and easy to work. We must take advantage of this and the mild spring temperature. Are there any questions or concerns?" Jonathan asked the group.

Samuel raised his hand. "Pa, what would ya like me to do?"

"Son, I want you to be my shadow." He smiled. "You must learn as much as you can because one day all of that'll be yours. This week we'll ride out and tag anything that needs to be cleared. We can start this afternoon after lunch. How does that sound to you?"

"Sure, Pa. I'll be glad to help." A broad smile stretched across Sam's face.

"All right, y'all are dismissed." He turned to Yung. "I'll see you and your men next Monday, bright and early."

"Indeed, Mr. Sower."

The superintendent bowed and followed Patrick out of the cabin door.

Throughout the remaining portion of the week, Jonathan and Samuel rode their horses around the property placing strips of red rags tied to sticks on boulders, shrubs, and trees. These items were to be cleared by the first four farmhands.

Staring at the ground, the farmer clenched his teeth, disturbed at several cow patties on the field. *Hum, not a good sign. This dung better be from last fall, before I purchased this land. I sure hope that the owner of this herd is aware that this is private property now. I won't have any cattle free-grazin' on my property.*

MONDAY MORNING, APRIL 15ᵀᴴ and the eight back-forties of wheat grew well in the warm California climate, the furthest forty acres being the tallest by about six inches. As Jonathan and Samuel prepared the horses for pulling the cultivators, a familiar faint noise from the distant fields aroused Jonathan's senses.

Um, um, um.

"What in tarnation?" Jonathan stopped moving the machinery and strained his ears toward the sound. "Did ya hear that, Sam?"

"Hear what, Pa?"

"Stop what you are doin' and listen."

Samuel put down the harnesses and listened intently.

Um, um, um. The low hum wafted in the gentle wind.

"Yep. I hear it. It can't be. I hope it isn't." Sam's eyes grew wide.

Father and son glanced up and scanned the crops. To their dismay, at the northern edge of the fields, about a half-mile away, they saw what looked like over fifty black, flat-bottom boats floating atop a sea of green waves.

"Oh no! Sam, get our guns. Cattle are in the field." Jonathan dropped what he was doing. "I'll fetch Yung and one of the farmhands."

"Right away, Pa."

Samuel ran into the cabin, returned with the gun belts and shotguns, and met his father and the two men at the corral to saddle their horses.

They galloped along La Grange Road over to the field's edge and did their best to scare the Black Angus away by shooting into the air. After the cattle scattered into the adjacent unclaimed territory, Jonathan and Samuel dismounted to inspect the remains of the devastated farmland. Much of the sprouts had been trodden upon and eaten.

Shaking his head in disbelief, the angry farm owner crouched down to examine the destroyed crop.

"Dang them cows!"

He plucked the shredded produce from the ground. Stubble. He threw it down, cringed, and huffed.

"What a darn shame. This is goin' to cost us. By the looks of the damaged field, the cattle must have been here all weekend long. I think we just lost a full back-forty."

Angry, Jonathan's blood boiled to his head, bringing heat to his cheeks. He stood and spoke stern words to the superintendent and the farmhand. "Yung, hire four more men. Instruct them to saddle up and stand guard along the edge of the fields until we can build a fence around the property. If any of the cattle trespasses, they have my permission to lasso them and put them in the corral. If anyone asks questions, give them my name."

"I understand. But, what should we do with destroyed wheat?"

"There is nothin' much we can do. It's too late to replow the field and re-seed. The crop won't be mature by the time winter arrives. Let's hope the damaged seedlin's will recover. Please inform the farmhands to continue cultivatin' as scheduled."

"Yes, Mr. Sower."

Yung yanked on the horse's reins and trotted back to the corral as the other farmhand followed.

"Sam, you're comin' with me," Jonathan growled.

"Where to, Pa?"

"I'm goin' to file a complaint to Marshal Warner at the courthouse."
Jonathan huffed and mounted his steed.

"He-yah." He kicked Jake's side with the heel of his boots, and
the horse reared upward and galloped into town as Samuel followed
close behind on Fire.

Jonathan and Samuel approached Marshal Robert Warner's
rolltop desk across from the county clerk on the second floor of the
Snelling Courthouse. Below on the first floor, the dull chatter of prisoner's
voices rose. The stocky built official leaned back in his wood chair while
cleaning his Colt revolver. His dark, neatly combed hair gradually blended
into his sideburns, and his lips were hidden behind his thick mustache.
His long duster coat draped over each side of the seat and revealed his
U.S. Marshals badge pinned above his heart on his vest. His black ten-
gallon hat hung on the wall beside his desk, and the spurs of his ebony
knee-length boots jangled whenever he moved his feet.

Excitement and chatter electrified the room. An urgent telegraph
had come in by transatlantic cable. A crowd formed around Margaret,
the county clerk, as she read the message coming from the San Francisco
County Office.

"President Abraham Lincoln shot in head. Stop. April 14th. Stop.
Died this morning. Stop. Assassin at large. Stop."

Pandemonium filled the courtroom after hearing the report.
The people rushed Margaret and tried to take the note from her hand
to read for themselves. Marshal Warner lifted his revolver packed with
powder and shot toward the ceiling because he could not calm anyone
down. The gun made a loud blast, which caused the crowd to cover their
ears and quiet down immediately.

"Listen, folks," the officer hollered. "Settle down. Once we receive
more news, I'll ask Margaret to post the note on the front door. In the
meantime, inform your family and friends of this tragic incident and

keep the President, his wife, and our country in your prayers. Please get business done here and go home, and don't involve yourself in any rioting or unlawful conduct because of this situation. Thank you."

As the crowd dissipated to their original dealings in the courthouse, Jonathan did his best to discuss his grievance, despite the inattentive response he received from the busy lawman.

"Marshal Warner." He began as the officer returned to his desk. "I'd like to file a complaint against whoever owns the livestock grazin' on my property. Do you know who these cattle belong to?" Jonathan snorted, pointing toward his farm.

Leaning back in his chair, the marshal cocked his head back, and his eyebrows scrunched together. "Are you kidding me?" he replied. "They are owned by Merced County's supervisor, Jackson Montana, of course."

"Is this the same fellow who owns 10,000 head of cattle?"

"Yes, sir. He's the biggest toad in the puddle."

"Dear God. Not only is he one of the richest men in California, but he is a government official too? What am I up against?" Jonathan crossed his arms and rolled his eyes upward toward heaven.

The marshal smirked at his hopeless remark.

Because of the politics involved and the timing of the President's assassination, Jonathan perceived that his complaint would fall short on the marshal's priority list. But a burst of boldness that could only come from the Lord caused him to stand up for his rights.

"Excuse me, sir. I just lost a lot of time and money on crops damaged by his cattle. Damage is damage, and there must be a law that protects property owners from someone else's neglect!"

Marshal Warner threw his hands upward. "You've got every right to complain. Here ya go, sir. Fill out this complaint form and return it to Margaret, and she'll notify Mr. Montana."

"You can inform Mr. Montana that his cattle will become mine if they continue to destroy my wheat, and anyone caught trespassin' will be starin' down the barrel of my shotgun."

Jonathan hoped the warning would expedite his request as he detected the marshal's quick response as a means to shove him aside. He grabbed the paper from the marshal's hand and stared sharp into his eyes before sitting down to fill out the form.

The disgruntled farmer filed the grievance to no avail. California did not have enough law officials, resulting in the wealthy cattle owners having a stronger voice at this time. Much of justice had to be dealt with through the integrity of the individual. Each person had to take the law into his or her own hands.

8

The New Rancho

Jonathan hired four more carpenters to build the wood post fence around the acreage. He estimated it would take a month to complete. The cattle kept returning the first few days of construction, forcing the farmhands to rope and corral the stubborn ones who refused to leave.

One morning, while trying to chase them away, Samuel found himself challenged by a bull. The mammoth beast clawed at the trampled wheat and prepared to charge at the young man and his steed. They stood frozen in shock to see the animal snorting and focusing on them intently.

About fifty yards away, Jonathan turned his head toward the noise and discerned the dire situation. He yanked on Jake's reins, and the horse turned toward the bull's direction.

"Sam, don't move!"

The startled father brought his rifle butt up to his shoulder and aimed at the enormous black mass of muscles charging at his son. He shot the bull, which tumbled to the ground, destroying more wheat stalks because of its weight and inertia moving forward before it died.

Alerted by the blast, Yung rode over to the carcass to check its branding. Jonathan joined the superintendent, dismounted his horse, and examined the beast. Together they identified the brand marks as belonging to Jackson Montana, confirming Marshal Warner's suspicion.

"Well, Mr. Sower, there's nothin' much you could do," Yung said. "It was either the bull or your son."

"This ought to get the cattleman's attention," Jonathan said with reluctance. "In the meantime, let's butcher it an' we can share it amongst ourselves."

So the men secured a lasso around its neck and tied the rope to the horn of their saddles. They dragged the carcass near the corral where they butchered it.

LATER ON IN THE DAY, two *vaqueros*, Juan and Miguel, Jackson Montana's cattlemen, rode about on their horses to some of the outlying farms around the unclaimed territory north of Snelling, looking for their lost livestock.

"Excuse me, *señor*. We are missing some black cattle. Have you seen them near your property?" Juan asked a farmhand cultivating a field on the far northern end of La Grange Road.

"Nope. Not here. But I've heard that a new farmer in Snelling had troubles with some cows destroying his crop."

Hearing this news, the *vaqueros* headed south eight miles on La Grange Road, passing their herd. For the first time, Juan became aware of the tall heads of wheat now growing at the southern end of the road, bordered by an unfinished wood post fence. The flattened stalks drew his eyes. He also found the pool of blood where something or someone once lay.

"*Aye, yi, yi* ... dis is not good." Juan peered down at the evidence on the ground.

"*Sí,* I think we'll find the *vacas*, cattle, at dis ranch." Miguel shook his head.

They kept riding with caution, holding their pistols in one hand and staying alert for angry farmhands, until the Sower's cabin came into view. Juan did not know what to expect from this new resident, especially since they found bloodshed on the property.

The *vaqueros* dismounted and tied their horses behind the shrubbery and oak that lined the creek. They crawled on their bellies to the crest of the creek's bank, removed their *sombreros*, and peered at the corral. There they saw several Chinese laborers sitting in the shade of a large tree by the cabin having their lunch.

"*Uno, dos, tres, cuatro.*" Juan counted the distinct Black Angus amongst the tan-colored oxen. "Four *vacas*, but no bull."

"*Sí.* I count the same," Miguel said. "Okay, we need to tell the boss. Let's go while they're still eating."

The *vaqueros* mounted their steeds and returned to where their herd was grazing. The following morning Juan rode out to their employer's ranch in Bear Creek, informing him of the situation.

THE FIFTY-ONE-YEAR-OLD JACKSON MONTANA leaned on the column of the patio archway of his 2,300-acre *hacienda*. He frowned while observing some of his cattle grazing near the stream. In his right hand, he held the opened letter of complaint from the Snelling county clerk he received in the mail earlier that morning.

He pushed away from the column, crumbled the paper in his hand, and started to walk back to his office in the house when a lone rider wearing a familiar *sombrero* galloped up to his private pathway. *That must be either Juan or Miguel.*

He had allowed this small group of *Californios* to live on his property, working as *vaqueros* and house servants, since they were the original owners of the *rancho*. The *mestizo* relatives of Spanish and Mexican descent were given a choice to stay on the ranch as workers or be forced to move to Mexico when California became a state fifteen years earlier. They chose to remain.

Juan brought his horse to the front of the *hacienda*, dismounted, and tied its reins to the post. He dusted off his suede, silver buttoned, embroidered *charro calzonera* and matching *pantalonera* and climbed up the steps to where his employer stood to stare down at him. He pushed his *sombrero* off his head, and it hung on his back from the strap wrapped around his neck. At the top of the porch, he extended a handshake.

"*Buenos días, Señor* Montana."

"*Buenos días,* Juan. What brings you back to the ranch so soon?"

"I am sorry, *Señor,* but I have bad news to tell you."

"Uh, all right." Jackson snorted like a bull. "Let's go into the house and discuss it in my office."

The heel of their boots tapped when they walked on the home's clay tile. Jackson sat behind his oversized oak desk as Juan removed his hat, placed it on a table, and positioned himself on a cowhide leather seat across from him.

Alerted by the men's footsteps, the housemaid dressed in a colorful Mexican frock entered the room. "Would you care for some refreshment, *señors?*"

"Yes, Teresita. Bring us some *horchatas* and *empanadas, por favor,*" Jackson requested.

"*Sí, señor.* Right away." She whisked away and closed the office door behind her.

"Okay, Juan. What is this bad news? Let me guess. Does it involve Snelling?" Jackson threw the crumpled letter on his desk, grabbed a cigar out of a box, and lit it. "Would you like one?"

"No, thank you." Juan sat back and wrung his hands together on his lap. "Yes, it has something to do with a new *rancho* in Snelling."

He looked up at the deep lines on the face of the seasoned cow rancher as he puffed a plume of smoke into the air.

"It looks like the cattle have destroyed a large portion of his crop. Miguel and I saw four of your *vacas* in their corral, and we think they might have killed one of the bulls."

Jackson paused, silently staring out toward the window as he took another long drag on his cigar and exhaled. He loosened his bolo and gulped, his Adam's apple bobbing underneath the skin of his sagging neck.

"You and Miguel must keep the herd away from Snelling. But before you do that, I want you to try to get my cattle back. I've got a bad feeling about this. This farmer has filed a complaint at the marshal's office. I think he can be trouble. Be prepared."

"*Sí, señor.* How do you expect us to do that and manage the herd?"

"Bring two buckaroos with you. They can tend to the herd while you and Miguel do what is necessary."

"*Señors*, your refreshments." Teresita placed the tray on the table beside the leather chair and handed the drinks to the men. "Is there anything else, *Señor*?"

"No, Teresita. *Gracias*," Jackson said.

As the men enjoyed the snack, they discussed other ranching matters. Juan returned to Snelling with two more wranglers.

THE COMPLETED WOOD POST FENCE around the property kept the cattle from coming near the wheat. The night sky fell on the farm like a dark, warm wool blanket trapping the heat of the day beneath it. The Chinese farmhands went home for the day, and the animals stood still and quiet in the corral.

Inside the cabin, Jonathan and the family finished their dinner and were preparing to go to bed when their hound dogs perked up. They ran to the door and began to scratch and growl.

"What is it, Boomer and Ann?" Sam turned his head from where he sat by the hearth.

Gurr. Arf, arf. The robust, floppy eared male dog growled and let out a deep throaty bark.

With haste, Jonathan blew out the oil lamp on the table. "Y'all get in the bedrooms." He grabbed his gun belt hanging from the mantel, and Sam did the same.

"Pa?" Sarah shuddered.

"Come on, children. Let's do as your father tells us." Mary gathered the girls and young David into the back bedroom.

"Hold the dogs back, son." The father crouched behind the front door.

Sam pulled the hounds' collars as Jonathan cracked the door slightly and peered out into the darkness. He could barely see the moonlit silhouette of two men grinding at something at the corral gate.

Um, um. The livestock became restless.

Jonathan closed the door and spoke low, "Sam, two men tryin' to steal the cattle. I'm goin' to sneak behind one of the sheds so I can get near and have a better shot. Before I do that, I need you to put the dogs in the bedroom then come back to the front door with the shotgun to cover me when I tell you to. You won't be close enough to hit anythin', but the blast should scare them. But don't shoot until I tell you to. You understand?"

"Understood." Samuel shoved Boomer and Ann into the room with the other family members and returned to the front door.

"All right, are ya ready?"

"Yes, Pa."

Jonathan cautiously opened the door, enough for him to squeeze out into the warm, dark night and for his son to kneel behind the wall and keep watch. Crouching in the back of one of the sheds, he could get a clear view of the two men trying to saw off the lock on the corral gate. He could hear Spanish being whispered between them.

"*Rapido, rapido,*" one *bandito* said to the other who sawed at the fixture.

Sweat formed on Jonathan's brow, and his heart started beating faster. A quick vision of being on the battlefield, aiming at Rebels dressed in gray, flashed through his mind. He pushed back the thought. A sudden rush of adrenaline pounded through his veins, and he cocked his revolver, aimed it at the two thieves, and shouted, "Stop what you're doin' and put your hands up."

Juan, whose back was facing Jonathan, immediately dropped the hacksaw and raised his hands.

Wide-eyed, Miguel's instincts prompted him to reach for his pistol hanging on his hip.

Not giving the cattle rustlers a chance, Jonathan squeezed the trigger, and the shot rang out into the night as it blew away the gun on Miguel's belt and part of his right hand.

"*Ai, yi!*" Miguel fell to the ground, holding his wounded hand close to his chest, writhing in pain. Juan stayed in his frozen position staring at his fallen *compadre.*

Jonathan cocked the revolver again and moved in closer. He took the bandana from around his neck and threw it at Juan.

"You." He kicked at Juan's shin. "Take off your gun belt

and throw it on the ground."

Trembling, Juan obeyed the farm owner, and then raised his hands in the air.

"Now, wrap his hand with the bandana. Then remove his belt and tie his wrists behind him."

"Sí, señor." Juan grabbed the scarf and wrapped it tightly around his friend's wound. Miguel sat up to allow Juan to unfasten his belt to use it to secure his wrists together then Juan quickly lifted his palms and faced Jonathan.

"Are there any more men with you? You better tell me the truth, or I'll shoot your foot off next." The farm owner growled.

"No, no, señor. Just us." Juan mumbled between his chattering teeth.

Still pointing his revolver at the men, Jonathan bent his knees, reached for the gun belt, and called out to his son. "Sam, come out and bring some rope with ya."

Within minutes, Samuel was at Jonathan's side and saw the two men sitting on the ground, one with his hands held above his head.

"Son, I want you to point this gun at the feet of the man with his hands tied behind his back while I tie the other feller's wrists. I'm goin' to lasso these two together back-to-back and lock them in the shed for the marshal to pick up in the mornin'."

"All right, Pa."

As his son took hold of the cocked revolver and aimed it at the wounded man's foot, Jonathan tied the other *bandito's* wrists. Then he walked the two men to an empty stall inside the shed, sat them on the hay covered ground, and lassoed them together.

"Sorry, boys. I wish I could've given you better accommodations. But this is the best I can do on such short notice." Jonathan grimaced, trying to make light of the frightening evening. "Enjoy your night's rest." He shut the stall door, walked out of the shed, and locked the door.

The following morning, Jonathan rode over to the Snelling courthouse to inform the marshal of the prior evening's event. The lawman returned to the farm in a buckboard as the farm owner and his horse gallop alongside him.

Handcuffing the *vaqueros*, the officer then placed them in the wagon. "I don't think these fellas will be botherin' you anymore, Mr. Sower.

They'll be locked up in jail for a long time." He shook Jonathan's hand.

"Thank you, Marshal. Let's hope Mr. Montana doesn't send any more of his *bandito vaqueros* this way."

"I'll be sure to warn him to stay off your property. I'm sure this isn't the last we'll hear from him. Just be prepared." The officer winked at Jonathan, boarded his wagon, and hauled down the wayside path toward town.

A FEW DAYS LATER, Marshal Warner made a special visit to the wealthy cattleman's ranch to inform him of his jailed employees in Snelling. His visits to the Montana estate of late had not been pleasurable. Sitting on the front porch of Jackson Montana's hacienda, they both remained cool and courteous. The smoke from their Cuban cigars masked the pungent scent of manure from the lowing cattle in the nearby field.

"I suppose you have an idea for my visit, sir." Marshal Warner cocked his head to the left, squinted his eye, and raised his right brow as he studied the proud and staunch rancher, sitting erect, gazing out into the untamed landscape. The precarious relationship he had with this man weighed heavily on his conscience. He was careful to be fair to him, being a notorious community figure, all the while doing the same for those who had filed complaints against him for using his title and wealth to push them around to get his way.

Jackson puffed on his cigar and held his breath a few seconds longer than normal. The smoke exited through his mouth and nostrils as he spoke.

"I reckon it's in regards to my two missing employees. They haven't reported to me the last couple of days, nor to their posts."

The marshal turned his sight to the field, avoiding eye contact before he delivered the bad news. "Yes, sir." He paused, trying to find the right words. "I have incarcerated two Mexican nationals claiming to be your employees. I arrested them recently for attempted cattle rustling at one of Snelling's wheat farms." He shifted his gaze to Jackson, hoping for a reaction. But Jackson's firm self-control, as if bracing himself for an expected storm, was evident despite the tension in the air.

"Go on." The rancher took another long drag.

"We have a serious matter on our hands, Mr. Montana, and it doesn't look good for these men. There are witnesses who will attest to their attempted thievery." The marshal tugged on his cravat as if to release some pressure from his chest. "These men claim they were trying to get your cattle back. By your orders." He cocked his head toward Jackson. "However, as stated in the letter of complaint sent to you, your livestock were retained by the wheat farmer as recompense for the damage they caused on his property. I do believe that was made clear."

Jackson's jaw muscles tightened as he flicked his cigar ashes onto the porch.

"The crop council has done their share of enacting the fence law. It's time the beef council does their part as well. Jackson, you're going to have to move your cattle east into the foothills or restrain them to your property, even if it means fencing them in. If not, the penalty is going to be costly for you."

Humph. A plume of smoke billowed from Jackson's nostrils and mouth. "And what about my men?"

"Well, I'll tell you what's fair. Since they only attempted and didn't actually steal the cattle, they won't have to hang for their actions. This farmer is a good and just man and is not going to press charges. But he is demanding that these nationals be deported to their country at your expense. I can have a posse escort them out of California and have them send their bill to you. The farm owner also demanded that your cattle not graze any longer in Snelling, as much of the land there will soon become cropland."

Jackson took one more drag, dropped his cigar on the porch, and smashed it with his boot's heel. His actions insinuated that this conversation was over. So the officer stood and adjusted his holster. The rancher turned to him, extended his hand for a shake, his eyes red with fire.

"I guess I have no other choice than to comply."

"Good. I hope we can put this matter behind us."

Humph. "I'll do my best, Marshal."

The officer nodded, mounted his horse, and returned to Snelling.

The wood post fence added a week's delay to the work schedule, which Jonathan felt would not affect the harvest's timing. However, other problems would arise for the new California farmer.

9

The First Harvest

The temperature rose during the first two weeks in June, from the low nineties to a sweltering 107 degrees. The heat took its toll on the farmworkers, as well as a portion of the crop.

Tap, tap, tap. Yung removed his bamboo hat, inhaled deeply, and exhaled slowly to calm himself as he waited for someone to open the cabin door. The farmworkers and carpenters went home for the day as he stayed behind to meet with Jonathan and give his weekly report.

Anticipating his superintendent's arrival, Jonathan placed the *San Joaquin Argus* on the table and stood to answer the door.

"Yung, come inside and sit down." He pointed to the wood-slat chair. "Can I get ya a glass of lemonade?"

"Yes, please, Mr. Sower."

"I don't think it is any cooler in the cabin than it is outside, even with all the shutters opened." Jonathan made light conversation while he poured the beverage. "Mary and the children had a hard time focusing on schoolwork today, so they decided to go to the creek and go for a swim instead."

"Ah. Very good idea. I do same when I go home. Go to river and cool down." He reached for the glass, and they both gulped down the tangy refreshment.

"So how are the men fairin' in this heat?"

"Not so good, sir. Despite added water breaks, some have fainted and many more feeling light-headed."

"I was afraid of that." He leaned back in his chair, crossed his arms, and rubbed the stubble on his chin, thinking of a resolve. "Would it help if they started workin' two hours earlier, say six o'clock and finish before the peak of the heat, at three?"

"Yes. I was about to make same suggestion." Yung grinned. "I inform men to start new schedule next week." Squirming in his seat, he shifted his weight with rapid momentum and bobbed his right knee from the ball of his foot.

"Is there somethin' else ya want to tell me?" Jonathan studied his nervous fidgeting.

"Well." He paused and stared at his half-empty glass. "I am afraid I do, sir." Making eye contact, Yung took a deep breath and continued speaking in a low voice. "It's back-forty on eastern edge of property."

"Yes, what about it?" Jonathan sat erect waiting for an assault of complaints.

"No matter how much water we give wheat, it does not thrive. It is green for a while, but it never produce heads. Stalks just wither, and now with heat, completely dried and dead, sir."

"What? Another back-forty lost?" He searched the superintendent's face for any sign of hope, perhaps a raised eyebrow or even a feeble smile. Not a flinch. He only returned a downcast and fearful gaze.

"Men think it is because of rocks and stone slab in that area. We clear land on surface, but we did not know what lay below plow's blades. Rocky soil cannot hold moisture, especially in heat."

Jonathan propped his elbows on the table and planted his face in his palms. "Ugh."

"Sir, that's not all."

Covering his nose and mouth with his hands to help control the sense of nausea creeping up from his belly, Jonathan forced himself to look at his superintendent.

Aside from the perspiration caused by the heat, sweat flowed from Yung's body like a leaky water pail, leaving moist sweat stains on his dust-laden shirt. He used his sleeve to wipe his face, then proceeded. "Plants along river grow very well."

Jonathan crossed his arms in front of him on the table and smiled. "Whew. That's good news."

Yung shook his head. "No, sir. You see … plants I speak of are wild blackberry bushes, poison oak, poppy, and dandelion. If we pull them, we pull out wheat too. It'll take several planting seasons before we completely remove weeds. Unfortunately, weeds crowd crop in this back-forty."

Jonathan's heart sank. *Perhaps, I was over-ambitious in tryin' to plant more than half of the 500 acres which have never been plowed before. Maybe I should have taken more time to prepare the land before I planted.*

With shoulders down, Jonathan slumped into his chair, shaking his head in disbelief.

"All right, Yung. It is what it is. Again, there is nothin' more we can do. Let's do our best with the crops that remain."

"Yes, Mr. Sower."

All of a sudden, Yung's downcast gaze changed to a brilliant smile as he stared at the half-full glass before him, which he drank to moisten his dry mouth. His eyes shined and his jaw dropped.

Finally, he has some good news.

"I almost forgot, sir."

Yung stood from the chair, reached down into his pant's pocket, and pulled out a small glass vial with a cork lid. "This is for you." He placed it on the table in front of his down-trodden employer.

Jonathan stared at the two-ounce, liquid-filled container, his eyebrows coming together, thinking hard. "What is it?"

"Look closer, Mr. Sower."

Leaning toward the table, Jonathan positioned his face level to the small bottle. Settled in the bottom, an eighth of an inch deep, flakes of gold shimmered.

"No, this can't be. Where did you find this?" Joy sprang from the same well in his belly where he felt despair a moment earlier.

"Carpenters found when digging trenches from river. Since it is your property, gold belongs to you." Yung's face glowed.

"Oh, my Lord, this is an unexpected blessin'."

Jonathan diverted his eyes from the glimmering distraction to his faithful employee standing beside him. "Yung, you must thank the men for me for bein' honest in their findin's. They could've pocketed the gold and kept it to themselves, but they didn't."

"It would've been obvious, sir, if you saw them with gold pans instead of shovels or hammers, now that they are building barn. Work more important to them. Besides, our camp also near river, and if they want, they pan there."

Jonathan started to imagine the endless possibilities the gold could bring: more land, a larger estate, more livestock. *Maybe this is why the Lord brought us here. What if...* Then like lightning flashes across a dark sky, First Timothy 6:9 streaked through his mind. *But they that will be rich fall into temptation and a snare, and into many foolish and hurtful lusts, which drown men in destruction and perdition.*

Remembrance of the scripture caused him to realize the test of temptation set before him. *More, more, more. What am I thinkin'? There are enough problems with the amount of land I have now. God sent us here as an answer to our prayers to rebuild our lives again usin' our God-given skills on farmland, which we can pass on to our children and their children.*

Jonathan stood from the table and walked to the front door, opened it, and stepped out into the heat as his superintendent followed. He crossed his arms over his chest and scanned the horizon of his property.

"Let's keep the gold between you and me, Yung. I don't want others to know it's there. Let's not cause any more headaches than we need right now. Do you understand my reasonin'?"

The superintendent stood to the side of his employer, stared out into the fields, planted his feet firmly beneath him, and locked his left wrist in his right hand behind his back.

"Say no more, Mr. Sower, and trust me to do same." He turned to Jonathan and bowed. "Now, my stomach aches to be filled, sir. I must go home. Until Monday."

"Yes. Thank you again for your hard work and effort."

Yung stepped into the warm orange glow of the sunset toward the corral to fetch his horse then trotted back to the Chinese camp on the west end of town.

"CHILDREN, GO CHANGE AND HANG YOUR WET CLOTHES on the line outside, please." Jonathan could hear Mary and the brood returning from the creek, giggling and looking refreshed. His family's laughter always brightened his day. Raising his slumped shoulders, he met his wife's gaze.

"How did your meetin' go?" She stood next to him as he scribbled numbers on a piece of paper at the kitchen table.

Jonathan had hidden the glass vial in his sock drawer and returned to the table to focus on the financial implications caused by the loss of some of his wheat. "Not good, Mary. I don't think this first harvest is gonna do well for us this year. Not only is there damage from the cattle, but part of the crop grew on rocky soil, withered and died, and another section is overwhelmed by weeds. All of this work and I think we'll barely break even."

"Now don't you go hangin' up your fiddle just yet, Jon. We both believe God wanted us to move here. We need to trust Him for His provision. Most likely, this isn't goin' to be the best year, but this is only your first. Don't give up already. There's much to be thankful for, thanks to the good Lord! The children and I love bein' here. We've met some fine people, and it's all been a blessin' so far. God never promised an easy path. You must be patient and wait on the Lord." Mary placed her arm around her husband's shoulders and squeezed him close to her hip as she glanced at the paper in front of him.

"Yep, you're right, dear. Perhaps I pushed myself too hard by workin' non-stop since we've arrived. I haven't had much time to sit down to thank God and ask Him for His help and strength. He is missin' in my life of late. I've forgotten who is in control. I do need to trust Him more." Nodding his head, he folded his notes and shoved them in his shirt pocket.

Mary shuffled into their bedroom and returned as swiftly as she left.

"Here, concentrate on this for a while instead of that piece of paper."

She placed their hard-bound family Bible on the table.

Jonathan chuckled. "Oh, darlin', ya do have the gift of encouragement."

She kissed him on his forehead and proceeded to make supper.

While Mary, Sarah, and Naomi busied themselves with cooking and the boys with unfinished homework, Jonathan felt compelled to read the book of Job. The story unfolded, stating how God allowed Satan to test Job's faith and love for the Lord. The enemy used difficult circumstances to take everything from this God-fearing man: his home, his family, and even his health. However, Job continued to acknowledge and trust God's judgment and goodness despite his misfortune. In the end, God restored all he had lost because of his proven faithfulness to God.

Surely, God must be testin' my faith in Him. I must remain faithful, trustin' in God's word and direction for us, even if the first crop did not do as well as I had hoped. Jonathan realized this would be one test amongst many from God.

THE FARMWORKERS BEGAN REAPING THE WHEAT in early August, and the carpenters finished building the barn and were ready to start the farmhouse.

The first harvest would be a disappointment. Twenty-five percent of the crops damaged by the cattle never recovered. Ten percent died on the stony ground on the far eastern side of the property, and weeds choked another ten percent that grew next to the river.

The remaining fifty-five percent was harvested and bundled, thrown into wagons, and hauled over several trips to Nielsen's Flour Mill in Merced Falls.

The milling factory stood close to the Merced River, using the natural forces of the rushing water to provide energy to move the heavy grinding wheel. Next to the mill were two grain silos, each with a long ladder used for baling and separating the chaff, and the three-story warehouse and office facility was adjacent to it.

Harold Nielson, the owner, swiveled around on the wood chair on wheels behind his L-shaped oak desk, which had bins stacked with paperwork on the wing to the right of him. Jonathan sat across from him waiting for the final measurement of the grain. The wood floor showed wear from the door to his desk from the daily traffic of people who came to do business with him. A foreman came in and handed him a piece of paper indicating the grain's weight, and then he exited the room. Nielson calculated the purchase price.

"You have 330 tons, Mr. Sower. Minus one-third returned to you for replanting next year, leaves 220 tons, which I will buy from you. My going rate is thirty dollars a ton. So that'll come to $6,600." The owner pointed to the figures on the receipt.

"Thank you, Mr. Nielson. Next year I plan on doin' better and doublin' this amount. This is my first harvest on virgin land, and I've come out on the little end of the horn."

"Well, I'll be ready for you." He handed Jonathan a note for $6,600 and shook hands. "Thank you for your business."

Jonathan's portion of seed was bagged and loaded onto his wagons. The factory workers heaved the remains into a long elevator where they baled the chaff, and the seeds ground into flour, bagged, then delivered to the general stores and bakeries.

Some profit came from Jonathan's first crop, but not nearly what he had hoped. He still praised God and thanked Him for His goodness and His provision for his family.

Driving one of the empty wagons home on Merced Falls Road, which ran parallel to the river, he fought the temptation of what its banks could offer.

No, don't even begin to think about it. Look away. It'll consume you: your thoughts, your time from the farm and family, and your money. Now is not the time. You must focus on establishin' the business first. The deep inner voice rattled in his head the entire drive home like a drummer boy's unwavering beat on his drum.

10

The Invitation

"Enjoy your evenin', men." Jonathan waved from inside the barn as the parade of farmworkers put away their tools and headed home. He and Samuel were settling the horses into their stalls when the sound of someone clearing his throat buzzed his ear.

"Hello, is anyone home?" The voice pierced through the dimly lit building.

"Hey, Pa, are ya expectin' someone?" His son whispered to his father while he closed the stall gate.

"Not that I know of." He kept his voice low as he studied the back-lit figure standing at the opening of the barn door with the golden sun setting behind him. The glorious beams surround him like a glowing halo. "Who's inquirin'?"

"Good day to you, sir! My name is Pastor Daniel McSwan. Please allow me to introduce myself and invite you to a camp meeting."

Realizing this was a friendly visitation, Jonathan proceeded toward the sunlit door as Samuel followed. He extended a hand to the unexpected visitor, who was neatly dressed in a brown vest, linen frock coat, tan trousers, and a wide-brim palm leaf hat over his dusty blond, short-cropped hair.

"How do you do, Pastor? I'm Jonathan Sower, and this is my eldest son, Samuel. Welcome to our farm."

"I'm doing well, thank you. My wife Ruth and I made it our aim to come out and meet you folks." He pointed to where she sat in the carriage and continued as they moseyed toward her. "I'll be preaching at a camp meeting Friday, September eighth through Sunday, the tenth at Branche's Ferry, in Tuolumne County, a short distance below La Grange. I realize it's about ten miles from your farm, but I figure since the harvest is over, a relaxing retreat might be enjoyable for you and your family."

Hmm. A warm smile, gentle eyes, kind spirit, neat appearance. All right, you got my attention. Jonathan sized up the pastor, as camp meeting memories of when he was a young boy filtered through his mind.

He recalled when his old hometown, Perryville, Kentucky, had only a handful of residential farmers. Traveling evangelists from large townships visited, calling all those living in outlying areas to rendezvous in a nearby open field to hear God's word. They preached under a brush arbor made from tree trunks with small circumferences for posts, branches used as crossbeams, and freshly cut bows stacked on top for shade. He still remembered the ache on his bottom from the crudely made pew benches and the pinch from an adult sitting behind him whenever he and his sister Nicole were noisy and wiggling too much. Overall, delightful memories excite him once again of singing worship songs with all the gusto he could muster, playing with other children, and eating all the delicious food during the Saturday evening dinner gathering.

Visions of his own youngsters flashed before his mind's eyes. *Other children! Oh, my Lord, mine have not met anyone their age yet since we moved here, nor have they been to a camp meetin'. This is somethin' they must attend and experience.*

The rest of the Sower clan scurried out of the cabin toward the corral. "Speakin' of family … Pastor and Mrs. McSwan, please meet my wife, Mary, daughters, Sarah, who is fourteen, Naomi, who is ten, and our youngest son, David, who is nine years old." Jonathan nudged David forward, and he extended his hand to the preacher as the girls curtsied.

"Pastor and his lovely wife are invitin' us to a camp meetin' in a couple of weekends from today in La Grange. Now that the harvest is over, suppose we get away and go have some fun before school starts."

"Oh, Papa, can we, please?" The children cheered and bounced happily around him as his wife smiled and nodded.

"Well, Pastor, it's been a coon's age since I've attended a camp meetin'. I believe you can be expectin' our family to be present because we haven't found a church yet in these parts," Jonathan said. "To tell you the truth, I've been feelin' quite thirsty of late, if you know what I mean. It's been too long since we've sensed the touch of God in our lives."

"Praise be to the Lord!" The Pastor clasped his hands together and raised his eyes toward heaven then at each of the family members. "I also preach every Sunday morning at nine o'clock during the late fall and winter months at the courthouse in Snelling. You folks are welcome to join us. In the spring and summer, I conduct the camp meetings in several foothill counties. I feel called to bring the gospel of good news to people living in remote places, especially to the border ruffians in the gold mining areas."

"Lord willin', we will be able to attend the Sunday services too." Mary nodded her head. "By the way, we are about to sit down for supper. We will love it if you stay awhile!"

"Oh, my! How thoughtful of you, Mrs. Sower," Ruth said as she turned on the carriage bench and repositioned the hoops under her amber-printed day dress to make eye contact with Mary. "Normally we'd take up your offer, but the hour is getting late and we have one more visit to make before dark. Thank you, though. Perhaps we might arrange another day to dine together."

The muted rays of the setting sun highlighted Ruth's strawberry-blond ringlets beneath her wide-brimmed, straw touring hat trimmed with white satin ribbon and wildflowers.

"Well, I'll leave you with this invitation with the details of the camp meeting. We look forward to seeing you folks and spending some time with you." Pastor McSwan handed the sheet of paper to Jonathan, shook his hand, and hopped back into the buggy. Naomi and David chased them to the end of the wayside path and waved them good-bye.

11

The Camp Meeting

"Sakes alive, I thought this day would never get here." Sarah finished packing the last basket of food with her mother and sister for the four-day trip.

"No joshin'. That was the longest two weeks of waitin' I've ever had in all my life," Naomi said as she gathered in each hand the wicker containers filled with the weekend's sustenance to bring to the Conestoga.

Sarah wiped her hands on her apron, raised her left eyebrow, and half smiled, humored by her young sister's naïve statement. *Well, enjoy every moment of this vacation before you and David start school next Monday, Naomi.* She did not want to ruin the excitement of the trip by reminding them the new schoolhouse awaits their return.

"Well, I think that's the whole caboodle, girls. Let's get these baskets loaded. I hope the boys are rarin' to go," her mother said.

THE FAMILY ARRIVED AT BRANCHE'S FERRY in the late afternoon, with time to set up and prepare supper. Sarah craned her neck from the wagon bench, combing the camp's crowd for others her age.

Pastor McSwan greeted them and directed them to their site. Two large circles of wagons formed one inside the other around a wooden platform stage in the center. Within the circle stood several brush arbors. As soon as her father parked, they disembarked and walked over to the pastor's family.

"I'm so glad you made it here safely! Y'all remember my wife, Ruth." The pastor turned to his spouse, who then reached over to her mother and gave her a big hug. "Now, you can meet our children. This handsome young man is Joshua, who is fifteen, and our darling little girl Rebecca, who is eight."

"Hello, welcome to camp." The bashful youth stepped out from behind his father and greeted them.

Sarah's eyes met with his, and she could feel a flush of warmth on her face. *Oh my, a boy. He is quite handsome too.*

Joshua shoved his fists into his brown linen trousers with suspenders and scuffed at some pebbles with the toe of his right boot.

Sarah took the opportunity to examine the timid fellow about her age while he diverted his attention away from her. The ends of his neatly cut, brownish-blond hair peeked from under his dark cap and brushed the collar of his russet-plaid shirt. She shifted her gaze when his sister approached out of breath from running around the camp with other children.

"Hi, there!" Rebecca waved to the family and turned to her father. "Can I go play now, Father?" Her gold ringlets tied in a ponytail bounced as she pleaded. The lace of her pant drawer peeked beneath her cotton printed day dress, which came to her shins, and her black ankle-high boots covered in mud gave warning to inevitable cleaning.

"Well, wait a minute, young lady. Why don't you take Naomi and David with you…if it's all right with their mama and papa." Pastor McSwan clutched his daughter's hand and waited for her parents' answer.

"I don't have any objections," her mother said. "They'll only get in the way while we're pitchin' camp." She turned to the young siblings. "Children be on your best behavior. Try not to get your clothes too dirty. We'll be eatin' supper in about an hour, so be back in time to wash up, you hear?"

Pearly whites glistened between a rosy pink smile as Rebecca grabbed Naomi and David's hand. "Come on. We're making a maypole down by the river." The children scurried away giggling.

"Joshua, why don't ya help these good folks set up camp while your mother and I continue to direct the other people arriving?" the pastor said.

"Sure, Father." He turned to her father. "Just show me what I need to do, Mr. Sower."

Sarah's soul seemed to reach out and touch his as he walked by her. Her knees felt like jelly.

Her parents went to work directing her, her brother, and Joshua.

"Samuel, will you gather some wood to start a fire and ready the stove?" her father asked. "Joshua, would you mind helpin' me to put up this canopy by the side of the wagon?"

"Not at all, sir."

"Sarah, you can help me by huskin' the corn on the wagon's tailgate and puttin' out plates while I make the fried chicken and biscuits."

"Okay, Ma." Before she fetched the basket, she peered at Joshua as he separated the wood poles, ropes, and stakes for the canopy next to the wagon.

Using her shadow, Sarah centered her straw hat correctly on her head and over her braided bun at the nape of her neck. She twisted, visualizing the silhouette of her apron's bow tied in the back of her floral-printed day dress. *Golly, where's my lookin' glass when I need one? Oh well, that'll have to do.*

Sarah realized this was the first time she had met anybody or regarded any boy her age since they left Kentucky. Her heart beat fast in her chest, and warmth rushed through her body like a soothing bath. The new experience pleased her senses yet frightened her at the same time, not knowing how to act or react in the presence of a possible suitor.

Okay, try to relax. Whatever you do, don't trip in front of him. Oh dear, I hope food isn't stuck in my teeth.

She stared at Joshua then at the basket, which beckoned only ten yards away but appeared to be a mile away. Her feet did not want to cooperate. She felt like a baby walking for the first time.

I can do this. I'm almost there. Oh, he's lookin' at me. I know it. Quick. Just grab the basket and go.

Finally, at the wagon, she used both hands to lift the heavy ladened container and underestimated its weight. "Ugh."

Joshua jumped to her aid and reached for the bushel, brushing her hand. "Do ya need help?"

Startled, she pulled her hand away and stepped back, locking her eyes with his. Two translucent topaz gems filled her senses. "I, uh, no, yes, maybe, I mean..." *Sarah, you oaf. Get a hold of yourself.*

"Where would you like it? At the table?" His sweet voice, like warm butter, melted one word into another as he lifted the basket and stood by her side.

Her mouth opened, but nothing would come out, so she nodded instead. The boyish grin on Joshua's face mesmerized her.

"Okay. I'll bring it over." He turned and began walking to the table.

Gawking at his backside, Sarah finally snapped out of her daze, cleared her throat, brushed her apron, straightened her hat, and scurried after him.

He placed the bushel by her mother, who stood dusting the chicken pieces with flour.

"Here ya go, ma'am."

Sarah noticed her mother pausing and staring at Joshua as he set the basket down. Then her mother's eyes met hers, watching her every move as she followed close behind him. *Oh no. I better wipe this smile off my face before Ma senses I am up to somethin'.*

"Why, thank you, young man. Would you like to join us for supper?" her mother said.

No, Ma! Let me catch my breath first. "Uh ... yes, mighty kind of you, Joshua, for carryin' that for me." *Please, don't stay, although I really wish you would. I'm not ready yet.*

"I'd love to, Mrs. Sower. But I think my parents already planned for me to help them this evening. Maybe another night?"

"Gladly. We have plenty of food to go around. Come over any time you are available."

The warmth of his smile sent waves of pleasant emotions within Sarah that she never felt before.

"I will try my best, ma'am. All right, I better get back to what

I was doing." He returned to the unfinished canopy.

"Are ya okay, dear?" Her mother's voice seemed distant as she stood gawking at Joshua as he moved further away.

"What?" She turned to her mother and gathered her thoughts. "Oh, uh, yes, Ma. I'm fine. I didn't realize the basket was so heavy. I'm so glad he offered to lend a hand."

She simpered and began husking the corn to avoid any interrogation from her all-knowing mother.

With their chores finished, Joshua bid good night to the family and glanced at Sarah one more time. "I'll see everyone tomorrow!"

AT NINE O'CLOCK IN THE MORNING, Jonathan helped his wife by carrying blankets to the center lawn area under the brush arbors around the stage as other families also gathered. There they sang songs and listened to the pastor preach. A two-hour break for lunch and dinner provided enough social time in between sermons. The evening services invited those who desired to pray and worship all night, or as long as they wanted. Jonathan found himself amongst the real pious of the faith worshipping until the sun came up, breaking for breakfast, getting a quick shut-eye, and starting again at nine.

The next two days marked milestones for his family as they experienced a spiritual awakening in their lives. They worshiped and sang hymns from the *Camp Meeting Chorister* hymnal. "Come All Ye Weary Travelers," "Great God, Where'er We Pitch Our Tent," "How Pleasant Are These Tents, Oh Lord."

They enjoyed every Spirit-inspired word Pastor McSwan spoke. Even Naomi and David seemed to glow when he explained what salvation through Jesus Christ meant.

The charismatic minister encouraged those who heard the gospel's message for the first time. "If you have not received Jesus Christ as your Lord and Savior, then I want you to come to the altar and I will pray for you. The Father is tugging at your heart telling you He loves you. Confess to Him, and He will forgive you of your sins and grant you everlasting life." He continued to preach, and many people came to the wooden stage platform.

Opening the hymnal book to Hymn 12, "The Invitation," he sang,
"Hark! The Jubilee is sounding
Oh the joyful news to come,
Free salvation is proclaimed,
In and through God's own dear Son,
Now we have an invitation,
To the meek and lowly Lamb,
Glory, honor and salvation,
Christ the Lord is come to reign."

Jonathan closed his eyes to worship and allowed the song to penetrate his soul.

"Jon." He heard his wife gasp and felt her nudge, but he was enjoying the blissful interlude with God.

Again, she prodded him. "Look, darlin'. The children."

He opened his eyes and turned in the direction his offspring sat, but they weren't there. His line of sight drew him to where the new converts gathered. At the foot of the stage, he beheld them standing with their hands raised to heaven and their faces shining with the glory of receiving Jesus as their Lord and Savior.

He embraced his wife as her eyes reddened and pooled with moisture. "Oh, darlin'. Now we know for sure our children are saved."

"Jon, I am so glad we came to this meetin'. Our old church never afforded them this opportunity to announce their faith publicly. I assumed they accepted Jesus Christ as their Lord and Savior because we mentioned the gospel so many times to them." She shuddered. "Maybe they were too young to understand or weren't ready. Perhaps they needed to hear it from someone else."

"Mary, Mary." He kissed his wife's hand and stared deep into her eyes. "We did our part, and so did our other church. All is good. Didn't Apostle Paul say in 1 Corinthians 3:6, 'I have planted, Apollos watered, but God gave the increase?'"

"You're right, Jon."

He embraced her, and they continued in reverence as they listened to the man of God.

"Now, recite after me this simple prayer of faith. Heavenly Father…" The minister addressed the new believers.

"Heavenly Father," The new converts said.

The pastor broke down the invocation, and the group recited along. "I come to You asking for the forgiveness of my sins. I confess with my mouth and believe with my heart that Jesus is Your Son and that he died on the cross at Calvary so I might be forgiven and be granted eternal life in the Kingdom of Heaven. Father, I believe that Jesus rose from the dead. I ask You to come into my life and be my personal Lord and Savior. I repent of my sins and will worship You all the days of my life. Because Your word is truth, I accept that I am born again and cleansed by His blood. In Jesus' name, Amen."

Jonathan would not take his eyes off of his children so that he could implant this memory forever in his mind. They looked like angels worshipping God with their hands raised to heaven. But then Sarah put her arms down and was craning her neck as if looking for someone. *What are you doin', child? Who are you lookin' for? Ma and I are right here.* Sarah's eyes caught his, and she waved back. However, she continued to survey the crowd about her when finally she froze, fixating her gaze on something or someone. Jonathan directed his sight to where she was looking, and there he saw Joshua, praying with the new converts next to his father.

SUNDAY MORNING SERVICE arrived sooner than they hoped. Everyone gathered by the stage to be filled with God's words one final time before returning home.

"In closing this glorious weekend, allow me to leave you with the passage from 2 Peter 1:5-11 to abide by," Pastor McSwan said. "And beside this, giving all diligence, add to your faith virtue; and to virtue knowledge; and to knowledge temperance; and to temperance patience; and to patience godliness; and to godliness brotherly kindness; and to brotherly kindness charity. For if these things be in you, and abound, they make you that ye shall neither be barren nor unfruitful in the knowledge of our Lord Jesus Christ. But he that lacketh these things is blind, and cannot see afar off, and hath forgotten that he was purged from his old sins. Wherefore the rather, brethren, give diligence to make your calling and election sure: for if ye do these things, ye shall never fall: For so an entrance shall be ministered unto you abundantly into the everlasting kingdom of our Lord and Saviour Jesus Christ."

After the service, the Sowers said their final farewells to Pastor McSwan and his family. Sarah tried her best to bury her feelings, should she never cross paths with Joshua again, as they glanced at each other for the last time. She relayed to him a desirous and hopeful smile and climbed into the wagon. Their ride back home passed quickly because they chattered on about the weekend and sang their favorite hymns along the way. However, Joshua flooded every corner of Sarah's thoughts.

12

New Routines

"Rise and shine, David and Naomi. It's seven o'clock. We'll be leavin' for school in an hour." Mary clanked her cast iron skillet with her wooden spoon as she scooped scrambled eggs into plates at the kitchen table. Placing the weighty cooking pan back on the stove and wiping her hands on her apron, she realized the new routine would require habituation. She stood at the children's bedroom doorway and shoved her knuckles on her hips.

The early morning sun filtered in through the cracks of the shutters, sending scattered beams into the log cabin, poking her ten-year-old daughter's eyes.

"Oh, Ma." Naomi flipped over to her other side away from the light and buried her face in the pillow. "Why can't we just have lessons at home like we've been doin'?"

"Come on now, children. We've discussed this. Imagine all the friends you'll meet. You'll be the first students at the brand new Snelling School. We need to support our community."

David sat up in his bunk and rubbed his eyes. "Why doesn't Sam and Sarah have to go?"

"Because they're done schoolin'. Besides, Pa and I need them workin' on the farm. Once you're old enough, we'll have you wakin' up at five in the mornin' milkin' the cows and feeding the animals. So if you think gettin' up early for school is hard, wait till your farmin' chores begin. Come on, lazybones. Up. Up." The goal-driven mother tugged at Naomi's quilt on the top bunk.

"Ugh." The lackadaisical young girl groaned.

"Naomi, you've been chompin' at the bit to wear your new olive-colored day dress and bonnet. Now's your chance," Mary said. "And David, I've set out your new gray trousers, suspenders, and blue plaid shirt. Don't forget your cap hangin' on the wall."

She turned toward the kitchen to pack their lunch baskets. "Come and eat your breakfast when you're done dressin'."

The children huffed as they put on their clothing. A few minutes later, they sat slumped at the table playing with the scrambled eggs on their plates and oat cereal in their bowls, without hurry.

"Come on, David. Don't dawdle." Mary tossed the dirty dishes into the washbasin. "Tie your boot laces, the both of you. We must leave now before we're late."

THE NEWLY BUILT SCHOOL sat at the edge of town closest to the farm, an easy quarter-of-a-mile walk from the cabin, along the wayside path of the wheat field. It was painted an eggshell white with brick-red trim on the shutters and door and surrounded by about two acres of leveled ground and four outhouses to the left of the building.

The class started at eight-thirty. Mary, Naomi, and David arrived at eight-fifteen, leaving enough time to meet Snelling's first instructor and become familiar with the school grounds and classroom. David swung the door open for her and his sister.

Standing at the entrance, mouth agape, mother and children surveyed the cheerful, well-lit room. It had two large windows on each side of the building, expelling an abundance of natural sunlight. Low shelves, fully endowed with stout books of different bright colors and sizes, sat beneath each window. Between the two windows on the left side hung an oversized painting of George Washington in a dark brown wooden frame. Hanging between the windows on the right was a map of the world, framed in the same color.

Two rows of five, two-person, oak and metal student desks with a honey glow filled the room. On each desk awaited an eight-by-ten slate with chalk and a textbook called *The New England Primer*.

The pungent fumes of fresh paint and chalk dust tickled David's nose. "Achoo!"

"Bless you." Mr. Cavern sat peering up at them behind his molasses brown desk, positioned in the front to the left. In one hand he held an opened Bible and in the other a steel-head ink pen. In the corner behind him proudly stood the United States flag and staff. Centered on the wall hung a large blackboard with his name and *Welcome to Snelling Grade School*. To the right corner, a stool with a dunce hat created fear for unruly students in front of a black wood-burning stove.

"Thank you." David rubbed his nose with his sleeve.

"Don't be shy. Come in." The middle-aged instructor stood from his desk, tugged at the wrinkles of his gray-blue Crocker vest, and adjusted his jacket with matching trousers. He moseyed toward them.

"Hello, madam, students. My name is Mr. Cavern. Welcome to Snelling School." A gold tooth glistened at the side of his mouth when he smiled.

"Good morning to you, sir. I am Mrs. Sower from the farm just behind the school." Mary extended her hand. "We live around the corner, on La Grange Road. These are two of my four children, Naomi and David. The two eldest, Samuel and Sarah, completed their education and are helpin' at home."

He tilted his head back and chuckled. Not one dark pomade curl fell out of place. "Ah yes. I am familiar with your farm and family, from a distance, that is. From my classroom window, I can get a glimpse of all of you working. Well, I am most certainly glad to have you as my pupils this first year, Naomi and David. Please find a seat and we'll begin class in a few minutes."

Muffled chatter transition into gasps when the schoolhouse door opened, and about a dozen students and parents rushed in. Her children's countenance converted from frowns to enormous grins and squeals when Rebecca McSwan entered with her mother. They waved and invited her to sit near them.

Ah, they will do fine in school. All worries are forgotten. Mary giggled.

"Please, do come in and take a seat, children. Parents, if you don't mind, will you kindly stand in the back of the room?" The teacher pointed as they found their places and settled down.

"My name is Mr. Cavern, and I want to welcome all of you to Snelling's premier grade school." He had his speech well-rehearsed, explaining classroom rules, etiquette, and the importance of punctuality. "I will gladly stay afterward if you have any further questions or suggestions. So until then, you are dismissed so that we may begin our day. Thank you." The parents shuffled out of the room, closed the door behind them, and returned to their homes.

AS MARY APPROACHED THE FARM, she viewed Sarah in the barn as she finished milking the cows. Samuel, Boomer, and Ann were busy wrangling the horses and oxen to the corral to be fed and watered. When she entered the house, she noticed Jonathan at the kitchen table working on the farmhouse plans.

"How'd the children do with their new teacher?" Her husband asked.

"Oh, they did fine. Mr. Cavern seems to be a gentle and self-controlled soul. I think they will enjoy his teachin'."

She wrapped her apron around her waist and pulled the jar of flour from the top shelf of the wood-framed pantry to make bread. In a large bowl she mixed the ingredients together and kneaded it into dough. Next, she covered the lump with a damp towel and placed it next to the stove to allow it to rise and double its size.

SAMUEL WAS FILLING THE WATER TROUGH in the corral when Patrick pulled up in his wagon. The free-roaming ol' man in dusty dungarees jumped off and hustled over to the fence, placing one foot on the lower rail and his arms on the upper.

"Hey, Sam. How'd you like to help me deliver some sacks of flour and barley the next few days to the general stores in Coulterville, Chinese Camp, and Jamestown?" Patrick's gruff sounding voice bellowed.

Samuel's ears perked up when Patrick mentioned Jamestown. Visions of prospectors panning at the creek and cashing in their gold findings flashed through his mind. He put the water buckets down and walked toward the fence.

"You bet I'd like to go." Samuel grinned.

"Well, let's ask your pa and ma. We'll probably be gone a li'l more than a week, so you'll need to pack a few things, like a blanket and a warm coat. We'll be camping along the way, so bring your shotgun so we can do some huntin'," Patrick said wide-eyed as he slapped his knee with his right hand.

Samuel's mind rushed with images of himself wading in the water, panning, and holding gold nuggets shining with brilliance. He felt as if he were floating on a cloud as he and the rugged cargo-hauling soon-to-be employer walked over to the cabin to talk to his parents.

"GOOD DAY TO YA, FOLKS," Patrick greeted as he sat at the end of the table next to Samuel's father.

"Well, howdy, Pat. Nice of you to drop by. How's things goin' for you?" Jonathan put his pen down and crinkled his brows, curious about Pat's unexpected visit and his son charging at his heels.

"Jon, you know this is a busy time of the year for me, deliverin' grain to the general stores in several counties. Sure could use some assistance, and I'm hopin' you would allow me to borrow Sam to help for 'bout nine days. My boy would've been helpin' me if he hadn't died of cholera five years ago. He'd be Sam's age now." Pat's eyes watered and face crumpled as he cleared his throat. After a brief pause, he collected himself and resumed his divulgence. "We'll be makin' deliveries in the foothill towns of Coulterville, Chinese Camp, and Jamestown. I'll give him a handsome wage if he lends me a hand."

Patrick laid his straw hat on the kitchen table and brushed the moisture from his face.

Jonathan paused for a moment and glanced over at Mary, who stopped wiping the flour off the other end of the table. They searched each other's eyes for an answer.

"Don't look at me, Jon. You'll have to make that decision. This would be a good time for Sam to go since the harvest is over. I suppose, between you, Sarah, and I, we can manage his chores for a week."

Jonathan realized that his son worked hard and always responded to his beck and call. Working a job outside of the farm would be an opportunity for his eldest to learn to be independent, proving he surpassed hobbledehoy.

"Hmm." The worrisome father placed his elbows on the table, folded his hands, and brought them under his chin. "Do you think you can handle things on your own, son, and take instruction from Pat as your boss?"

"Yes, sir, Pa. I'll do anythin' he tells me to do."

"Well, Pat, he is all yours, for nine days, that is. How would you like to bring Boomer along with you boys?"

"I can't thank you enough, Jon! Yes, we'll take your hound with us and Sam's rifle in case we plan on doin' some huntin'... if it's all right with you, of course."

"Sure. Why not? You may need it for protection, too. Sam knows how to handle his guns." Jonathan grinned, feeling the pride swell in his heart.

"Okay, I have to make a delivery to the mercantile today, then I'll come back in the mornin' to get ya, Sam." Patrick shook Jonathan's hand and patted Samuel on his shoulder. "Thank you too, ma'am. Good day to y'all." He tipped his hat, exited the cabin, climbed back into his wagon, and left for town.

After finishing his chores, the eager youth collected the things he needed for the hauling journey. He rolled up his feather mattress, gum blanket, and his mother's old, thick quilt. In a canvas sack, he packed one linen shirt, his long underwear, and a heavy wool coat. The Colt revolver, gun belt, and his Winchester rifle secured in its leather sleeve leaned against the wall beside his belongings.

Mary could hear Naomi and David's footsteps on the cabin steps as they returned home in the late afternoon. They could not stop chattering about the friends they met and the new things they learned.

"Okay, y'all. Supper is ready, so why don't you wash up, and we'll discuss everythin' at the kitchen table." Mary arranged the dishes on the table as Jonathan removed his work. Her heart filled with warmth reflecting upon each family member's progressive stations in their lives.

They sat down, and Jonathan bowed his head. "Dear Lord, we thank You for Your provisions and this delicious food prepared by the loving hands of my wife. Bless it now to nourish our bodies. Amen."

As the children passed the meal around the table, she and her husband interjected comments and parental guidance while Samuel, Naomi, and David cheerfully shared their happy news.

Samuel petitioned his brother and sisters. "I'm gonna be leavin' tomorrow for about nine days with Patrick to make deliveries to some general stores in the foothills. Would y'all mind doin' my chores 'til I get back? If you'd do me this favor, I promise to return it one day."

"Samuel, don't make any promises ya can't keep," Mary said. "We're family here, and we're to assist one another unconditionally, as long as it is for somethin' good and not evil."

"Well, I would appreciate your help." He grimaced. "This'll be a grand outin' for me. We'll be goin' to Jamestown. Do y'all remember the gold prospectors? Maybe Pat and I will have time to do some pannin' while we're there."

"All right, Sam, if you strike it rich, I expect you to keep to your promise to pay us back." Sarah chuckled.

"What about you two, Naomi and David? How was your first day of school?" Jonathan asked, staring at them intensely while he ate.

"It kinda started out scary." The young boy shifted in his chair and stared at his plate. In an instant, like a strike of a matchstick, his face lit up and returned his father's gaze. "Then we saw Rebecca, and she sat right next to us, and I wasn't afraid anymore. I thought Mr. Cavern was gonna be mean, but he is a real dandy, and he's teachin' us our alphabet by memorizin' things from the Bible."

"Yes ... like what?" Mary asked. "Why don't you recite somethin', David?"

"Well..." He stared upwards as if searching his brain for the day's lesson. "A ... In Adam's fall, we sinned all. B ... Heaven to find, the Bible mind. And C ... and C..."

"And C ... Christ crucified, for sinners died." Naomi interrupted her little brother.

"You show off."

"How about you, Naomi? What was your favorite subject today?" Jonathan asked.

"I met three new girlfriends my age. Their names are Ruby, Della Mae, and Abigail. The thing I enjoyed best about school is recess and lunch break." Naomi grinned like the Cheshire cat and wiggled her eyebrows up and down several times as she chomped on her green beans.

"Now, sweetheart." Mary balked at her daughter's shortsighted comment. "You better had paid good attention to your schoolin', unless ya want to grow up beggin' on the streets somewhere when you get older."

"I know, I know. You told me that a hundred times."

"Young lady, if I hear you talkin' to your ma like that one more time, you'll get the rod." Jonathan pointed his index finger at his frivolous minded daughter. "You owe her an apology."

"Sorry, Ma, I'll pay better attention at school."

Mary nodded, accepting Naomi's admission when a scraping sound came from Sarah's plate, diverting her focus. Her heart sank a notch to see her eldest daughter frowning, sitting quiet, and dragging her fork around the food while she listened to her sibling's gaiety. *Oh, dear. What's troublin' Sarah? Maybe she's feelin' left out.* Her mother's intuition reminded her of a certain young fellow who brought a glow to her daughter's face.

Hmm, I bet she would love to spend time with Joshua McSwan again. How can I do this without embarrassin' her? I'm sure she doesn't want me to know about her feelings for this boy.

All at once, the answer came to her mind. She placed her palm over her eldest daughter's hand holding the fork to stop her from mindlessly playing with her food.

"Sarah, since Naomi and David will be in school, an' Samuel gone for a week, why don't you and I go into town tomorrow and pick up some material for a new dress? Pastor McSwan told me he will be preachin' at the county courthouse two Sundays from now. I thought we all ought to go to hear him again once Sam is back. Fourteen days is plenty of time to sew the latest fashion."

Sarah's long face glowed once more as it did at the camp meeting. "Okay, Mama. I would love that." She sat up straight, finished her dinner, and entered into her brothers' and sister's conversation, encouraging them in their new endeavors.

13

The First Leg

Samuel and Boomer sat by the hearth ready for Patrick Tuesday morning at eight o'clock. The gold panning opportunity in Jamestown and the weeklong hauling to the Sierra foothills kept him awake most of the night. Finally, the long-awaited rap came and he flew to the cabin door to greet his new employer.

"Good Morning, folks. Thanks again for lendin' your son. I really need his help," Patrick said to Samuel's family, who were seated at the table having breakfast. "Ya ready to hit the trail, Sam?"

"Mornin', Pat. Yep. Let's ramble." Samuel flung his rifle on his back.

"All right. Throw your things in the wagon."

"Love you, Ma and Pa. Don't worry none." The sprightly youth gave them quick hugs. *I've gotta get outta here before she asks me another question about what I packed and what we are plannin' to eat on the trail. Ma, you drive me crazy sometimes.*

"We love you too, son. Have a great time," his father said.

"Be sure to stay warm now and mind Patrick's instruction," his mother said.

"I will, Ma." Samuel turned on his heels and whistled for his hound. "Come on, Boomer!"

They climbed into the Prairie Schooner and drove six miles

to Nielson's Flour Mill. Sam stayed in the wagon at the loading docks as Pat went into the owner's office on the third floor to receive the delivery schedule and the first payment installment. After the foreman loaded the sacks, Patrick signed the Bill of Lading, and they headed north on Merced Falls Road toward their first destination. Coulterville was more than twenty-five miles away, a two-day ride.

The gently rolling hills masked with low-lying shrub brush began turning a dark shade of green and gray as the sun set below the horizon. After a short distance, Patrick found a place to stay overnight.

"We'll camp by the creek under that big oak tree. Why don't you water the oxen, and I'll get a fire goin' and make us some sausage and beans."

As they ate, his employer reviewed the itinerary for the week as they sat around the warmth of the campfire.

"The first leg of our journey will be to the lower foothill towns. We'll stay overnight at a hotel in Coulterville, and push out the next day to Chinese Camp, and find a campsite outside of town. The upper foothills will be our second stop, an' we'll spend a couple of nights in Jamestown before we head home. We must always be prepared since we're carryin' cargo. You never know when some bandit will try to rob us of our goods. So keep your guns close to your gum blanket at night." Patrick placed his rifle and gun belt in a strategic location under his bedding on the ground.

"We'll never be cartin' any money with us, just freight. Most outlaws know that. They would have to steal this slow movin' wagon to cart off the goods. So, more than likely, they won't bother with us." He chuckled.

"Pat, do you suppose we can spend some time in Jamestown?" Samuel asked. "I'd like to try my hand out at pannin'."

"Now, how did ya read my mind?" Patrick grinned. "It can't be all business, you know. Gotta enjoy your hard labor too. Of course, we'll have time. But for now, how 'bout I teach you how to play poker?"

"Uh … I don't know, Pat. Ma says gamblin' is a sin."

"Only if you allow it to control you. Ah besides, we ain't goin' to gamble. It's just a game." Patrick cracked a grin.

"All right. I guess a little fun won't hurt."

After playing a hand, they tumbled onto their gum blankets. They lay flat on their backs watching the embers of the campfire float into the night sky and fade against the glow of the stars. With the warmth of the night air and the sound of the crackling wood, they soon found themselves drifting off to sleep.

AWAKE AT THE FIRST LIGHT OF DAWN, they drank coffee and ate biscuits and sowbelly. After hitching the oxen, they headed north on Merced Falls Road for twelve miles and turned east on John Muir Highway for another four. Samuel played "The Days of 49," "Life in California," and "Prospecting Dreams" on the fiddle to idle away the hours on the trail.

The small town called Granite Springs, comprised of three residents, became their next campsite and hunting grounds. After they settled, Boomer's nose went to work sniffing the ground for the scent of raccoon as Samuel and Patrick followed, shotguns in hand. Not surprisingly, the tawny hound was barking up a twisted oak tree.

Ssss. The four-legged bandit cried out. His eyes glared behind his black mask, permanently affixed upon his furry face.

"Good boy!" The eager young hunter patted his hound's rib cage.

"All right, Sam. Why don't you shoot him down? Is your gun ready?"

"Yep." He positioned his rifle to his eye. His heart beat fast from the thrill of finding prey. With a steady hand fixed on his target, he aimed and fired.

Bam! The critter tumbled down between the branches to the base of the tree. Boomer stood barking at his prize until Patrick claimed it.

"Whoo-hoo! Raccoon stew tonight." Pat broke off a sturdy branch and tied the coon's front and back paws around the pole. The men carried one end each on their shoulders and brought the critter back to camp to be skinned and cooked. A long hard day and full bellies bade a good night's rest for the tired huntsmen.

THURSDAY'S TREK TO COULTERVILLE stretched six grueling miles of a consistent steep grade. The four oxen snorted and huffed, pulling the fully laden wagon. Walking by their side, Samuel and Boomer helped move them along, while Patrick hollered commands and shook the reins.

Exhausted, they arrived at Coulterville in the late afternoon and pulled up to the mercantile. As Sam tended to the packs, Pat went inside to settle business with the owner and purchase some provisions. He returned to the Schooner, where they began unloading some of the sacks.

After they made their delivery, they headed for the livery stable. Patrick traded the oxen for fresh ones and left the wagon in the barn overnight. They walked into town and checked into the first hotel while Boomer waited on the porch.

The short, bald-headed clerk standing behind the front desk greeted the weary travelers. "Hey, Pat … Welcome back. Will it be your usual room? I see a new partner helpin' you this time."

"Howdy, Chester. Yep, this here is my good friend, Sam. He's the son of one of my customers in Snelling. We'd like a room for a night, sir, if we may?"

"Surely. How about room 204 on the second floor? Our dinner special tonight is Elsie's porterhouse steaks. And, of course, you can expect our usual game of poker in the saloon."

"Thank you, ol' man." Patrick winked as he took hold of the keys. "How 'bout we get some grub, hey, Sam?"

"I'm starved." Samuel rubbed his stomach. "It's a pleasure to meet ya, sir." Tilting his slouch hat at Chester, he followed his employer.

They proceeded to the dining room where Elsie, a middle-aged woman dressed in a forest green printed day dress and apron, greeted them. "Well, hello again, Mr. Fay. A table for you and your partner?"

"Yes, ma'am."

The courteous waitress seated them in a booth. "What can I get for you gentlemen today?"

"Well, I would like the steak special, medium well, along with a tall glass of your finest on tap," Patrick said.

"And you, young man?"

"Uh, yes. I think I'll get the same thing he's havin', except with a sarsaparilla, please."

After Elsie took their order, Patrick leaned forward. "What do ya think about the work so far?"

Samuel sat back and gazed upward, recollecting. "I've truly enjoyed the last few days. Thanks for considerin' me to come along with you. Now I know why you love haulin' freight. It's 'cause you can travel an' see all these places, plus get paid too."

He clasped his hands together on the table, pressing his chest into the table. "I appreciate my parent's havin' concern for my future, but I'm curious 'bout what's goin' on around me, especially in the minin' towns. I'd help ya any chance I could to get away from the farm. Don't get me wrong. I don't mind farmin', but I'm not sure I want to do that for the rest of my life."

"Well, Sam, when I was your age, I thought the same way as you do. I wanted to get out an' explore. That's how I ended up in California. Many people were talkin' 'bout the golden treasure in these hills, so I fixed to come with my kinfolk. For a while, I panned an' mined. It was good while the gold lasted, but that's it, it didn't last. At least not for me. Patience is not my virtue. Prospectin' is a lot of hard work. However, it only pays if you can strike it rich. You'll have to find out for yourself.

"Ev'ry generation of the Fay family lived by one rule: Never be idle. If your hands can't be usefully employed, attend to the cultivation of your mind." He tapped his head and winked. "I discovered serving the mining community to be more profitable."

Samuel took the opportunity to bombard Pat with all kinds of questions about the gold rush instead of the hauling business. Soon enough, Elsie returned with their supper. Because of his persistence, Patrick promised to teach him how to pan.

After dinner, Samuel untied Boomer, gave him his leftovers, and went to their room. It had two single beds on each side, with soft quilts and fluffy pillows. A ceramic washbowl, pitcher filled with water, a bar of soap, and towels were on tables beside the beds, and in between them was an armoire.

"Well, Pat, I'm purdy darn tired. I think I'm gonna wash up, read some, and go to bed."

"Sure is somethin' that you can unwind so quickly. I'll do the same, but I'm goin' to head back to the saloon for a game of poker first. Don't wait up for me." He skedaddled out the door.

Samuel went to bed and was so tired he did not hear Patrick come in around the wee hour of one o'clock.

SUN RAYS PEEKED THROUGH THE WINDOW SHADES Friday morning. Samuel woke up to what he thought was his ma kissing his cheek. But when he opened his eyes, to his surprise, Boomer stood over him licking his face, anxiously trying to wake him. For a moment, he didn't recognize his surroundings until he peered over Boomer's head. Asleep in the bed across from him, Patrick lay snoring, still dressed in his dusty trousers and dark, linen, plaid shirt. *At least he had the mind to take off his dirty boots before climbin' into the clean sheets.*

"Oh, Boomer ... all right ... hold on. I've gotta go too." Crawling out of bed, Samuel put on his shirt and dungarees over his underclothes. He grabbed the rope for Boomer's collar and, with stealth, exited the room and headed to the hotel's outhouse.

When they returned, Patrick began stirring. He sat up in his bed, rubbed his eyes, stretched his arms upward, and took a deep breath.

"Ooooh! Good mornin'. Lord, what time is it? We better be hittin' the road soon. I'm gonna run to the Irish shantee too. Why don't we meet in the dining room for breakfast, then we'll head out?"

"Mornin', Pat. Yah, Boomer and I are ready. How'd you do in poker last night?"

"Well, I'm not a millionaire yet. There's never a dull moment with them good ol' boys. They nearly started a brawl after the game. Something 'bout someone cheatin'. Sure am glad Elsie was nearby to calm things down. Sometimes the gentle persuasion of a woman is the remedy to defuse a sit'ation. Okay, well, I've got to run an' do my business. Meet you for breakfast?" Patrick put on his boots and left in haste.

"Yep, I'll be there." Samuel headed to the dining room with Boomer trailing behind him.

After the morning meal, they went to the livery stable to pick up the wagon and the fresh oxen. Their next stop was Chinese Camp, about fifteen miles away. On their way, they took the Don Pedro Ferry to cross the lake. They also encountered some rolling hilltops to climb and shallow creeks to tread. The magnificent views of the flat and widespread San Joaquin Valley could be seen from the foothills.

The late afternoon sun barely touched the black oak treetops when they arrived at the general store. The owner, Mr. Chung, an older gentleman wearing a high-neck collared black shirt with frog buttons and light grey trousers, bowed to Patrick and said in his interspersed English and Chinese accent, "Come in, Mr. Pat, come in. You bring me eight sacks of flour today?"

"Good day, my friend. I sure have. Please sign this delivery receipt, and Sam will start unloading them for you." Patrick craned his neck toward the savory aroma coming from the back door leading to the kitchen.

"Ah, pleasure to meet you, Mr. Sam." The cheerful store owner stepped away from the counter and graciously bowed, his long pepper-colored hair, braided from his nape to his waist, swayed as he moved around. "You gentlemen join me for dinner? I will cook delicious Chinese food for you. You hungry, I bet. long way from Coulterville." Pointing his index finger at both of them, he grinned.

"Well, I was hopin' you'd ask." Pat laughed. "Ya know I love your cookin', Mr. Chung."

Samuel smiled and bowed according to their cultural tradition. *Chinese food? I guess it must be good if Pat likes it. All I know is I can eat a bear. Ew ... I hope that isn't what's in the pot.* He began unloading the heavy sacks of flour as Patrick helped.

The jolly little man straightened the longevity cap on his head and summoned them to the kitchen when they finished.

"Come, come. You sit at table. I bring you food." He brought out one bowl after another of savory ethnic cuisine. "You want fork or chopstick?" Grinning, he held up both utensils.

"Fork," the two said simultaneously.

Samuel had never tasted such style of cooking before. Tender pieces of meat stir-fried with chopped broccoli. Chunks of bok choy cabbage and shrimp intertwined with soft, thick noodles, and the rice fried in soy sauce burst with salty flavor. The food seemed to dance on his tongue, and he could not stop himself from going for second helpings. The Asian meal faired far different from the meat and potatoes his mother prepared at home.

After dinner, they said their farewells to Mr. Chung and brought the wagon outside of Chinese Camp. By now, the sun had sunk below the horizon, and darkness engulfed the hills. So they lit a lantern and searched for the towering rock where Patrick normally camped.

Trees surrounded the eight-foot granite wall. Patrick hid the Schooner behind it for protection and shelter. They started a small campfire, rolled out their mattresses, fell asleep with their guns beside them, and Boomer curled up by Samuel. The fire dwindled while they slept like logs.

Boomer's low growl awakened Sam. He focused on the dim glow on his hound's face. Boomer lifted his head, twitched his nose, and got up and ran to the base of the wall and fired ferocious barks upwards.

14

Catching the Fever

*A*rghhh! The beast lunged down at Boomer and they wrestled on the ground. Sam squinted, trying to wake up and focus on the flurry of barking, growling, scratches, claws, and bites.

"Mountain lion!" Pat jolted out of his blanket, grabbed his gun, and shot into the dark sky to avoid hitting the aggravated hound dog.

The oversized cat fled as the vigilant hound chased after it. Samuel stopped short of a sprint, realizing he could not keep up with his faithful friend.

"Boomer. No," he called out. "Come back here!"

Once the creature distanced itself far enough away from camp, Boomer returned, moaning from the cuts and scrapes on his torso.

"Good boy. Good boy. All right. You're safe. I've got ya." The courageous dog breathed heavily as Samuel embraced him and gave him an extra portion of jerky and fresh water. "Come on. Let's take a look at you and get you mended." He began washing his faithful friend's wounds with rags and wrapping them with therapeutic cloth from Pat's makeshift medical emergency box.

Pat threw more wood on the fire. "How's our boy?"

"Ah, he'll live." Sam rubbed Boomer's head against his chest. "He's a tough ol' hound."

"All right. Why don't you both try to get some shut-eye, and I'll stay watch the rest of the night? Then you can drive the wagon to Jamestown in the mornin' while I get some shut-eye."

Samuel nodded in agreement, snuggled beside Boomer, and eventually drifted off into sweet slumber feeling safe as his boss kept watch.

THE COLD, CRISP MORNING AIR pained Samuel's nostrils, forcing him to wake up and throw another log on the fire. Sometime in the night, sleep caught up with Patrick as he lay snoring with his shotgun lying next to him. *I can't believe it's Saturday already. This trip is halfway over and goin' by too quickly.* He wrapped himself in his blanket and stayed warm by the flames as Boomer curl up next to him.

Pleasant memories of the six-month expedition coming out to California drifted through Sam's mind: cooking over an open fire, sleeping on the hard ground under the stars, and hunting wild game with his father and hound.

The night sky changed from midnight blue to pale azure, amber, and then mellow yellow as the sun came crawling over the horizon. The choir of birds burst into unison when the first rays touched the tips of the trees' branches, turning the leaves a translucent lime green. *Ah, how I love bein' outdoors.*

Finally warm enough, Samuel inhaled the mountain air and decided to make breakfast. The aroma of sowbelly, biscuits, and coffee, as well as the fire's warmth, woke Patrick and a slow grin appear as he wiped the dust from his eyes.

"That was some night, wasn't it?" The gruffy cargo man sat up, scratched his head, and scraped at the warm food on his plate. "Ya never know what to expect out here in the wilderness. Thank the Lord Boomer is okay. You did good, boy." He patted the dog's head and handed him a piece of sowbelly.

After breakfast, they pulled up stakes and hit the trail again. Samuel pushed the oxen to move a little faster toward Jamestown, an easy six miles away from Chinese Camp. They left around seven in the morning and arrived at their next destination by noon.

Prospectors bustled to and fro in the friendly frontier town. Many headed to Woods Creek, where gold was discovered in 1848. Some of the miners hiked further up the road about five more miles to Sonora, and another ten more to Columbia, to find work at the hydraulic mining companies.

Patrick dismounted after Samuel parked in front of the busy mercantile. "I'll make it quick since I know you're eager to go pannin'."

While Samuel watered the oxen, he could see his employer through the store window as he nudged his way to the owner, shoved the Bill of Lading on the counter for his signature, and returned to the wagon. They unloaded the last of the sacks of flour, which included the freight for the stores in the surrounding townships. After unloading, they took the Schooner to the livery stable. Rustling around the wagon-bed, Patrick found a canvas bag, which contained two small spades, metal plates, and mason jars with lids.

"We're goin' to need these for pannin'." He threw the pack over his shoulder. "Let's get some lunch first at the Willow Hotel and Saloon and check into our room."

"I'll follow you," Sam said. "Come on, Boomer. Let's go."

"Not too long ago, a mine shaft collapsed under this hotel, and twenty-three men died. Buried alive, they say." Patrick's face contorted while walking toward the two-story building. "Some believe it's haunted. But don't let that spook ya!" He chuckled, making ghostly sounds. *Ooooooo.* "No matter, they make the best barbecued ribs in town. You must try some since we're here."

"Well, this ought to be good." Sam's voice trembled.

After they were fed and settled into the hotel room, they headed for Woods Creek, with the canvas bag in tote, to where many prospectors already claimed a small section of embankment.

"Whoa. Sure are a lot of prospectors. Do you think there are any good spots left, Pat? Maybe we should've started earlier?"

"Don't worry. We'll find a place. Let's walk up the creek some."

As they went further upstream, the muddied gold-seekers glanced at them with angry, steely eyes, warning them to stay away from their claim. Finally, they came to a shallow pool of water, which collected before tumbling downstream amongst the rocks into the next level.

"This is a good spot. No one around." Pat surveyed the area. "Okay, let me show you what to do." He removed his boots and socks, rolled up his pant legs, and rustled through the canvas bag gathering the tools he needed. Getting into the water about ankle-deep, he bent down, grabbed his spade, scooped a small amount of gravel, and placed it in the large metal dish, along with some water.

"You simply tilt the pan side to side an' shake an' swirl so the mud suspends in the water. The gold will separate from the muck then sink because it's heavier. Let the muddy water wash gently out of the pan. Keep doin' this until all that remains is black sand and hopefully gold." Patrick demonstrated as shimmering flecks appeared, some swirling with the water and some settling fast in the pan's bottom.

"Whoo-hoo! Looky here, Sam." Pat sunk his index finger into the water, pushing the small slivers to the edge and into Sam's right hand. "These are gold flakes. Feel how heavy they are compared to these little shavings."

"Yep. I feel the difference, although they're 'bout the same size and color."

"The lighter flake is known as *fool's gold*. It's worth nothin'. So be careful." Pat opened the jar as Sam dropped the real gold flakes inside. "Now sometimes gold forms in clusters around the rocks. So be sure to check them too." He swirled some more.

Samuel kicked off his boots and socks, snatched his pan and spade, and sank his toes into the muddy creek. After several attempts, Samuel's eyes grew large, experiencing the same results.

"Yahoo. Good, Lord. Is this gold, Pat?"

Grinning from ear to ear, Patrick peered into Sam's platter. "Eureka. I think you've got gold fever."

Boomer began barking as he stood at the edge of the creek. The whooping and hollering made him excited, too, so he decided to jump in and splash around. After his swim, he went back to the bank, shook off the excess moisture from his fur, plopped himself down under a pine tree, and took a nap. The two men spent the rest of the afternoon panning. They placed their riches in their jars of water and twisted the lids shut.

The prospectors would not go home until the sun set. For Sam, he could not bear the thought of possibly missing a piece of gold in the next scoop of mud. He and Patrick hardly spoke a word to each other as they focused on establishing a rhythm in their personal method of panning. At the last ounce of amber glow and the first bite from a pesky mosquito, they decided to call it a day and head back to the hotel, where they could eat some supper, wash up, and go to bed. They agreed to wake early and spend one more day panning before returning home to Snelling.

THE MOMENT THE SHADES IN THE BEDROOM WINDOW showed a hint of light, they woke up and went downstairs for breakfast.

"Well, did any ghosts bother ya last night?" Patrick asked as he rolled up his sleeves.

"If they did, they didn't do a good job of it. I slept like a corpse." Sam laughed at his joke. He sat down in the third booth on the left side of the dining room. Caught off guard, he felt a tug on his hair on the back of his head. Not thinking anything at first, he assumed it snagged upon the high-back wooden bench where he was seated.

The waitress delivered their breakfast, and the pull came again, but stronger. "Ow!" Sam rubbed his head. "That's the second time somethin' pulled my hair."

He turned around to inspect the booth. The smooth wood finish had no splinters for his tresses to become snagged.

For a moment, Patrick stopped chewing and locked eyes with Samuel. "Are ya serious?" Goosebumps appeared on his arms.

"Yes." The startled youth ate at a faster pace. This time, the tug came strong. "Ow!" He applied pressure to his scalp and stared at his fingertips. "Blood?"

The whites of Patrick's eyes engulfed his pupils, and he reached over to his partner. "What's goin' on? This strand just fell on your shoulder."

Sam jumped to his feet, afraid to sit down.

The waitress heard the commotion and high-stepped over to their table.

"Are you okay?"

"I'm not sure. Somethin' keeps pullin' on my hair. It's not funny. It hurts."

"Oh, dear." Nervously looking around, the other guest's eyes met hers. "This is goin' to be an interesting day."

"Why? What do ya mean?" Patrick asked as he sat at full attention.

"Well." She shifted her weight from one foot to the other. "For some reason, this particular booth you gentlemen are sitting in has had the most supernatural phenomena of late. A few of our guests mentioned their silverware levitating, or they felt something kicking them in the shins. I can move you to another table if you like."

Patrick and Samuel, faces distraught, simultaneously answered, "No, thanks." They wrapped up their food in their napkins and shoved it into the canvas bag, paid their bill, and ran out with Boomer behind them.

"Ooowee, that was weird." Samuel walked briskly toward the creek. "Do we have to stay there tonight?"

"Well, I guess not. Another hotel is down the street. We can register after we get back."

"Yeah, let's do that."

The rest of the day dwindled as they found small nuggets of gold between the cracks of the rocks. During the last hour of sunlight, Patrick said, "Hey, Sam. Let's go back to town, cash in, and check into the other hotel."

Samuel lifted his jar against the setting sun and shook it so the flecks sparkled from the golden rays. "Okay, but I think I want to keep mine for now so I can show Pa an' Ma. If it's all right with you."

"Oh, of course you may, son."

MONDAY MORNING THEY WOKE UP WITH BODY ACHES from

stooping down panning all day on Sunday.

"Lord, am I sore." Patrick rubbed his lower back.

"Yeah, me too. But we sure had loads of fun." Samuel stood and stretched. "Can I come with you again on your next delivery?"

"You betcha." He gleamed. "However, right now, I would rather be home in a hot bath with my lovin' wife's arms around me." He winked. "Let's get some breakfast and go home."

Traveling back proved faster as they coursed downhill carrying no cargo. Instead of four days, they returned in three. They spent their last day of travel hunting, and Patrick shot a six-point buck as a goodwill gesture for borrowing Sam. They roped it and used the oxen to pull it up into the wagon bed.

The flour mill in Merced Falls was the last stop. The fatigued cargo-hauler dropped off the signed Bill of Ladings in exchange for a note for the balance due.

They reached Snelling midday, elated when the farm came into view. Their sore, tired bodies longed for a delicious home-cooked meal.

WHILE TENDING TO THE ANIMALS, Jonathan recognized the Schooner at a distance turning right on La Grange Road. He remembered his conversation with Patrick at the kitchen table and recalled the time it would take to make the deliveries. "Yep, it's been nine days."

They pulled up to the barn and jumped out of the wagon to greet him, as he stood with his arms crossed over his chest, grinning profusely, happy they had arrived home safely.

Samuel grabbed the small jar with the gold flecks and nuggets and walked with haste over to his father. "Hey, Pa, I had so much fun. Look what I brought home." He hugged his father and shoved the container into his hands.

Jonathan inspected the contents in amazement and also caught a glimpse of the dead buck in the Schooner's bed. "Whoa, seems like ya fellows did more than deliverin' flour."

"Yep. Samuel proved himself to be of valuable service to me on this trip. We had a grand time in them hills!" Patrick gave Jonathan a firm handshake. "Your young man can work with me anytime."

"Well, that is mighty good to hear. But you know he's got plenty to do around here on the farm. In fact, I'm ready to start buildin' the farmhouse next week. So both your timin' couldn't be better," Jonathan said with a tinge of envy in his heart. He did not recall ever spending as much time alone with Samuel, doing father and son bonding. "I'm so glad you're home again. Let's get some of this venison cooked up an' the rest made into jerky. You boys can tell us about your trip durin' suppertime."

His wife and the other three children's smiling faces appeared in the cabin window. They ran outside to welcome them home. Samuel took the jar from him and passed it around for everyone to stare at and gawk.

"Ma, this is for you. And I know where to get more too. Patrick is plannin' several deliveries before the end of the year. He said I could go with him. I can't wait!" Samuel handed his mother the glimmering spectacle.

"Oh my goodness, Sam." Mary gasped as she held the container. "Sounds like you've already made plans." Her countenance changed from dropped jaw to a forced smile as she peered at the yellow flecks. "Whoa, this is real gold in its purest form. Thank you, son."

The family entered the cabin and chatted as Mary prepared a sumptuous venison supper and listened to Samuel. Patrick relaxed at the kitchen table and chuckled to hear Sam's tales of grandeur.

"That mountain lion was as big as a horse. Nineteen hands high, I'd say. You should've seen how Pat near shot him and Boomer chased him off." Sam stretched his right hand above his head. "And the creek in Jamestown was like a river of gold. Next time we go back, we're plannin' to stay longer. Right, Pat?"

Patrick nodded and flashed the family a huge grin.

If there is a next time. Jonathan smirked. *It looks like I'm goin' to have to pile more work on my son to keep him from wanderin'.*

15

Autumn Services Begin

"Sure am lookin' forward to this mornin's service." Mary tugged on the corset laces as Sarah held on to the bunk bedpost. "Do you realize we haven't been to church since we left Kentucky? It'll be refreshin' to listen to Pastor McSwan preach."

"Mama, I think it's too tight. I can hardly breathe." Sarah tried to expand her lungs.

"Sorry, dear." She loosened the laces. "How's that?"

"Much better." The teenage girl tugged, wiggled, and adjusted her body until the corset contoured to her frame. Giggling at her new form, she peered down at her heaving, youthful bosoms and hourglass-shaped waistline. *Oh my, I am quite bodacious in this contraption. Joshua is sure to notice me now.* "I agree. It has been far too long since we've been to church. Although, it ought to be a bit strange to attend service at the courthouse, with the jail beneath us an' all."

"Well, think about it, though. Who better than a bunch of outlaws to receive the gospel of salvation through Jesus Christ? I reckon Pastor McSwan knew what he was doin' when he chose to conduct services there. Killin' two birds with one stone, my opinion of course. The courthouse will have to do until he and the Lord can raise funds to build a proper church." Mary tied a bow in the corset. "All right, let's try on your new day dress that we both worked so hard to complete for this day."

Sarah turned on her boot heels to face her mother. The crinoline lay furled on the ground as she stepped in the center of it, lifted the cotton-shrouded birdcage to her waist, pulled on the waistline cord, and tied a knot.

"Petticoat first." Mary hurled the delicate, lacey, white layers over her daughter's head and positioned it over the hoops. "Skirt next." She unfastened the hook and eye of the rose-colored gathered yardage ruffled at the hem. Sarah reached in through its center and adjusted the skirting over the petticoat as Mary refastened it in the back. "Now for the bodice." The excited mother held the boned, lined blouse as her daughter inserted her arms into the sleeves and buttoned the front from the collar to the waistline. "Now, for the *pièce de résistance,* your bonnet."

Sarah stepped toward the dresser mirror and placed the satin spoon headdress of the same color over her soft brown ringlets, which draped over her shoulders.

Moisture filled Mary's eyes. "Turn around, dear." She gasped. "I do believe you're officially a young lady now, Sarah. No longer a little girl. Now go present yourself to the rest of the family."

The bodice boning and skirt pleats accentuated her sprouting ladylike figure, and the budding young lady beamed as she pranced into the kitchen where the others sat finishing their breakfast. Gasps filled the room as she entered and twirled on the balls of her feet.

Jonathan stood from his seat. "Lady in the house." He bowed as his sons followed his example. "My daughter, you are a picture of beauty. You and your mama outdid yourselves with this raiment."

"Thank you, Papa." Sarah's cheeks turn a pinkish color and her eyes glisten.

"Gentlemen, I do believe we must escort these fine ladies to church." Jonathan extended his left elbow to Mary, Samuel to Sarah, and David to Naomi as if exercising formality to a grand ball. Giggles and laughter commenced as they boarded the Conestoga and headed into town.

Upon arriving at the Snelling Courthouse, Sarah could see Pastor McSwan waving to them from the top of the steps, motioning them to come in. A staircase ascending from the front yard walkway to the second-story porch led them to the courthouse's double doors. Only the marshal accessed the jailhouse on the first floor.

"Welcome, folks." The pastor shook her father's hand. "Thank the good Lord, you are able to attend service today. Come inside and find yourselves a seat, and we will be starting off the reel. My family is sitting in the front row. I'm sure they would love to know you've arrived."

"We are delighted to be here, Pastor," her father said as he motioned the Sower clan into the building. The ladies walked in first with the lads following.

Sarah noticed the McSwans turning in their seats toward the entrance. Simultaneously, she and Joshua's eyes met. Warmth flushed her cheeks, and she thought her face turned as rosy as her dress. After passing a smile at the young man, she focused on the back of her mother's hat, trying not to make her intentions obvious.

Mary greeted Ruth and motioned for her daughters to come forward to do the same and sit behind them.

"My goodness, how beautiful you are today." Mrs. McSwan gaped at Sarah's new day dress. "You're blossoming into a fine young lady."

"Thank ya, Mrs. McSwan." Sarah curtsied. "You are so kind." She glanced over at their son, whose eyes fixated upon her as if in a trance.

Walking over to the second row behind him, she whispered, "Good mornin', Joshua. It's a pleasure to see you again."

Face reddening, he could not find the right words to come out of his mouth. "Huh, oh, hello, Sarah. I'm glad you can be here. You look really pretty today." He placed his fingertips over his lips as if trying to retract what he said and gazed down at his shoes. "Uh, oh, I mean…"

The naïve yet flirtatious young lady interrupted before he could utter anything more and become tongue-tied. "Thank you, Joshua, and you're quite dapper yourself," she said in a demure but warm gesture.

Her father and brothers followed Naomi and her mother. He waved to her to scoot over a few more seats. Sitting three chairs over to the left behind the young man who consumed her thoughts of late, she beheld his every move and features while she listened to his father lead the parishioners in singing hymns, proceeded by his sermon.

PASTOR MCSWAN INHALED AND BEGAN. "Today, I am going to talk about a topic, which most of you in this congregation are familiar with since you are farmers. Sowing seeds." He chuckled, glanced about the room, and seemed to set his eyes on Jonathan intentionally. Adjusting himself in his seat, the local wheat baron loosened his cravat, readying himself for a message directed at him.

"Let me read to you from Matthew chapter thirteen." The minister began. "'Behold, a sower went forth to sow; and when he sowed, some seeds fell by the wayside, and the fowls came and devoured them up. Some fell upon stony places, where they had not much earth: and forthwith they sprung up because they had no deepness of earth. And when the sun was up, they were scorched; and because they had no root, they withered away. And some fell among thorns, and the thorns sprung up and choked them. But other fell into good ground and brought forth fruit, some a hundredfold, some sixtyfold, some thirtyfold. Who hath ears to hear, let him hear.'"

The pastor captured Jonathan's attention, at least during the reading. *How can he know what my crops produced? He probably prepared this sermon for me since he set his gaze in my direction.* He fidgeted, trying to stay focused. His thoughts betrayed him as they drifted to his discouraging first harvest destroyed by cattle, wild blackberry bushes, and the scorching sun. *Thank God I broke even, enough to pay my employees and feed my family until next season. Next year I'll do better. I must.*

Before too long, the pastor closed the service asking everyone to bow their heads in prayer. "Lord, we give you the glory for the bountiful harvest. We pray for the seed of Your Word planted in our hearts to grow and be fruitful in our lives. May each of us do our part to sow the seed of Your gospel with our neighbors. Bless these good folks with Your goodness, mercy, and love. In Jesus' name. Amen."

He dismissed the congregation and hastened to the front doors to shake church members' hands as they exited.

Ruth stood and turned to talk to the Sowers. "Thank you for coming to service today, and we hope you would come next week too. We will conduct services here through the winter until the weather permits us to resume camp meetings again."

"We appreciate your invitation," Jonathan said with a smile. "That was an encouragin' message meant for me."

Face aglow, Mary turned to him. "Now, darlin', what would you think about having the McSwans over next Sunday before candle-lightin'?"

"A wonderful suggestion, indeed!" The witty farmer shifted his gaze from his wife to the minister's spouse. "What do you say, Mrs. McSwan? Do you think your family would be available to come over for supper next week after church?"

"Now, you both can call me Ruth." She smiled. "I can think of no reason to decline your invitation. In fact, we would love to. Should the date not be fitting for Pastor, I'll be sure to send word. I do believe that afternoon is open for us, however."

"Wonderful. Is three o'clock convenient, Ruth?" Mary asked.

"That'll be fine. Thank you again."

Out of the corner of his eyes, the intuitive father saw his eldest daughter and the minister's son smiling at one another. Soon enough, the young man's father joined him and their spouses.

"An appropriate sermon, Pastor. The good Lord must have inspired you to write it with me in mind," he said as he did his best to hold a conversation and keep an eye on the teenagers.

"Ah, the credit is certainly not mine, but the Holy Ghosts for placing that scripture on my heart for the entire congregation. I'm well pleased the message stirred your soul."

"Daniel, dearest, Jonathan and Mary invited us to sup with their family after church next week. May we accept their invitation?" Ruth squeezed her husband's elbow.

Pausing for a moment to think, he said, "I do believe we shall."

"Yippee!" Snickering at Naomi and David, Rebecca peeked over her chair and turned to her parents. "Can we go outside and play?"

"Yes, dear. Stay on the front lawn and be mindful of the adults," Ruth said as the young children scurried out of their seats and through the double doors.

WHILE THE PARENTS CONVERSED, Sarah, Joshua, and Samuel sauntered down the aisle.

"So, I guess we'll be visiting you next Sunday." Joshua initiated the conversation.

"Hey, maybe we could take the horses out for a quick jaunt around' the farm. We'll show you the tree fort we made by the creek." Samuel's eyes widened.

"I'll be looking forward to it. Will you be coming too, Sarah?"

"Of course. I can ride a horse as well as y'all." She sensed an urge to start a playful challenge.

"Yeah ... sure you can, Sis." Samuel teased, perusing her prim and proper attire.

Joshua's smile displayed appreciation for her appearance rather than agreeing with her brother's jousting comment. Before Samuel could notice his response, the handsome young man glanced across the street to conceal his amorous attraction for her. "Hey, you want to see what Mr. Jacobi has for sweets at the Mercantile?"

Her brother shoved his fist into his right pant pocket and jingled the loose coin he earned from Patrick. "Sure, let's go."

The congenial German proprietor was waiting for them from behind the counter. "Hello, young folks. I bet you have a sveet tooth. Look vat I have here. Rock candy, gumballs, cherry lollipops, peppermint sticks, and chocolate fudge brownies."

They peered into the round glass jars filled with goodies. Serendipitous pursuit caused the heart struck youth to reach into the rock candy jar, Joshua's hand holding hers.

"Here, why don't I buy this for you, Sarah?" he said, gazing into her eyes.

Sensing the warmth of his touch, Sarah's knees became feeble. This little moment of time seemed to last an eternity as she fixed her eyes on him.

"You mustn't, Joshua," she said and lavished his name rolling off her lips.

"Oh no, I insist!" He removed her hand from the candy jar, holding her gaze to his.

"Thank you." She allowed him to hold her hand a moment longer but pulled away as she became aware of her bub approaching them after he purchased some sweets for the younger siblings.

"Have you two decided yet?" Samuel inquired, trying to assess the moment.

"Uh, yes. I'm going to purchase some of this rock candy." Joshua grabbed a handful and gave them to Mr. Jacobi along with his money. The jovial storeowner put the confections into two bags, thanked them, and continued his business.

They returned to the wagon where the family sat waiting, and Sarah and Samuel climbed on board. The horses began to strut away, and waves of farewells were exchanged. With one last inconspicuous glance, she indulged herself in the feverish adoration emanating from Joshua's pining blues.

Chapter 16

First Kiss

The week seemed to blow by like a swift breeze through a mountain pass as Sarah, her family, and the farmhands' preoccupy themselves with building the farmhouse. All she could think about the past few days was Joshua and how she might conduct herself when his kin visited their farm today after service.

What am I goin' to wear? Standing barefoot in her cotton chemise and drawers, Sarah cringed as she stared at her dismal collection of day dresses hanging on the rack in her shared bedroom's corner. The brand new attire she wore to church the previous Sunday beckoned to be worn again. *I can't possibly wear that again. It's too soon.* "Well, I guess the pale blue dress will do." Holding the faded garment, she sighed. *At least, I don't have to suffer the hoops and corset again.* She rummaged through the clothes to find her corded petticoat and linen stay.

"Ma, may I borrow one of your crochet collars and cameos today?" She hollered toward the kitchen where her mother was serving breakfast to the others.

"Go right ahead, dear. Hurry now so you can eat somethin' before we leave."

"I'll be right there." Sarah dressed and added a dark blue silk ribbon around the crown of her straw bonnet. After tossing her hair into a hairnet, she fitted the hat on her head and fussed at her reflection in the dresser mirror. *Ugh. A far cry from last week. Lord, help me.*

"Good mornin'. Sure am lookin' forward to visiting your home this afternoon." The minister shook Mary and her family's hands as they entered the courthouse.

"Good mornin', Pastor," the family chimed in.

"We can hardly wait for y'all to come over. Your visit is all the children spoke about throughout the week. Oh, and goin' to church, of course," she said as she shuffled forward while other members filed inside. "I do see your wife callin' us to sit by her. Shall we talk after the service?"

"Indeed." He smiled as he extended his hand to the next person.

Mary moseyed over to the seats behind his family, followed by her own.

As soon as the congregation was seated, Pastor McSwan continued his discourse from the previous week about farming. He turned the pages of his Bible and straightened his back. "Please turn in your Bibles to Matthew 13:24.

"'The kingdom of heaven is likened unto a man, which sowed good seed in his field: but while men slept, his enemy came and sowed tares among the wheat, and went his way. But when the blade was sprung up and brought forth fruit, then appeared the tares also. So the servants of the household came and said unto him, 'Sir, didst not thou sow good seed in thy field? From whence then hath it tares?' He said unto them, 'An enemy hath done this.' The servants said unto him, 'Wilt thou then that we go and gather them up?' But he said, 'Nay; lest while ye gather up the tares, ye root up also the wheat with them. Let both grow together until the harvest: and in the time of harvest I will say to the reapers, Gather ye together first the tares, and bind them in bundles to burn them: but gather the wheat into my barn.'"

He continued by expounding the scripture. "The enemy plants the bad seed in the field amongst the good, unbelievers among the believers."

"Sure hope there aren't any tares growin' in our crops next year," Jonathan whispered in her ear.

"Nor in the bread I baked for this afternoon," she murmured through clenched teeth.

"Rebecca, turn around and be still." Ruth snapped as her daughter smiled at Naomi and David behind her then twisted in her seat to face forward.

"Looks like we're not the only ones havin' a hard time concentratin'." Mary brought her index finger pointed upward to her lips to signal her family to be quiet. Sarah's discreet fixation on Joshua told her where her daughter's mind dwelt. Thoughts drifting back to her preparations for their visitors, Mary directed her gaze at the pastor half listening.

I sure hope I prepared enough food for all of us. I would hate to make any bad impressions.

After service, she gathered the children and headed to the wagon after confirming the time of the McSwans arrival.

"Okay, we'll see y'all at three o'clock."

"Can I bring anything?" Ruth asked.

"Oh no. Everythin' is ready. Just bring your appetites."

Mary and her family climbed into the buckboard and sang hymns on the way home.

THE FOYER CLOCK RANG THREE O'CLOCK when Sarah heard the McSwans carriage arriving outside. She rushed to the window. *Oh, they're here.* Her heart leaped. She watched as her father greeted them and gave them a brief tour of the farm.

Her father had prepared ribs, steaks, and corn to be grilled outdoors, and her mother baked beans and assorted fruit pies. They had brought the kitchen table outside in front of the cabin under a towering twisting oak. Sarah dressed it with a delicate, white crocheted cloth and a vase of sunflowers picked from her mother's garden.

The warm autumn day enhanced the golden wheat stubble's pungent scent coming from the harvested fields. The enormous trees provided plenty of shade. David, Naomi, and Rebecca took turns on the swing dangling from under a branch, which her father constructed out of rope and a scrap plank from the barn. He had also made some stilts for each of the children.

The adults conversed around the table, as Sarah, Samuel, and Joshua stood by the corral, making plans for the afternoon.

"Do ya think we have enough time to head over to the tree fort, Sam?" She leaned into the fence and fed a carrot to her horse Belle. She glanced over at her parents to see if they were watching them. *Sure would like to get away from their watchful eyes.*

"I hope so. I'd love to see what y'all built." Joshua pat Belle's head while keeping his eyes on Sarah.

Samuel had one foot propped on the fence's lower railing and his chin resting on his hands on the upper. He seemed to snap out of his daze and turned his head toward their parents. "Looks like Pa is just startin' the grillin', so I think we have time. Let's go see if it's okay with them." He pushed away and sauntered over to the table as Sarah and Joshua trailed behind.

"Pa, Ma, Pastor, and Mrs. McSwan, may we take a quick horseback ride over to the creek? It's only about a half-mile away. We won't be long." Samuel pointed in the direction they planned to go.

The pastor glanced over to her parents. "Well, I don't mind."

"Yep, I suppose that'll be all right." Jonathan turned the meats on the grill. "Please, make sure to be back in an hour for dinner. Sam, you're the eldest, so you are responsible."

"Yes, Pa. I'll be careful." Samuel turned to Joshua. "How well do ya ride?"

"Pretty good, I reckon, for a pastor's son." He snickered as they walked to the corral. "In fact, it's routine for my father and me to take our horses around the camp meeting area, into the towns, and even into the deep mountain forest to invite people to come. We've actually been chased out of areas by some Mi-Wuk Indians."

Sarah's eyes widened as she entered the gates and held Belle's head as Sam adjusted the saddle. "You've been chased by Injuns here in California? Weren't you afraid? Isn't that dangerous for the two of you alone?"

"Well, my father and I believe our lives are in God's hands. If it's our time to depart to Heaven, then it'll be while we are in His will and doing His work. We have the peace of knowing we'll go to be with the Lord forever," Joshua said, gazing at the blue expanse, a shine to his eyes.

Sarah shook her head and bit into her bottom lip, thinking of the dangers Joshua would face as he and his father shared the gospel in Indian territory.

Samuel didn't flinch when he mentioned Indians. He began saddling Jack, the gray steed. "Funny, I've never encountered any on the trail yet. Most of them seem friendlier now and never desire to confront anyone unless they feel threatened. Or in your case, Joshua, bein' preached to." He winked. "I'll let you ride Jack. He's a good horse who knows his place and follows instructions very well."

Samuel handed Jack's reins to Joshua then whistled, calling his steed, Fire. The molasses brown stallion trotted to his owner, nudging his back with his nose, and scuffed at the ground with his hoof. "Hey, boy." He turned and rubbed the face of his feisty, sleek friend. "You ready to ride?" Fire snorted and kicked the ground with his front hooves.

They meandered down the wayside path toward La Grange Road, and her brother led the way.

We don't have time for this slow trottin'. Let's see who is the better rider. Sarah kicked Belle's ribs and snapped her rein. Belle jolted. "Race ya to the creek."

"Ha! Hee-ya!" The boys followed, cracking their reins. The horses dashed and darted through the dusty road, over a wooden bridge, then onto a path along the banks. Samuel took the lead at the bend, Sarah a tail's length behind him, and Joshua taking the rear.

Upon arriving, they pulled up to a sturdy bush, dismounted, and tied their horses.

Samuel chortled and knuckled Sarah's shoulder. "Good ridin', sis. But you'll never beat me."

She rolled her eyes and cracked a lopsided grin. "Yeah. Well, let's hope I never will. It would be a cryin' shame if a prissy girl, like me, did."

"Hey, wait a minute. What does that say about me?" Joshua huffed and stomped his foot. "I came in last because I didn't know where this place was." He grinned. "Now that I do, I betcha I'll get back to the farm first when we return."

"All right. I'll hold you to that bet." Samuel chuckled. "Come on. The fort is right over there."

He pointed at the enormous oak, which had huge roots reaching deep into the soil, working their way over to the water's edge. Half of its branches hovered over the creek and the other over the bank. In the center, her eldest brother had built a rugged platform made of scraps of wood from the barn. Small planks, used as steps, were nailed to the tree's trunk.

The fort beamed ten feet wide by eight feet high and included one side without a wall where one of the large branches reached over the creek. They could use this strong limb to crawl or scoot on top of till they sat above the water. From this branch, Samuel tied a rope with knots every two feet, which dangled into the water. Pulling up this makeshift ladder to the open edge, they could swing into the chin deep stream and climb back into the hiding place. This little fort lured as a relaxing getaway for the Sower children on weekends, after they completed a hard week of work on the farm.

"Wow, this is amazing!" Joshua said, gawking at the structure. "You actually built this, Sam?"

"Yep, with the help of my bub and sis. Nobody else knows about this fort other than you and our parents. Promise me you won't tell a soul."

"Yeah, sure. You have my word. So, can I come out here too?"

"Yes, as long as you check with us first. You can't bring anyone else, okay?"

"All right, I promise I won't." Joshua chuckled, placing his hand over his heart.

Inside the fort nestled four small wooden vegetable crates, used for seats, and one large wood crate for a table. On top of the makeshift table, an oil lamp, a bag of marbles, a couple of children's books, and some opened peanut shells evidenced recent visits. In the corner stood a fishing pole contrived of a long, thin switch attached to a line and a hook.

Joshua and Sarah placed a crate near the open edge where the limb extended and sat watching Samuel as he climbed out upon the sturdy, strong branch, straddled it, and stared down into the water.

"I'm goin' to pan in our creek and riverbank one day," Samuel said, his back to them. "The Sierra's are loaded with gold, and the Merced River is bound to be carryin' some downstream."

"That's all you ever think of these days, brother." She shook her head.

"So, how do you like living in Snelling, Sarah?" Joshua asked.

"Oh, I suppose it's all right. Work on the farm is hard and gets kinda lonely with only my bubs and sis to talk to. I haven't met many people my age, until you came along." She faced him and fluttered her long brown eyelashes. "How 'bout you?"

"Yeah. The same goes for me when helping my father and mother with the ministry. The camp meetings are a lot of fun, and we'll meet an occasional family or two, but they all live far away. You're the closest person I've met my age too." Joshua stared into her eyes. "And I sure am glad we did."

Warmth rushed to her face. She held her composure as ideas popped into her mind. *What did he mean by that? Is he glad to meet my acquaintance, or does he want a deeper relationship?*

"I share your sentiment. Do you suppose your parents will allow you to come out to the farm an' visit on occasion? Perhaps you might tell them that you'd like to help. I'm sure my Pa can arrange for you to work on buildin' the farmhouse, or maybe you can assist me in tendin' to the animals. Only if you want to, of course."

"Yeah. I'd enjoy doing that, Sarah. I know my mother and father have been hounding me to start working at the Mercantile, now that I'm sixteen."

"Well, we'll just have to mention this idea tonight." She smiled, thinking about the possibilities of being with him more often. "Speakin' of which, we better be headin' back."

Samuel sat daydreaming on the branch of the tree.

"Sam, we should get home, don't you think? We don't want to hold up supper. Ma an' Pa would be upset."

"Yep, okay." He snapped out of his daze. "I'll meet you both at the horses." Reaching down to grab the rope, he swung down to the bank and sauntered over.

Sarah led Joshua toward the fort door. Unexpectedly, he grabbed her hand, and as she turned her head toward his, he gazed deep into her eyes, drew her close to himself, and kissed her.

After their lips had parted, she opened her eyes and sensed her body go limp when his eyes, like the fierce gaze of a lion, invaded her soul, tingling every nerve in her body. So she leaned into his arms as he spoke. "Sarah Sower, I think we'll be seeing each other more often. Is this okay with you?"

"Oh, Joshua, I'm hopin' so." Warmth filled her senses and her knees weakened. Time seemed to stand still at that moment. "I guess we better go."

Although her body resisted, she pried herself from his embrace and took a deep breath trying to regain composure as he climbed down the steps. She straightened her straw bonnet and dress and allowed him to assist her down the tree and onto her horse.

"Is our bet still on? You two don't seem much in a hurry." Samuel shook his head as he pulled on the reins to keep Fire from galloping away.

Placing his left boot into Jake's stirrup, Joshua then swung his right leg over his back. Settling in his saddle, he gave Jake a swift kick, which caused him to leap forward. "It sure is!" He yelled as he darted back to the ranch.

17

Courting

Jonathan placed the platter of meats on the table when Samuel, Sarah, and Joshua arrived from the creek. "Good timin', ya'll. Why don't you go an' wash up before we eat?" he said as his wife poured sweet tea into the glasses. "Call your brother and sisters to do the same."

The siblings washed their hands at the Artesian pump and sat down. Daniel and Ruth McSwan seated themselves at one end of the table sipping the refreshment, and he and Mary at the head of the table.

"Pastor, we would be honored if you would say grace," Jonathan said.

"I would be glad to pray for this bounty," the minister said as they joined hands. "Dear Lord, we do thank You for Your love, mercy, provision, and this amazing meal set before us. We are ever grateful for this wonderful family that You brought into our lives and community and do pray for Your blessings upon them. Bless our time together this evening. In Jesus' name. Amen."

Both families passed the plethora of plated food and shared stories about their adventures of moving to California. The children discussed school, and Pastor and Ruth dispensed riveting memories about the people and places they had encountered at previous camp meetings.

Sarah and Joshua sat beside each other. With his peripheral

vision, Jonathan studied them hoping he would not get caught staring. They displayed fondness between themselves. Rose-blushed faces, whispers, and a warm glow emanating from their smiles, all contained in an invisible bubble. *Hmm. Sarah and Joshua. Why didn't I see this comin'? Of course. No wonder she's so concerned about her appearance when she goes to church. Mighty fine choice, daughter, if I say so myself. He seems to be a respectful young man.*

He glanced at Daniel, Ruth, and his wife, who sat observing the budding young couple as well. Mary locked eyes with his. He raised his brows and grinned. Without saying a word, the congenial parents turned to the minister and his spouse, who return a contented smile. Pastor McSwan shrugged and nodded, and Jonathan returned the gesture. *Hmm, I guess that was Pastor's nod of approval.*

As Joshua emerged from him and Sarah's private conversation, he cleared his throat to speak. "Mr. Sower, sir. Your farm is beautiful and well, uh, if there is a need for some extra help … well, I, uh, will be turning sixteen soon and, uh, well, I want to let you know I'm available to work."

Upon hearing his suggestion, Ruth and Pastor McSwan turned to each other, mouths agape. They glanced over at Jonathan for his reply.

The solicited farm owner inhaled, leaned back in his chair, wiped his mouth with a napkin, and squeezed it on his lap. His intuition told him that the proposal's purpose deemed two-fold; one for employment, the other an excuse to be near his daughter. He paused for a moment, stared down at his plate, and thought about Joshua's proposition.

Lord, this is more serious than I imagined. Whoa. He contemplated the work he needed to do on the farmhouse. *Gosh, should I do this?*

Their relationship is happenin' much too fast. Sarah is only fourteen. Hmm. But, I was a hair older than Joshua when I fell in love with Mary. But she was sixteen like me. He rubbed his chin and grinned at the thought of his early courting days.

He seems like a nice young man, grounded in the Bible. What could go wrong? I must be vigilant and keep a watchful eye.

"Joshua, I could use another farm-hand. There is plenty to do around here. When would you like to start?"

Sarah squirmed in her chair and stared down at her plate, grinning. The love-struck teenager held his breath then let out a sigh after hearing Jonathan's answer. He sat erect. "Well, sir, I'm ready anytime." He then turned to his parents. "Is this okay with you, Mother and Father?"

Still in shock, Pastor McSwan stammered, "Oh, uh, well sure, son. Making this offer is a responsible thing to do. I'm impressed by your motivation. We give you our blessings." He and Ruth smiled at their maturing young man.

"All right. Well, that settles that." Jonathan slapped his knee. "Why don't you plan on comin' by tomorrow in the mornin', and I'll get ya started." All the while, he knew where Joshua's request was leading. He turned to his wife, who nodded in approval.

Mary grabbed the peach pie and scooped a portion onto her plate. "More dessert, anyone?" She passed a piece to Joshua.

Nearing six o'clock, the families were finishing the sweet confection when the ground trembled beneath them. The table shook, and circles formed in the glasses of sweet tea. The horses neighed and whinnied, the cows and oxen lowed and stomped, and the hounds barked.

"What was that?" Mary blurted out, wide-eyed.

Jonathan analyzed the moment as he stared at the ripples in his glass. "I do believe that was an earthquake." He glanced at everyone around the table, the whites of their eyes enlarged.

Everyone kept quiet and did not move a muscle as they watched the liquid in their glasses settle. Jonathan waited for an aftershock to occur. After a couple of minutes, the animals quieted and calmed down.

"I think it's over." Pastor McSwan offered a warm and assuring grin. It seemed to set everyone at ease, and they returned his smile. "You all must get used to California earthquakes. They don't happen often. Sometimes God will find an opportunity to remind us who is boss around here."

The sun hung low on the horizon, and a glowing, golden radiance cast upon everyone's faces and over the fields, a remarkable contrast to the earthquake.

Mary said, "Oh Pastor, and yet the Lord demonstrates to us how much He loves us through His creation."

"Amen to that, sister!" Ruth lifted her glass of sweet tea to toast the occasion.

AFTER THE SUN HAD SETTLED BELOW THE HORIZON, Mary arose from her chair and started gathering the plates. "Please continue visitin'. I'm gonna clear the table."

Ruth also stood. "Oh, let me help you, and I will not take *no* for an answer." She began collecting the chinaware and followed the giddy farmer's wife into the cabin. She placed the dishes into one of the two large metal tubs on top of the counter near the black iron stove.

Mary grabbed the kettle filled with warm water and poured half the liquid over the plates in one tub and the other in the second container for rinsing. She took some soap and began washing the china and handed it to Ruth, who rinsed, dried, and stacked them.

Oh dear, this is an awkward moment. Am I supposed to say somethin' about Sarah and Joshua? How do they view our family? Is my daughter good enough for a clergyman's son? Are we Christian enough for them?

Thoughts rattled through Mary's mind as she stood next to the woman that could be her future in-law. She had full awareness of Sarah's secret affection for their young man. However, she wasn't prepared for the confrontation so soon.

Maybe I should ignore the subject until their relationship becomes more solid. Ah, but he has already made his intentions known by offerin' to work at the farm.

"Mary, this was a most delightful day spent with all of you. And the meal was outstanding. I believe it has been a long time since someone invited us for a home-cooked feast as grand as what you prepared today," Ruth said.

"Why, thank you, Ruth. It's our pleasure to bestow kindness and generosity to a very well deservin' family. You do so much for our community and our neighborin' towns. Y'all deserve far better than what I've cooked for you. I know our good Lord has a great banquet and reward waitin' for you in His kingdom."

After they finished their task, the women headed toward the front door when Ruth faced Mary, her face beaming with happiness. "I do believe we will see each other more often than we had imagined.

Daniel and I are ever grateful to you both for offering Joshua this job."

Understanding the meaning behind her statement, Mary reciprocated. "I agree with my whole heart, Ruth, and I can't wait to spend more time with your family too. Oh, what pleasure it will be." The two women giggled, locked elbows, and walked out to the table where their husbands leaned back in their chairs, watching the older siblings assist the younger ones in mounting the stilts.

"Well, Daniel, we ought to be headin' home before we lose the sunlight," Ruth suggested.

"Yes, my dear. I agree." Pastor McSwan leaned over his seat, stood, and stretched.

"This was a lovely day, a fantastic supper, and a most enjoyable visit with you folks. We do appreciate you taking the time to do this for us." He shook Jonathan's hand then cupped Mary's hand in his. "Mary, my dear sister-in-Christ, you make a mean peach pie. Not only will Joshua be around more often, but you might be visited by Ruth and me begging at your doorstep for another taste of your delectable cooking."

"Oh, Pastor, our home is always open to you. We expect ya'll to visit anytime."

Ruth gathered her children playing by the oak tree. After putting down the stilts, they walked over to the horse and buggy and hugged their hosts.

Joshua whispered to Sarah, "I'll see you tomorrow."

She returned a smile and nodded. "I look forward to your return."

The McSwans climbed into the carriage and headed for home.

JONATHAN STOOD REVIEWING THE FARMHOUSE PLANS at a table outside the cabin when he noticed Joshua approaching along the wayside path the following morning. Naomi and David already departed for school, and the remaining family and farmhands were busy about the new home.

"Hello, Mr. Sower," Joshua said.

"Good mornin'. You ready to go to work?" He chuckled.

"Sure am."

"Okay, I hope you can handle a saw 'cause I'm gonna have ya help Sam cut some planks." He proceeded to the farmhouse with the eager youngster at his heels so that his son could instruct him.

"Now, if you need a break, come on in the kitchen, and my wife will get you somethin' to drink. You know where the outhouse is. Lunch is at noon for about an hour. Most of the farmhands bring their own or go home, but you can eat with us in the cabin. The day starts at eight o'clock, and under normal circumstances, we are done by four. Now, how does five dollars a week to start sound to you?" Jonathan asked.

"That's mighty fine, sir," Joshua said, trying to contain his excitement.

"All right, I'll have Sam show ya what to do." He turned to his son. "Sam, train him up well." After a couple clicks with his mouth, he winked, and turned to Joshua, "If ya need anythin', I'll be around the cabin." The ambitious farm owner returned to overseeing the plans. His heart leaped at the dual opportunity before him. Not only would he be training his eldest to take on more responsibility on the farm, but he might also be gaining a future son-in-law who would be learning the trade.

SARAH WAS BUSY TENDING TO THE LIVESTOCK in the barn when she saw Samuel and Joshua heading toward the cabin. She could count on her brother's timely hunger pangs to alert her for lunch or supper. However, today was different. Never had she felt so giddy, and her chores seemed easier and more delightful, knowing her beau was nearby. She put down what she was doing and hustled outside.

"Josh, Sam!" She called. "Wait up for me."

"Sarah, there you are." Joshua stopped, and his face brightened as she approached.

"Well, how is your first day of work?" she asked.

"I couldn't have asked for a better job anywhere else. Sam's teachin' me how to frame a farmhouse. Perhaps one day I'll be able to build my own."

His eyes seemed to twinkle when he said those words to her.

Sarah's thoughts raced with the imagination of them living in their home filled with their children.

"Sorry to break up the moment, but I'm starvin'," Samuel said. "Let's go."

Her mother had prepared some sandwiches and lemonade for the hungry crew. "Great to have ya here, Joshua."

"Likewise, Mrs. Sower. I believe I'm goin' to enjoy working here."

"Josh seems to be a natural at carpentry." Samuel winked at his new sidekick.

Joshua chuckled. "I'm just trying to follow Jesus' footsteps."

"Or maybe somethin' else is motivatin' you." A smirk escaped the older boy.

Sarah felt her face warming at her brother's remark.

"Well, whatever the case, Sam needed the extra hand if we are goin' to finish the farmhouse in time for Christmas." Jonathan reached over and patted Joshua on his back. "Sure glad to have ya on board, Josh."

The family chattered on about their chores for the week. Afterward, the love-struck teens had a little time left to talk before going back to work. They strode over to the horses by the corral fence.

JONATHAN, MARY, AND SAMUEL watched the young couple from the cabin window as the son said out loud, "I think my kid sister is in love."

"I think you're right, Sam." He laughed. Being in a giddy mood himself he said, "An' she beat you to it!" They returned to the kitchen.

Sweet memories reflect upon his face, and he turned to his wife, who was gathering the dishes. He took the dishtowel and flicked it at Mary's hip with a crack. "Reminds me of when we were young."

Mary laughed at Jonathan's teasing. "All right, ya two, best be on your way back to work before things get outta hand here."

The rest of the week moved by with efficacy. On Friday during lunch, Joshua showed the Sower family the headline in the Merced Herald Newspaper. Jonathan read it out loud.

"*The Earth Quake.*"—"*The earthquake which took place here on Sunday last, seems to have been a general thing all over the southern part of the State. In San Francisco and Santa Cruz, it was particularly severe, creating great alarm among the people and not a little damage to property. In San Francisco, there is scarcely a brick building in the city uninjured, while in Santa Cruz, says a dispatch to the Bulletin, 'there was a general tumbling down of chimneys, and those left standing were turned partially around. The losses are estimated at $10,000, but may exceed that amount.' We (the Herald) have not heard of any person having been killed though in San Francisco. At this place, it was felt by very few, and those who did feel it describe the shock as being very light, but corresponding in the main with the accounts given by the San Francisco papers.*"

"Imagine that," Sarah said. "This happened while we were together last Sunday evenin'. That's gotta mean somethin'."

Everyone laughed at the thought.

Jonathan turned his gaze to Joshua, who sat swooning at his daughter on the other end of the table.

"Yes, it does mean something," Joshua replied. He stood and locked eyes with Jonathan. He cleared his throat. "Since we are all gathered here together, I have somethin' I need to ask that might shake things up a little." All eyes were on him as he trembled. "I, I…"

"Go on, son," Jonathan smiled to encourage Joshua, having the idea of what he was about to do.

"Sir, I would like to have your permission to court Sarah."

Jaws dropped and eyes enlarged. The family bent their gaze from the nervous young man to the patriarch for his reaction.

Jonathan straightened himself and volleyed his gaze between the lovebirds and settled upon his future son-in-law again. "Joshua." Pausing, all eyes on him now. "You have my permission."

Drowned in relief, the young man turned to Jonathan's daughter with a grin that stretched from ear to ear, and he released a huge sigh. "Thank you very much, Mr. Sower." He sat down and cupped Sarah's hands in his. "I do believe the ground is trembling beneath my feet, Sarah."

"Mine too, Joshua. Mine too."

NOW THAT BOTH FAMILIES KNEW Joshua was courting Sarah, they seemed more relaxed around each other during Sunday service. They visited one another often and saw Joshua almost every day.

On Monday, October 16th, Jonathan peered out the cabin window and saw his foreman walking up the wayside path with three farmhands instead of the usual dozen. He strode over to meet him outside.

"What happened, Yung? Where are the carpenters?"

"Sir, there was accident in Rio Vista. The steamer, *Yosemite*, blew up last Friday at six-thirty in evening. It discharged freight and was departing wharf on Sacramento River when boiler burst. Killed one hundred people and scalded more. One dozen white people, thirty Chinamen, and one Chinese woman were rescued. Most were blown in river and will never be found."

"My Lord." He shook his head. "What does this have to do with our workers?"

"They had family and friends on board who travel daily on the steamer. They go to Rio Vista when they heard news. Many have not returned yet."

Jonathan realized the implications the tragedy held for his deadline. "You men do what you can in the meantime. Keep me posted, will you, Yung?"

"Of course, sir."

The heavy-hearted farmer was thankful he had taken on Joshua's help. Upon the return of the farmhands a week later, they worked without tiring and were able to meet the deadline so the Sower family could move into the farmhouse in time for Christmas.

18

The First Farmhouse Christmas

Jonathan and his family huddled on the front porch of their newly constructed, two-story farmhouse on a chilly Friday afternoon in mid-December. "Before we go inside, let's join hands in prayer." He stretched his arms to the side, grabbing hold of Mary's hand to his right and Samuel's to his left. The other children completed the circle.

Upon bowing their heads, he began. "Heavenly Father, we thank You for the love and mercy You've given to our family this year. We ask for Your blessin' and protection for the beautiful home you've provided, which is more than we deserve. I pray we can be good stewards of the entire property for the glory of Your name. May You also bless us with many happy years of new memories. We ask this in Jesus' name. Amen." He opened his eyes and admired the glowing faces surrounding him.

"Allow me the honor of opening the front door, and then y'all can follow your Ma and me inside." The fresh scent of paint greeted the family. Light flooded in from the window at the end of the hall, illuminating the foyer. To the right, the staircase ascended to the bedchambers upstairs, and the door next to the foot of the steps led to the living room. To the left of the hallway was Jonathan's office, and next to it was the dining room and kitchen.

"May we look for our bedrooms, Pa?" David asked as he climbed.

"Of course, boys. I believe your room is the first one to the right at the top of the stairs with a window facin' the backyard. And girls, yours is down the hall with the window lookin' out to the front of the house."

The children raced up the steps, and Jonathan turned to his wife, whose eyes sparkled.

"What would ya like to see first, my love?"

"Oh, Jon, let's start with your office, then the family room, and then the kitchen. Let's save our bedroom for last."

"All right, after you. Lead the way, dear." He delighted in his family's joyful laughter as they explored the house. They would spend the weekend moving in their furniture and belongings from the cabin.

THE FRIDAY BEFORE CHRISTMAS, the family took the wagon up to Mariposa to chop down a perfect six-foot cedar to grace the new living room. Mother and children spent Saturday afternoon baking sugar and gingerbread cookies for ornaments and popping corn to string for garlands. Jonathan topped it with the shining tin star he crafted the previous year. The tree gloried in its sugary delights.

Mary had removed the lower branches and created a magnificent wreath with an oversized claret bow. She sprinkled it with red winterberries and dangled a garland of small pinecones and bells in the center. The pine-scented creation hung on the front door. Pine trimmings, evergreens, and more berries accented the staircase, fireplace mantels, and dining table.

"The home is beautiful, darlin'. I think you outdid yourself this year," Jonathan said as he and Mary sat by the warm, stone hearth in the living room.

"I've waited a long time for this day, darlin'. I wanted to make Christmas special, bein' our first holiday in our new home. I believe our preparations are ready for our first Christmas Eve dinner and housewarmin' party tomorrow. I can't wait till the McSwans, Patrick, and his wife, Ingrid, will see it. It'll be nice to meet her finally," Mary said, embracing her husband.

THROUGHOUT THE HOUSE THE NEXT DAY, the aroma of baked ham, green beans, sweet potatoes, pumpkin pie, spices, and pine permeated the rooms. Jonathan peeked out the window of his office when he heard the familiar sound of Patrick's rumbling wagon wheels and clogging oxen hooves coming up the wayside path in the late afternoon. He watched the couple park, help his wife from the buckboard, and grab a hefty basket from the back. Closing the drapes, he listened for the bells at the front door.

Jingle, jingle, jingle.

"Someone answer the door, please!" He heard Mary holler to the family from the kitchen.

"We'll get it, Ma!" Samuel and David called from the living room.

Jonathan turned his head toward the boys' boots stomping on the wooden floor. He threw some more logs in the dual fireplace between his office and the galley as they entered. Peeking through the flames to the other side, he beheld the warm scene of Mary, Sarah, and Naomi busy plating the bountiful holiday dinner.

"Happy Christmas!" Patrick's raspy, deep voice bellowed.

The boys returned the greeting, their voices bolstering with joy.

Through the office door, Jonathan watched as David hurried to the kitchen to tell his mother and sisters. "Mr. and Mrs. Faye is here!" The clanking sounds of dishes ceased as the girls put down what they were doing and paraded to the foyer.

Then the young boy scurried to his office. "Pa, come an' meet Patrick's wife."

Jonathan removed the dust from his hands and joined them by the front door.

A tall, slender beauty of Norwegian descent, the middle-aged woman had touches of gray blended in her blond, braided hair tucked in a bun under her bonnet. She had accessorized it with sprigs of holly. "Happy Christmas," she said with a gentle hillbilly accent like her husband.

"Hello, Patrick. And this must be Ingrid. And the same to you, ma'am!" He extended his hand to shake hers. "I'm Jonathan, and this is my wife, Mary. These are our children, Samuel, Sarah, Naomi, and David."

"I'm so glad to meet y'all finally. Patrick's told me so much about your family." She inhaled deep, taking in the excitement.

"Can I take your coats?" Mary said as Ingrid removed her hat and cape, and Patrick his overcoat. A petite woman, she wore a hooped, dark-plum colored day dress with a white crocheted collar and matching cuffs on the wrists.

The gruff cargo-hauling associate cleaned up nicely in his dark wool trousers, gray vest over an olive-green plaid shirt, and charcoal color frock coat. He even tidied up his beard for the festive occasion. "Thank you, and this is for y'all!" He handed a bountiful basket covered with fine lace to Jonathan.

"May I peek inside?" Sarah asked.

"Please do. We might even be able to use some of it this evenin'," Ingrid replied.

Sarah removed the delicate covering. "Oh, my. Jams, jellies, bread, and cookies. I thought I smelled somethin' absolutely divine."

"Ah, thank you," Jonathan said. "Well, come into our cozy family room and sit by the fire. Would you care for some eggnog or wassail?" he asked as he gave the basket to his eldest daughter to bring to the kitchen.

"Oh my. Wassail for me please, to start. That ought to warm me up," Ingrid said sweetly.

"I'll take one of those too." Patrick stood by the fireplace rubbing his hands over the glowing flames.

Mary hurried to the serving table at the back of the family room and poured the hot beverage from the kettle into her fine china cups.

"Here you are." The merry hostess handed them their beverages. "Now, if you'll excuse me for a moment, I have to finish settin' the dinner table. When the McSwans arrive, we can sit down and get to know one another more."

"Oh, please. By all means. Do what you need to," Patrick said.

Samuel, Naomi, and David sat down on the hand-woven carpet near the fireplace next to their first guest as they relaxed on the winged-back chair. Patrick situated himself next to his wife on the couch and began sharing his stories about being on the trail and hauling cargo from one town to the next. He had them laughing at some of the extraordinary encounters he had with people from different places.

"Just a few weeks ago, I visited a small almond farm in Hughson to pick up firewood from cleared trees. That's when I saw a hunched-back ol' man, wearin' a tattered straw hat, holdin' a twig in his hands, walkin' in circles out in the fields." Patrick rubbed his chin. "Square, Richard Square was his name. At first, I thought the fellow was lost or confused. I figured he must be the owner of the property since no one seemed to mind him bein' there. I jumped off the wagon and hollered over to him. But he just kept shufflin' his feet, holdin' this Y-shaped branch in his hands."

"Didn't any hounds come after you? Usually, these ol' farmers have for themselves some guard dogs to alert them of strangers," Samuel said.

"Nope. But when I finally approached him from behind, he near jumped out of his skin when I said hello. He cursed me to high heaven for frightenin' him." Patrick snorted as he laughed aloud. "He was so focused on what he was doin' that he paid no attention to his surroundins'.

"Well, after he calmed down a bit, he explained to me his method. He told me he was practicing the ancient art of dowsing. He was lookin' for water to build himself a well. The nearest creek was almost three miles away, and he needed water for his orchards. He showed me how he became one with the branch by holdin' it a certain way so that he could feel its vibrations. Supposedly, the piece of wood will point him to the water when it found it. When I told him I didn't believe in that mumbo-jumbo, he near chased me off his property with that thing." Patrick swung his arms around him, imitating the old man swinging the rod. The children rolled in laughter.

Jingle, jingle, jingle. David and Naomi raced to the door to greet the second guests.

"Happy Christmas!" The McSwan family cheered.

"Yeah!" The children screamed as they grabbed Rebecca by the hand and rushed her into the living room to play some games by the fireplace.

"Indeed, it is! Come on in." Jonathan greeted the festively attired family.

"The McSwan's are here," Samuel yelled.

Mary and Sarah had finished what they were doing and came into the foyer. The guest removed their coats and hung them on the coat rack by the front door. Everyone flowed into the living room, and more chairs were brought in as they gathered around the fireplace, chatting for a while and sipping on some refreshment.

"My lovely ladies prepared a grand Christmas dinner of ham, sweet potatoes, green beans, cranberry relish, hot cross buns, gravy, cookies, and pecan and pumpkin pies. Whew," the proud husband and father said.

"Well, I hope y'all are hungry," Mary said over the chatter and laughter. "Let's go to the dining room and enjoy supper."

They followed his wife and sat down at the expanded table where everyone sat together. Pastor McSwan did the honors of blessing the home and the meal. Jonathan's heart swam in sheer delight to have all his loved ones under one roof in the home of his dreams.

AFTERWARD, THEY GATHERED IN THE LIVING ROOM where the Sowers brought out their instruments and played carols. While the families merry around the tree, Joshua and Sarah quietly exited the room and went into her father's office by the dual fireplace to exchange gifts.

"Happy Christmas, Sarah." He grinned as he reached in his coat pocket and handed her a small box wrapped in red paper.

She caressed the pretty little package and peered up at her beau.

"Well, go ahead and open it," he said.

Inside the small container was a heart-shaped locket on a gold chain with a small picture of him fixed to one side.

"Oh, Joshua … it's beautiful. You shouldn't have." Her eyes welled with tears. *He really does love me.*

"I worked hard to get something special for my gal. It's all worth it for you, Sarah. Here, turn around and let me put it on you." Joshua fastened the necklace around her slender neck.

Touching the locket over her beating heart, she turned to Joshua. "I'll never take it off." Feeling warmth rush to her cheeks, she lifted her other hand that held a medium size box. "This is my gift to you, but I'm afraid it is not as amazing as yours. I did put a lot of love and care into it though."

She handed Joshua the present wrapped in red ribbon. Inside was a wool scarf, matching mittens, and socks, which she had meticulously knitted for him.

"Sarah, this is beautiful. You made this for me?" He felt the soft texture before he put them on.

"Yes, I did them for those days when you'll be away from me at the camp meetings. I hope they'll keep you warm and thinkin' of me." She adjusted his scarf.

"Oh, I don't need these things to remind me of you. You're always on my mind. But because you made them with your own hands, I will treasure them with my heart and wear them as often as I can on those chilly nights away from you." Joshua kissed Sarah, and they returned to the living room to join in the laughter and the merriment.

19

New Friends

January 1866

The fizzling sound of a lucifer being lit streamed into Naomi's ears. *Phosphorus*—the repugnant odor pinched her nostrils, stirring her from her sleep. A subtle glow from the oil lamp penetrated her closed eyelids and increased to its brightest, disturbing her dreams.

Grr. Naomi pulled her quilt over her head. "Put it out, Sarah! It's too early. The roosters ain't even begun to crow yet." *Just because you get up every mornin' at the crack of dawn to milk the cows and feed the chickens, doesn't mean you gotta wake me at the same time. Why don't you dress in the dark like you normally do?*

"Get up, Naomi. You need as much time as you can to prepare for school. You don't want to be late on your first day back." Sarah tugged at her blanket. "Your friends will be there," she said with a glimmer in her voice.

Naomi's thoughts drifted to her classmate's happy faces and laughter as they played with trundle hoops on the playgrounds. *Dirk, Ruby, Della, Abigail, and Rebecca.* She flicked the quilt away from her face, sat up in her bed, and swung her legs over the side. "All right, I'm up."

"Good. Get dressed and come down for some breakfast."

Sarah grinned as she donned her day dress and apron. "Sure is nice to finally have our own room. Now we don't have to worry 'bout changin' in front of Sam or David." She reached for her wadded, wool-lined bonnet and proceeded downstairs.

Naomi rolled her eyes and planted her feet on the cold, wood floor. *Whew. The winter chill in California is far more bearable than the winters in Kentucky. My toes used to freeze on the floors over there. That time seems so long ago.* She shuffled to the small stove in the corner of her room to warm her face, hands, and feet. Then she trudged to the dresser where her wool socks, pantalets, day dress, and pinafore had been set out before bedtime. She dressed, braided her hair, and moseyed downstairs to the kitchen.

"*Cock-al-doodle-do!*" Samuel crowed and flapped his arms like a rooster. "Mornin', chickadee. Good to see you up with the rest of us." He mocked and grinned like a fool.

"*Ssss.*" Naomi sneered, twisting her lips and gritting her teeth at her brother's snide remark. She plopped herself on the wood chair, grabbed some toast with jam, and placed it on her plate.

"Aren't you excited to go back to school, sis? I am," David said while chewing.

She peered up at her mother, who scooped a heaping spoonful of scrambled eggs onto her dish. "Yes, of course I am." *Yes, I can't wait to see my friends again. Ugh, but to sit and listen to lessons all day ... boring!*

"I've packed your favorite sandwiches in your baskets, turkey with sweet pickled cucumbers. Oatmeal cookies are in there too," her mother said, taking the skillet back to the counter.

"Sounds scrumptious, Ma." The corners of her lips curled up a slight degree. Food seemed to be the catalyst for improving her mood. Her conversation at breakfast became lighter and more jovial as she ate.

"Did you finish your winter break assignment, David? What was your New Year's resolution?" she asked.

"I wrote about my goal to read one Bible chapter a day." He sat erect as his legs swung beneath him.

Naomi imagined a halo above her sweet brother's head. She snickered. "Well, my essay is about how I'm goin' to make more friends and become the most popular girl in school." Her chin jutted up, and she fluttered her eyelashes.

"Oh, my. Look at the time." Mary glanced at the cuckoo clock hanging on the wall. "Be sure to wear your heavy cape, Naomi, and your wool coat, David. Take the umbrellas too. Give yourself a little extra time to walk to school. The clouds are about to burst open."

The siblings cloaked their outerwear and grabbed their lunch baskets.

"You ready, little brother?"

"Sure am, sis. Let's go."

They opened their umbrellas and stepped down from the front porch onto the muddy wayside path, which led to the school a quarter of a mile away.

Naomi shook off her umbrella and hung her cape on the dowel at the entrance, then scanned the cramped schoolroom, looking for her friends amongst the twenty children of various ages. Rebecca and Abigail were already seated and waving at her.

"Please be seated children, and let's begin." Mr. Cavern threw another log in the potbelly stove and returned to his desk. "Welcome back, students. I hope you had a joyful Christmas. The weather does not appear too welcoming on our first day back. The winter season is upon us. Expect recess to be indoors." He paused waiting for her classmates' groans to subside. "Not to worry. There are plenty of puzzles and rainy day games to play. Try to get along with one another, please." Giggles returned. "Let's begin by reciting our alphabets, starting with the first row."

The first student stood and recited, "A … in Adam's fall, we sinned all."

The next pupil followed. "B…," He stopped, distracted by a gust of cold air rushing in as the door opened wide. The Edgar siblings, Bert who was thirteen, Chad eleven, and Lizzie who turned nine, walked in dripping wet. They wore no outerwear, were shivering, and had miserable frowns.

The instructor pulled out his pocket watch to check the time.

"The three of you are tardy again."

"But Mr. Cavern ...I..." The eldest boy spoke for the group.

"Never mind. Sit by the stove and dry off. Take turns wearing the dunce hat, starting with you, Bert. I want each of you to write, 'I will not be late,' ten times on your slates. You can go to your seats after you've finished. Understood?"

"Yes, Mr. Cavern," they answered.

"Let's continue." His stern focus displayed his perturbance as he pointed to the second student.

As the students took their turn reciting, twelve-year-old Abigail whispered in Naomi's ear, "I wish the Edgars would stay home. Nobody likes them anyways. People talk. Rumor tells us their father works at the lumber mill in Merced Falls all week and comes home on the weekends. He doesn't spend time with his family. Instead, he goes to the saloon and gets drunk. When he does go home, he beats on his wife and children. That's why they're covered in bruises and are absent a lot. Besides, they're kinda smelly. Their mother never washes their clothes. I bet they haven't taken a bath in days." A belittling laugh escaped her breath.

Naomi, who was now eleven, became aware of these things about the siblings. She knew most of her classmates were afraid to befriend them because of their unruly behavior. Or, maybe they were prejudice toward them because of their social status, being poor and neglected. How could she blame the others? But what came out of Abigail's mouth infuriated her. It's one thing to think badly about someone and not say a word. Yet it's another thing to poke fun of that person when they are down.

Being the third and insignificant child in her family, so she thought, her heart sank at the disparagement. Her eldest sibling, Sam, is the male heir; her sister, Sarah is smart and beautiful; and the youngest, David is spiritually gifted. Who was she? Just miserable, clumsy Naomi.

"Be quiet, Abigail, before ya get us into trouble." Naomi glanced over at the Edgars, empathizing with them. The snickers of the other classmates seemed to reverberate louder in the small classroom. *This is horrible. The dunce hat adds more to their humility. They are distressed and injured enough as it is.* She could sense the sibling's tension and outrage, especially coming from Bert as he glared at the class. His eyes seemed to be flashing darts of fire.

Something about the Edgar siblings' rough exterior intrigued Naomi. She was not able to determine if she felt compassion for them, or if, by some strange reason, she was attracted to the challenge of gaining new friends of an unlikely kind. She hoped to talk to them during recess to win their friendship.

The brothers and their sister sat in the corner of the room, disrupting class as they teased and fought one another. Naomi cringed at the vulgar words expelled from their mouths. On many days, Mr. Cavern quite often had to separate them in different corners of the room, but he had not done so yet.

Lunch break came quickly, and the only subject Naomi could focus on was the Edgars. She had built up the courage to approach them. After devouring her meal, she excused herself from her friends, grabbed a bag of marbles, and advanced toward the siblings with caution. Their faces appeared bewildered at first, brows furrowed and eyes narrowed. Chad and Lizzie turned to Bert for a gesture to ward her off.

Bert's dirty blond hair dipped over his left eye, so he jerked his head to move his bangs. Naomi imagined she was crossing enemy lines. Dark, squinty pupils focus on her every move, and his lips tightened over clenched teeth.

"What do you want?" Bert glared at her.

At first, she jumped back but took a deep breath. "I was wonderin' if y'all would like to play a game of marbles."

"Heck, no! Why should we want to play with you? Go away, sissy girl." Bert's sharp tongue jabbed at her. Feeling warmth rush to her face, she glanced around and viewed a room full of wide eyes glued on her uncharacteristic behavior.

His abrasive response motivated Naomi all the more for the challenge. So she lifted her chin and crossed her arms over her chest. "Why? Are you afraid I'm going to beat you? Who's the big sissy now?"

The ruckus caused Mr. Cavern to stand at his desk and reach for the paddle. *Oh no, not that.* She shifted her gaze to Bert. *Now, look at what you've done with your hot temper. You better do somethin' or else you'll get a lickin' on your behind.*

He sneered at her and snatched the bag of marbles out of her hands. "Gimme that."

He scooted the desks around to make enough room for them to play on the ground, then he selected the huge, clear, cerulean shooter he called "Blue Moon." Next, he drew a twenty-four-inch wide circle on the wood floor with chalk and placed his marble in the center.

Naomi followed his lead and found a place to sit down. She chose the large white-and-green shooter she named "Limeade" and positioned it in the center also. They would use their marble to target their opponent's and push it out of the ring. The winner was the person with the fewest shots.

She could hear the students, including Chad and Lizzie, gathering around murmuring amongst each other. "Hey, Naomi is challenging Bert to a match."

"Why would she want to play with him?"

"She's brave."

"She's stupid."

"She's crazy!"

Well, think what you like everyone. I'm gonna prove that you have nothin' to fear about the Edgar siblings. Y'all are a bunch of chickens and gossipers. She realized they were curious about the strange encounter and wanted to see what would become of her.

Since she called the challenge, she allowed Bert to go first. He grabbed his large marble and centered Naomi's in the circle. He aimed, and Blue Moon tapped the right side of Limeade, and it rolled about three inches to the left.

"One!" The children counted together.

Next, he repositioned himself to the right of the ring and targeted. Again it hit the lime-green marble on the right, pushing it two inches to the left.

"Two," the students shouted.

He aimed again, and this time it bumped Limeade on the left, which made it roll back to the same place to the right.

"Three!"

"Darn it." Bert pounded the ground with his fist. He laid stomach down on the floor, lowered his chin, and positioned his aiming hand beneath his right eye. With his four knuckles down, thumb behind his curled index finger, and Blue Moon resting in front of his thumbnail on top of his index finger, he situated his marble so that Limeade was directly in his line of sight. He flicked his thumb. Blue Moon rolled with force and made direct contact with Limeade, ricocheting her marble pass the circle.

"Four!" The crowd cheered.

"Try to beat that." Bert sneered.

"Humph." Naomi turned her nose at him.

She centered Bert's cerulean marble in the ring. Kneeling down and sitting on her feet behind her, she positioned her right hand, knuckles on the ground in front of her knees to get a bird's eye view of the straight path her shooter was to travel. With a flick of her thumb, Limeade rolled with speed and slammed into Blue Moon dead-on, positioning itself within three inches from the circle.

"One," the classmates shouted.

If she stayed in the same place, she would simply have to repeat her tactic, but with a little more power. The maneuver should cause his shooter to go past the ring. So she aimed and flicked her thumb, but oh! Limeade took a slight turn to the right and missed Bert's marble.

"Two," her friends said sadly.

Hmm, maybe his marble is too far away at this angle. She repositioned herself to the right of the circle. From this vantage point, Blue Moon seemed further from the line, but closer for Naomi to reach. So she aimed and *smack!* Limeade collided dead-on again, and his marble went rolling past the circle.

"Three!"

Bert stood, stomped the ground, and pushed the desk next to him. But at that moment, Mr. Cavern rang the bell.

"Lunchtime is over. Return to your seats please."

The angry boy glared at her and gritted his teeth as she began gathering up the marbles. "I'll challenge you tomorrow."

"I'll be ready," she sassed with a teasing grin.

As she returned to her desk, David nudged up beside her. "Sis, are you sure ya want to be doin' this?"

"Look, little brother." She glanced at his disturbed countenance. "I know what I'm doin'." Her tone caused him to step back, and he whimpered to his seat. When school ended, she could tell he was careful not to mention anything more about the Edgar siblings as they walked home. He hung his head low as they discussed the homework for the next day.

The following days were rainy, so the game of marbles continued between Bert and Naomi indoors. They both won and lost. The Edgars seemed to enjoy the new, highly competitive friendship, although it would not be obvious by their mean-spirited behavior toward her. After they had become bored of playing marbles, she challenged them to jacks.

So far, so good. Visions of shared lunches dance in Naomi's head. *I wonder what it will be like next week.*

20

Torn Between Friends

The low winter sunlight spilled through the clouds enough to rid the chill in the classroom's looming dampness. Naomi imagined playing tag outdoors with her old friends at school this week. When she sat next to Abigail, she appeared to be quiet and unfriendly. No hello, no chattering.

Naomi sensed her friends' irritation the previous week when she played with the Edgar siblings. She saw the displeasure in their eyes as they glared at her and frowned. Now that the rain had stopped, she hoped to make amends with Abigail, Rebecca, Dirk, Della, Ruby, and her brother David.

"Hey, Abby, you want to play tag at lunchtime?" she whispered while they practiced their penmanship.

"Humph." Abigail snorted and kept her eyes on her slate. "Aren't you gonna play with your new friends? What happened? Are they no longer good enough for you? Are you going to throw them away like an old rag as you did to us?"

"Oh, Abby. Y'all will always be my best friends. I just felt sorry for the Edgars. They need someone to play with too. Maybe one day you'll join us in a game."

"Oh, and who appointed you to be their savior?" She grunted.

"No thank you, Naomi. My parents told me to stay away from their kind."

"All right. Have it your way. You still didn't answer my question, though."

Upon turning her head, Abigail made eye contact with Naomi and inhaled. Her angry frown relaxed into a forced, half-grin. "I guess so. After all, I do miss you. We haven't played together since before Christmas break."

Chalk on the table, Naomi reached over and squeezed her friend's hand. Abigail's smile lengthened across her face, and she squeezed back.

"I'M BACK, Y'ALL," Naomi said as she sat down to eat lunch with her six friends.

"Yeah!" Arms raised, Rebecca cheered. "We thought we lost you forever."

"Are you kiddin'? You can't get rid of me that fast." A cackle escaped her, and she bit into her sandwich.

"I told you she'd return," David said. "She was just practicin' her Christian duty to love her enemies."

"I'm not done with them yet. Before too long, y'all will be friends with them too."

Gags and snickers rebound from amongst her classmates.

"Spare us, Naomi. You can keep those friends to yourself," Ruby said.

Disgusted at their comments, Naomi shook her head. "Well, I guess they'll have to be my rainy-day friends then." She finished her sandwich. "Y'all want to play tag? You're it!" After slapping Dirk's back, she raced away with hopes to be chased.

The Edgar siblings kicked a leather ball between themselves and glared at Naomi on occasion, which made her cringe. *Should I go over and, at least, say hello?* Hesitation kept her from going because her heart tore to leave her old friends for fear of angering them again. *No, I better not.*

Arms crossed over his puffed-out chest; Bert stared at her, his pride would not allow him to ask her to join them in a game.

He probably expects me to go over there. Bert will need to figure it out.

She caught up to Ruby and slapped her back. "Tag, you're it!" Screams and laughter rang through the grounds. As Naomi paused, her eyes caught Bert's harsh gaze as he bounced the ball hard against the ground. *I bet he thinks I've abandoned them.*

Bert spun to kick the ball around with Chad and Lizzie. He had mentioned to her last week that he enjoyed soccer, but they needed one more teammate to even both sides. She didn't think anything of his comment because her thoughts were on marbles at the time. Just as she pondered this thought, Bert grabbed the ball from his brother and sister. "Wait here while I ask Naomi if she wants to play."

She could not believe her eyes as Bert approached to ask her to join them. He never asked anyone for anything, especially a girl. *Although he doesn't show any emotions with his chest puffed out and chin held high, he has to be scared or nervous.*

"Hey, Naomi! I need you with us to play soccer." He commanded rather than asked.

Torn between their new relationship and her old friendships, Naomi had to make a decision. She turned to her old friends who sneered at her. "No, Naomi! You're playing with us. You can't quit now."

She tried her best to respond to Bert as kindly as possible. "Sorry, Bert. I promised my friends I'd play with them today. Maybe tomorrow."

Fear crept into her heart as Bert's face turned beet red. *Did I just embarrass him in front of everyone? Oh dear, he's angry at me now. Great, Naomi, now you're as rotten as his father tellin' him he is a good for nothin', filthy brat. What have I done?*

Face contorted and eyes filled with fire, Bert yelled, "Ah, forget it, you traitor. I hate you. Don't ever come around' us again. You hear?"

He took the ball and slammed it hard on the ground. He stormed off, leaving Chad and Lizzie standing with wide eyes and dropped jaws, staring back at those around them.

"What happened, Chad?" Lizzie stood shaking. "Where is Bert going?"

"I don't know, Lizzie. It doesn't look good. I'm goin' after him," he replied. "I knew we should've never got involved with that no-good, snake of a girl," he said loud enough for Naomi to hear. His stare pierced like sharp daggers thrown at her.

"Well, I'm goin' with ya." Lizzie whimpered.

Before Chad and Lizzie fled the school grounds, they charged over to Naomi and cursed at her. "You traitor!" They spat and ran away.

Naomi's heart sank to her stomach. Nobody had ever spoken to her in that way, nor had she ever witnessed anyone talk like that before. Their words cut straight to the bone. Paralyzed and speechless, a lump formed in her throat, and big alligator tears filled her eyes.

David walked up behind her and wrapped his hand around her elbow while watching Chad and Lizzie run away. "Naomi, are you okay? Come on. Don't you mind them. That's why no one wants to play with them. I still love you, sis."

"Yeah, and we do too," Ruby, Della, Abigail, and Rebecca said as they crowded around her to bring comfort.

"Dirk ran to tell Mr. Cavern about the Edgars leaving. I'm sure he'll talk with their mother," Abigail said. "Come on. Let's go inside."

You traitor! I hate you! Bert's words rang in Naomi's mind the rest of the school day. *This can't be. What did I do to him to deserve this treatment?*

As time passed, hurt turned into anger. *I'm not scared of them.* Naomi was not going to stand for Bert's lousy conduct, so she decided to search for him after school and confront him. Her first step was to tell her brother to go home without her so she could deal with Bert alone. *Hmm, what shall I tell him so that he doesn't tell Ma and Pa where I am?*

After school, Naomi spoke to her brother. "David, why don't you go on ahead without me? I'm goin' over to one of my girlfriends' house to play, and I'll be home shortly, okay?"

"Ah … can I tag along with you?"

"No. This is girl's stuff. I'll catch ball with you later, okay?"

"Oh, all right." Frowning, David turned and walked home.

Naomi had an idea of where to find Bert. He had mentioned to her about a shortcut on the way to school through the cemetery, and a relative, Uncle Bob Edgar, who had been buried there. Some said that this uncle had shot one of the Snelling brothers back in December of 1858 over a dispute while playing a game called Crack-loo. It consisted of tossing a half-dollar at a crack in the floor at the Snelling Saloon. The person whose fifty-cent piece landed closest to the crack without falling in became the winner.

The town's people hung him with no judge or jury and buried him with a simple headstone in the back of the cemetery. She recalled Abigail gossiping about how Bert would often go to his Uncle's gravesite and throw rocks at it after his father had roughed him up a bit. Bert's family became ashamed of this story. Others believe that this was why his father became a mean, bad seed.

At the cemetery, Naomi located Bob Edgar's gravesite. It didn't take long to find it hidden from public view. There she saw Bert sitting down beside the grave marker with his head hung low. As she crept up behind him, the dried leaves crunched under her boots causing Bert to jump to his feet.

"What the heck are you doin' here? I told you not to bother us. Go away!"

He bent down to pick up one of the rocks to throw at her, but Naomi rushed in and kicked it from his hand. The dirt on his face tracked his tears and sweat.

"No, I'm not leavin', Bert. You can't talk to me the way you did. You don't own me, you know." Shouting with her hands clenched beside her, Naomi reasoned with him. "I've had those friends long before you. They'd be yours too if you let them and if you stop actin' like some bully."

"Who needs them or you anyway? Oh, go back to your silly friends and your big, cozy farm, little rich girl. We have nothin' in common, so leave me alone or else I'll…"

"Or you'll what, beat me up as your Pa does to you? Well, come on then." Naomi threw her books down, took a wide stance, and put both her fists up in front of her. Working on the farm helped to develop her muscular strength. *I can beat this bully.*

She could tell her comment about his father hit a nerve. The fiery darts in his eyes returned. He rushed at her, hoping to push her to the ground and punch her in the stomach. But before he could, Naomi pulled her arm back and swung at his eye.

He flew backward onto the dirt. He sat up, shook his head, and held it between his palms. "Whoa, I just got my butt whooped by a girl. My Uncle must be rollin' in his grave."

"You get up, ya coward," Naomi yelled at Bert, ready to slug him again.

"Okay, stop … I give up," he said humbly. As he glanced around the cemetery, he was thankful no one had seen what had happened. "Dang, Naomi! Where did you learn to punch like that?" Bert rubbed his eye, which began to swell.

"As you've noticed, Bert, I live on a farm." She put her hands down. "Now would you stop actin' like a big baby and come to your senses? My choice of friends is my business, and you can't do anythin' about it 'cause I can be just as tough as you," she replied snidely. "So don't you ever talk to me that way or else I will never play with you or your brother and sister again."

Naomi sensed Bert, Chad, and Lizzie enjoyed their friendship, and now she turned the tables on them. She controlled their relationship now.

"You better be at school tomorrow' with an explanation from your ma 'cause Mr. Cavern will be lookin' for y'all."

Gathering her books, she turned and walked away, leaving Bert still stunned on the ground. Her hand hurt from punching him in his eye, but she wasn't going to fess up to him. Her biggest concern now would be the fib she would tell her parents about her bruised knuckles.

21

Bad Discernment

"What happened to your hand, dear?" Mary pointed to the swollen redness on Naomi's knuckles as she lifted her fork to her mouth at breakfast.

Naomi gagged, dropped her utensil, withdrew her hand, and placed it on her lap. "Oh, uh, it's nothin', Ma. I hurt myself playin' tag yesterday with my friends. I slipped and fell." The lie spilled past her lips, smooth as butter, followed by a crooked grin. *Please believe me.*

Mary's eyes narrowed as she sat at the other end of the table sipping her coffee.

"You ought to be more careful, dear. Young ladies don't behave in this manner."

"Yes, ma'am." Avoiding eye contact, she looked down at her plate hoping her mother believed her. *My behavior seems to concern her more than my lie. May heaven forbid she finds out the truth that I slugged a boy yesterday. I wouldn't hear the end of the 'young lady' lecture. Stay calm, and don't overdo it. Hurry up and finish breakfast and get outta here before she asks more questions.* "I'll be more careful next time."

She turned to her brother. "Are you almost finished, David? We best be goin'."

"Yep. I'm done." He stood and put his dish in the sink.

"Don't forget your lunches. Enjoy your day in school," Ma said as she and her sibling shuffled out of the kitchen.

ARRIVING BEFORE THE OTHER STUDENTS, Naomi was seated at her desk when the Edgar siblings arrived and approached Mr. Cavern. The instructor sat at his desk peering over his bifocals. Bert locked eyes with her as he passed by. The sight of a dark purple crescent around his right eye made her jaw drop. As he placed a note in front of the teacher, Chad and Lizzie stood close behind him.

"Good morning, children. Glad to have you back. What happened yesterday?" Mr. Cavern wasn't smiling.

Bert cleared his throat. "This letter from our ma will explain everything, sir," he said in a low voice.

"All right." Mr. Cavern unfolded the crumpled piece of paper and began to read. His brows came together, and a frown became more apparent on his face.

Lizzie clenched her skirt. Chad stared down at his boots and shuffled his feet while Bert crossed and uncrossed his arms.

"So, all of you had stomachaches after eating lunch?"

What the teacher said seemed more like a statement than a question. He glared up at them, his left eyebrow cocked. His suspicious expression was similar to her mother's this morning.

Mr. Cavern must not believe their note. I betcha Bert forged it. I've seen his awful handwritin'. There is no way he can pen like an adult unless, of course, his ma is uneducated and he has to write for her. Well, that would make sense. Naomi kept her eyes glued on the situation.

"Yes, sir. Must've been somethin' we ate." Bert said as Lizzie and Chad nodded.

"If this ever happens again, you must come and report it to me before I dismiss you. I need to be aware of your whereabouts at all times. I am responsible for you, children. Your parents must meet with me about this matter."

"Uh, well, um, sir," Bert said, his voice shaky. "Ma's not been well lately. I'm not sure how soon she'd be able to come by."

"Is she all right? Last time she visited, she seemed distressed." He lowered his tone. "I couldn't help but notice the rips on her dress and bruises on her face. Much like the one under your eye." Although Mr. Cavern's glare softened, he still had an inquisitive look, eyebrows creased together. "Well, I pray she gets better. Please give your parents this note. I want to meet with them at their earliest convenience." He scribbled on a piece of paper and handed it to Bert.

"Thank you, Mr. Cavern, uh, sir." Bert shoved the slip into his pant pocket as they returned to their desks with their heads bowed.

DURING LUNCHTIME, NAOMI APPROACHED THE EDGARS, hoping to come to some agreement.

"Ooo-wee. I got you good din't I?" Hushed, she teased him so the other students could not catch wind of their conversation. She did not want to hurt Bert's feelings or ruin what little friendship they had by belittling him in public.

"Humph." Bert leaned back in his chair, crossed his arms over his chest, and looked away. "Yeah, if you weren't a girl, you'd have a black eye too."

"Don't ya care what the other kids will think?"

"Heck no. It'll only make them more fearful of me. They'll think I had it out with my ol' man again."

At first, Naomi grimaced at the thought, but then she chuckled because he did not want others to know she had planted his shiner. "What are y'all doin' after school? I know you don't care much about my silly girlfriends, but I do. So I'll spend time with them durin' lunch, and maybe after classes are over, we can do somethin' together. How's that sound?"

"Yeah … like what?" Chad asked. "You're such a little goody-two-shoes. We ain't got nothin' in common. You wouldn't be able to keep up with us bad boys anyways." Sneering, he lifted his chin.

The challenge ignited Naomi's competitive spirit. "I can do whatever y'all do, an' probably even better."

"Oh yeah? We'll see about that. All right, why don't you meet us after school in front of the Snelling Saloon, then we'll know the stuff you're made of," Chad said.

"Okay, I will." Naomi pushed her shoulders back. She turned on her heels and went to where her brother and friends stood watching with immense curiosity.

"Are you sure ya want to be talkin' with Bert after what he said to you yesterday?" David asked.

"Oh, I'm not afraid of him." She realized she must think of an excuse to send him home without her after school. "Hey, little brother, I'm gonna go over to one of my girlfriend's home to visit and work on a project together, so don't wait up for me, okay? Let Ma know, and I'll get home in time to do my chores before supper."

"Yeah. All right." He bought into her lie.

MID-AFTERNOON, SHE SAW THE EDGAR SIBLINGS walking toward the Snelling Saloon across the corner from Mr. Jacobi's store.

Naomi did not want David or her girlfriends to see her going into town. So she hastily said goodbye to her brother, excused herself to the outhouse, and waited till everyone disappeared. When they left the school grounds, she hurried to the three siblings who sat waiting on the saloon's front porch. She walked up to the foot of the steps.

"We din't think you'd show up," Lizzie said, shifting her gaze from Naomi to her brothers and back again. She seemed jittery, pacing back and forth, as if she knew something bad was about to happen. If not for the reputation of the dastardly boys, she could easily make friends with others.

"I'm a woman of my word," Naomi remembered her mother saying this whenever she made a promise. "Now what do y'all want to do?"

"Well." Chad stood, crossed his arms in front of him, and stared down at her. "First, you have to prove to us you can be trusted. You can't go squealin' like a baby an' tellin' on us."

Naomi shifted her weight over to her right foot as she held her books in her arm. She placed her left hand on her hip, waiting to hear the challenge.

"We've been kinda hungry these days 'cause our pa's not been around' and our ma has no money for food," Chad explained his family's situation as he glanced over at Bert, who stared elsewhere.

He turned to Naomi and fixed his eyes on hers. "We want you to go into Jacobi's Store and steal for us some bread and a few cans of corned beef, and afterward meet us at the cemetery by our Uncle Bob's gravesite."

Sweat beaded on her face, down the back of her neck, and under her thick, winter cape. Her heart started pounding fast in her chest. Caught up in the challenge, her pride did not allow her to reason clearly. A small voice in her head kept saying, *Don't do it. It's illegal. You'll get into a heap of trouble.* However, something seemed to dominate her will power, and the words rolled out of her mouth. "Here, take my books, and I'll meet you at the gravesite."

AS SHE PEERED INTO THE WINDOW, Naomi waited until the owner was occupied with a customer at the counter before she entered. *I can do this.* She shoved her hands under her cape and into the deep pockets of her skirt to check if they were empty. *All I have to do is walk around the store, slip things into my pocket, and buy an apple or somethin' small so Mr. Jacobi won't suspect anythin'.* She peered into the window again. *Okay, he's busy.* Her heart raced. *Be calm, Naomi. Act normal and be ever so quiet.*

The door hinges creaked as she opened it, and she kept her head down. *I'm in. Now to find the canned goods.* Walking past the first aisle, she scanned its shelves. *No, not here.* She moved onto the next. *There they are.* The bold labels popped out at her. *Corned beef.* She cast her gaze down both ends of the corridor to be sure no one was around. *Whew, the coast is clear. Do it now.* She grabbed three cans and withdrew her arm into her cape and her pocket.

Okay, that's done. Now for the bread. Naomi sauntered over to the next aisle. *Ah, this will do ... rolls.* She stuffed them into the other pocket. Her skirt seemed to drag from the weight of the goods so she lifted it a few inches to avoid tripping. As she turned the corner to go to the produce aisle, she nearly bumped into Darryl, the clerk, who was carrying a crate of potatoes.

"Whoa, young lady. Is there something I can help you with?" he asked.

Her heart pounded so hard she thought it might jump out of her throat. Perspiration dripped down her face and neck. "Oh, uh, no … no. I was just looking for somethin' to nibble on. Maybe one of those apples over there."

"All right. Let me know if you need anything."

"I will. Thank you." Naomi stepped to the side and scurried to the fruit barrel, her heart pounding and body shaking. *Gosh, that was close. Okay, let's get this apple and go.* The red fruit glistened in her sweaty palm as she walked toward the counter. *I don't think Mr. Jacobi will remember me, even though I've roamed these aisles before. He's only met Samuel and Sarah when they paid for things.*

"Good afternoon, young lady. Good to see you. Will dat be all for you?" The proprietor greeted her as she showed him the apple.

What does he mean by 'good to see you'? Does he recognize me? Hopefully, he doesn't put two and two together.

"Yes, sir."

"Okay, den. Dat vill be five cents, please." He opened his palm as Naomi, trying not to make eye contact, handed him a nickel.

"Thank you." She flashed a coy smile, bolted out the door, and rushed straight to the cemetery.

Whew! What a relief that's over. She found the Edgar siblings at the gravesite as they promised. Pleased with her accomplishment, she pulled out the food from under her cape. "Voila! Supper is served." Naomi shoved everything in Bert's hands.

He had a smirk as he examined the rations and glanced over at her. "Well, you guys," he grinned at his brother and sister, "I think we can trust her."

Chad opened one of the cans of corned beef hash with his camper pocket knife and used his dirty fingers to scoop out a little and put some in between one of the rolls. Taking a big bite, he closed his eyes and moaned as he chewed. "Ummm. You did good, Naomi. Here, you want some?"

"No thanks, it's all yours." She knew how much they needed the food. Plus, she didn't have the desire to eat after what she had done.

"Oh, and here, this one's on me." She handed Lizzie the apple. "Well, I gotta run 'cause I told David to tell Ma I'd be back before dark to do my chores."

Feeling queasy, Naomi wanted to get out of the cemetery and heave somewhere. So she grabbed her books and dismissed herself. Too busy eating, the siblings were not aware of her crouching behind the schoolhouse heaving.

Wiping her mouth with her sleeve, she regained her composure. As she walked home, she tried to push her bad deed out of her mind to no avail. *Ah, this is gettin' worse by the minute.* The voice in her head returned and seemed to get louder. *Thou shalt not steal, thou shalt not lie, thou shalt honor your mother and father.*

22

Reprimand

"Here, y'all. This is all I could muster up from leftovers last night without my ma noticin'. She is already suspicious because her pantry keeps goin' bare. Evenin's are spent countin' her canned jars over and over again." Naomi opened her basket and pulled out a cloth napkin filled with three fried chicken pieces and some corn cobletts.

"That'll do, I guess." Chad divvied the food between his siblings under the shade of an oak tree on the school grounds.

"Hey, she's doing her best," his sister said. "She's been doin' your dirty work for a month now. Leave her alone."

"Thanks, Lizzie. In fact, I think maybe one of you guys may want to do the stealin' in the store soon. I get the inklin' Mr. Jacobi is on to me. He's been greetin' his customers as they enter while Darryl's been watching the counter."

"Well, I suppose he's forgotten us by now." Bert kicked the dirt on the ground. "Can you do it one more time? Maybe we can take turns next week."

"All right, one last time. I'll meet you at the gravesite as usual." Naomi grunted. Her gut feeling told her today was not a good day for stealing. *Ugh, why do I give in to them? I guess someone has to help them out if no one else in this town will.*

"VELCOME, YOUNG LADY. You are becoming a regular customer, I see." Mr. Jacobi extended his hand as he tried to lock eyes with Naomi.

Letting go of his hand, her smile quivered as she turned away. "Good day to you, sir. I'm goin' to grab my apple, and I best be on my way home."

"All right. Let me know if you need anything."

She sensed his cold stare following her as she slipped behind the canned goods aisle. *I better make this quick. I think he is expectin' me to be at the fruit barrel.* The weight of the corned beef cans became too much for her day dress pocket. As she walked to the next corridor, the tattered stitching gave way, and the tins crashed on the wood floor from under her skirt. Before she could bend down to pick them up, Mr. Jacobi came rushing over.

"Ah-ha! Caught you red-handed." He grabbed her shoulder. "So you are the one who's been stealin' my groceries." He wagged his finger under her nose and picked up the cans. She felt her blood rush to her feet, and the room began to spin.

"I…I…I," Naomi's body shook, and sweat poured from her temples.

"You are in big trouble, young lady." He placed the product back on the shelf and dragged her behind the counter. "Sit down on zat stool in za corner and don't move a muscle." He turned to his clerk, who was shaking his head. "Darryl, go fetch za marshal."

"All right, boss."

Tears rolled down Naomi's cheeks as the employee whisked away, and the door slammed behind him. She realized it wouldn't take long since the courthouse was across the street.

Her eyes widened and jaw dropped when the door swung open a few minutes later. A chill ran down her spine as a tall, broad-shouldered man in a long duster and dark ten-gallon hat walked in, spurs jangling at every step. He towered over the counter. "Word's come to me you caught the culprit, Jacobi." His voice was deep and raspy.

"Yep. Here she is, Marshal Warner." The store owner winked.

"All right, young lady, you're coming with me." He reached around his side, revealing the hefty Colt revolver hanging on his hip between his gun belt bullets.

Naomi began bawling uncontrollably. *Why did Mr. Jacobi wink? They must've figured it was me, and now the marshal's goin' to execute me.* "No ... no. Don't shoot. I'm sorry!"

Clink, clink, clink. In his back pocket, he pulled out handcuffs and rattled them in front of her. He walked behind the counter and snapped them on her wrists. "All right, young lady, let's go."

"Where ... where are you takin' me, Marshal? I wanna see my parents."

"We're goin' to the courthouse. Oh, you'll see them, all right, behind bars for what you've done. Since you're a minor, they'll be held responsible."

Tears flowed, and her knees trembled and knocked. She stumbled across the street and up the steps of the familiar multi-use building.

The month she'd spent stealing and lying to her parents about being too sick to attend church had finally met its consequences. *What would Pastor McSwan think if he saw me paradin' down the road in handcuffs? He'd banish my family from the congregation for good. Hopefully, Mr. Jacobi doesn't make the connection between my brothers, sister, and me. He would never allow them in his store after service anymore. I'm in big trouble for sure.*

The marshal and the frightened girl sat down at his desk. He removed his hat, grabbed a piece of paper and his steel-tipped pen, which he then dipped into the inkwell. "Tell me your name and where you live."

"Naomi Sower, sir. I, I live at Sower Ranch," she said between sobs. "Please, don't put my pa and ma in jail."

The marshal grimaced. "Hmm, I'm familiar with the place and your parents." He scratched his head. "Now what is a nice, well-bred young gal like you doin' stealin' from a poor store merchant?"

"I...I..." She bit her lip. *"First, you must prove you are trustworthy, and you ain't gonna go squealin' like a baby an' tellin' on us."* Chad's words battered her thoughts. *The marshal must not know about the Edgar siblings. I gave them my word.* "I just like doin' it," she said. "I don't know why. I can't help myself."

"Well, then your mother and father will have to find help for you." He handed his deputy the piece of paper. "Jamison, I need you to go to the Sower's ranch and fetch this gal's parents and bring them here."

"Right away, sir." The officer snickered, put on his hat, and walked away.

"Would you care for some water? Your mouth must be plum dry after crying a bucket of tears." The marshal poured her a tepid drink. "Let me take these cuffs off of you. Can I trust you not to run away?"

"Yes, sir." She whimpered.

After removing the handcuffs, he handed the glass to her. "Relax until your parents get here. I'll be at the judge's bench discussing your case." He turned to the county clerk. "Keep an eye on her for me, Margaret." He winked at her.

"Will do, Marshal." She walked over to the tear-stained face adolescent, giving her a handkerchief. "Why don't you dry your eyes and wipe your nose, dear." She returned to her desk.

Naomi took the hanky and wiped her tears. She had never felt so embarrassed in her life. *What am I goin' to tell Ma and Pa? I know they won't believe the same lie I told the marshal. They'll want the truth. Golly, what did I get myself into?*

The tick-tock of the wall clock seemed to get louder. Fifteen minutes passed, then thirty. Naomi chewed on her fingernails. Forty-five long minutes might have been an eternity. *When are they goin' to get here?* Almost an entire hour had gone by when the sound of the door opening and her father's voice disturbed the hushed murmurings.

"Where is she, Deputy?"

"She's up there in the front at the marshal's desk." He pointed her way, and they rushed toward her.

Tears flowed once more. "I'm sorry, Pa and Ma."

Before her parents could get to her, Marshal Warner intercepted them. "Folks, I need you to step over to the judge's bench please, to discuss this matter."

"Yes, sir." Jonathan glanced at Naomi. His melancholy eyes matched his frown while her mother's enlarged with fright.

Hands moved in the air as the judge, the marshal, and her parents talked low and occasionally shifted their gaze her way. It seemed like another hour had passed before they finished, and her mother, father, and the officer returned. The marshal pulled two more chairs for the distressed couple and sat them beside their daughter. Mary reached over and held Naomi's hand as they listened.

"Naomi Sower, it is my duty as the marshal of Snelling to inform you of your sentence based on the misdemeanor charges of theft from the local merchant, Mr. Simeon Jacobi, of Jacobi Mercantile." He locked eyes with hers. Her heart pounded so hard she thought it would explode in her chest.

"The store owner agreed to drop charges as long as the sum of fifty dollars is paid to him for his losses, and your parents take appropriate disciplinary measures." He turned his gaze to Jonathan and Mary then back to Naomi. "We have conceded to remove you from public school for the remaining year, and you will be taught at home by your mother. Also, you will not receive any visitations from any friends during this time. Instead, your afternoons will be absorbed with house and farming chores. Do you have any questions?"

"No, sir." Her lips quivered.

"All right. Then I release you to your parents, young lady." They stood. "Don't let me catch you doing that again, you hear?" He winked at her and grinned, flashing a couple of gold crowns.

He winked again. What does that mean? Did he forgive me? Thank You, God. He's not goin' to shoot me after all. A slow smile crept onto her face. "Never again, sir. I've learned my lesson."

"How 'bout we go home and you can explain everything?" Mary squeezed Naomi's hand.

"All right, Ma." Naomi took a deep breath and walked hand-in-hand with her parents to their horse and carriage. *I guess I won't be seein' Bert, Chad, and Lizzie again. I might as well tell Ma and Pa the truth.*

THE NEXT DAY, JONATHAN HAD DAVID STAY HOME from school with Naomi as he paid a visit to the Edgar family that morning. He spoke to their mother and explained the situation. She agreed to keep her children away from his daughter.

The bewildered parents visited the teacher around mid-afternoon. They waited until all the students exited before entering to talk to the instructor.

"Hello, Mr. Cavern." Mary greeted somberly. "Can we take a moment of your time? This is Jonathan, my husband."

"Yes, of course. It's my pleasure to meet you, Mr. Sower, and to see you again, Mrs. Sower." He shook Jonathan's hand and pulled up two chairs. "Please, sit down. Your children were absent today. Does this meeting have anything to do with that?"

"Yes, unfortunately," Jonathan replied, leaning back with a frown on his face. "A terrible incident happened, which we are rather ashamed to discuss. Apparently, Naomi had been caught stealin' from Jacobi's store. We were visited yesterday in the late afternoon by Deputy Jamison informin' us that Marshal Warner had our daughter at the courthouse, awaitin' our arrival to claim her. He informed us of their reason for restrainin' her … thievery. As a minor, they couldn't hold her in custody, and as her parents, we were held liable for her actions." Jonathan humbly reported.

Mary continued. "Well, Marshal Warner explained to us that Mr. Jacobi would be willin' not to press any charges as long as we paid for the cost of the stolen items. He further suggested we reprimand our daughter in a manner suitable to us. So this is what we did. We paid our fine and settled with the store owner and brought her home where she is to be denied school privileges and visitations from friends for the rest of the year. I'll continue educatin' her."

Shifting in her seat, Mary leaned forward. "Naomi told us everythin' and how she had been involved with the Edgars and that they dared her to do their thievin'. It seems Mr. Jacobi suspected it was our daughter because she appeared after the Edgar children stopped frequentin' his store and stealin' from him. He never could prove it was them. But the groceries still kept on disappearin'. He notified the marshal, and they both devised a plan to teach her a good lesson once he caught her in the act. They never had any intention of puttin' a child behind bars … or us, for that matter, knowin' our good citizenship. They just wanted to scare her a little."

She sank back into the seat and inhaled. "Mr. Jacobi is a good man. He just wanted the cost of the stolen goods. My husband and I did the right thing and covered all the items the children stole. It's been rumored the Edgar family is in a bad situation."

"I met with Mrs. Edgar this mornin'," Jonathan said. "I told her we would not mention to the marshal their involvement as long as she reprimanded her children and kept them away from our daughter. I also offered her a little financial help, but she refused it."

Mary focused on Mr. Cavern's eyes. "As you might imagine, this was shockin' news to us. Our child knows better. However, she is still young and naïve. The matter which concerns us now is David's attendance. This is why we are here to talk to you. We need to know how Naomi became involved with these children and whether or not David should exercise caution when attendin' school."

Shaking his head, Mr. Cavern folded his arms on his desk. "I am so sorry to hear this news, Mr. and Mrs. Sower. I do want to make it clear, I was not aware of the depth of Naomi's relationship with the Edgar siblings. A few weeks ago during the rains, she attempted to become friends with them. I actually thought it a kind gesture on her part to try to include these children socially with the other students, or at least with herself to start. When the sun came out, it appeared everything went back to normal since the Edgar's kept to themselves, and Naomi returned to her friends."

He shifted in his chair. "But this week, I became aware of Naomi's grades dropping, and her homework and projects were delinquent. I also noticed she was not going straight home with David after school. So yesterday, I did a little investigating myself and followed her. As I suspected, she was meeting the Edgar children in the cemetery. I planned on visiting you this afternoon to discuss this matter, but it seems the Lord had a different plan."

Mary inhaled and exhaled, slow and steady. "Naomi informed me she'd been workin' on a project with one of her friends after school, and she'd be home before supper time, and I believed her. I also thought I was losin' my mind because food kept disappearin' from my pantry. What do you suppose you're gonna do about this, sir?"

"Well, Mr. and Mrs. Sower, I believe the proper measure would be to expel the Edgar children. This is serious, indeed. Trust me, this is not the first incident I've had with them in this classroom. This situation draws the line. I'll make an effort to visit their family today. I do understand you must do what is necessary to correct your daughter, and I'd gladly provide her curriculum so that she may finish the year with you. Will this solution help you in making your decision for David?"

"Yes, indeed, sir." Jonathan agreed and stood with a sigh of relief as he extended his hand to Mr. Cavern. "David will return to school tomorrow'. Well, we better not take too much more of your time. We've a young lady we need to reprimand. Thank you for understandin' our situation."

23

Directional

After leaving the schoolhouse in their horse-drawn carriage, Jonathan and Mary pulled into the wayside path leading to their farm. The clouds burst open, and the late February rain poured down in pea size drops. *Splitter, splatter, splitter, splatter.* The rain's rhythm rolled on the canopy.

"Well, if this ain't a sign from God of what is ahead this season." Jonathan flicked the reins and stared up at the gray, heaving thunderhead. "There must be a reason for all this happenin' with our children."

"As I see it, dear, whenever there's a major dilemma in our lives, its purpose always seems to be directional. God is simply tryin' to orchestrate things to get us to the place He wants us." She pulled her cape tighter and snuggled close to her husband. "For example, our home in Kentucky. Of all the farms in Perryville, why was ours chosen for a temporary Union hospital? I think God meant that to happen, so we'd desire to leave and ask for His guidance. He wanted to move us to an area of His choosin' where He can use us for His glory."

"Hmm ... that's an interestin' observation, Mary." Jonathan's brows creased as he searched for supportive scripture. "Proverbs 16:9 does say, 'A man's heart deviseth his way: but the Lord directeth his steps.' True. It was God who chose California and landed us in Snelling.

Now that we're here, things still don't seem to be goin' in the right direction. Sam doesn't want to farm, Sarah is thinkin' of marriage at fifteen, Naomi is grounded for misbehavior, and David…" Jonathan paused. "Thank the Lord, one child is without troubles." He belted a hearty laugh, the steam from his breath lingering.

"What do ya mean by Sam not wantin' to farm?" Mary's gloved hand tugged at his elbow.

"I meant to tell you that he and I butted heads the other day in the barn about his plans to haul freight with Patrick. I think it's an excuse for wantin' to go gold pannin' along the small creeks in Hornitos, Aqua Fria, Mariposa, and Coulterville while Patrick deals with his customers and visits the saloons for poker." Jonathan cracked the whip as the horse snorted at the rain pelting their face. The carriage bumped along the muddied path.

Mary cringed. "I'm thinkin' we made a bad decision allowin' him to go with Pat."

"Pat's not the enemy here, dear." Glancing at Mary, his eyebrows knit. "We can't stop Sam from his heart's desire. He's seventeen. He'll be a grown man next year. He's got to be able to sort things out on his own and make decisions for himself."

"So you are really goin' to let him go? But we need him here. He isn't an adult yet."

"Yes, dear, I know, and he does too. So we compromised. I agreed to allow him to help Patrick through the end of April while Joshua is available to take up the slack from his workload. Accordin' to Pastor McSwan, he'll need his son from May through September when they conduct their camp meetin's in the outlyin' counties. So Sam must come back because we'll be gettin' busier with the crops."

"Well, it's lookin' more like Joshua plans to be part of our family. He might as well learn our trade."

"I wouldn't be too sure about that, Mary. He must fulfill his callin' in ministry too. I'm not sure how Sarah will do with him gone for three or four months, let alone bein' a pastor's wife."

"Did you mention the McSwan's schedule to Sarah? Is she aware Joshua will be gone that long?"

"No. I was hopin' Joshua would."

"Oh, my." Mary held her hand to her heart. "I guess this time apart will be a good test of their love for each other."

"Yep. A lot of changes are about to take place in the next few months, which'll affect our entire family, includin' you, dear."

"Oh?" Mary cocked her eyebrow.

"Sure. Someone must take the slack for Sam on the weekends. Sarah already has her chores, and so do I. This means you and Naomi must help. I understand you aren't as strong or knowledgeable as Sam in his duties. So it may take you all weekend to maintain the farm equipment and livestock. I will assist, of course. In fact, you can give Naomi some of your chores as part of her correction. She is almost twelve. It doesn't hurt to start trainin' her a little earlier. I believe she can do it. You might have to miss church for a while until Sam gets back."

"Miss church? Oh, Lord. These are big changes. What about David?"

"Well, he must learn to stand on his own two feet. Go to school on his own, find friends on his own, and go to church on his own … well, with Sarah. I don't think she'll miss church, especially when Joshua will be away a few months. David is ten years old. It's time you stop babyin' him, Mary."

"I suppose you're right, dear."

Jonathan parked the rain-soaked carriage in the barn. "It's time we had a family meetin'. Why don't you gather the children into my office?" He pulled his pocket watch from his vest. "Say, in an hour, at four-thirty, before supper? We need to discuss these changes so that we're all in agreement."

"Yes, dear. Good idea. I'll let them know." Mary tightened her bonnet and adjusted her cape.

Jonathan jumped off the carriage and assisted his wife down its step. She opened her umbrella and returned to the house.

After unhitching the horse and putting him into his stall, Jonathan sat down on a bale of hay and prayed. *Father, if it's true as Mary stated and all these complications are a part of Your plan, then I pray You would help me to make the right decisions accordin' to Your will. One day You'll reveal Your ultimate plan for my family and me, and I'll be able to look back and understand why You allowed these things to arise. In the meantime, give me the strength to trust You and the wisdom to move forward.*

I ask for Your continued care and protection over my wife and children. In Jesus' name. Amen.

THE FIRE IN THE DUAL STONE HEARTH ROARED, casting a warm golden glow on his family's faces as they sat in a semicircle in Jonathan's office. The aroma of beef stew boiling in the pot over the flames on the kitchen side lingered in both rooms.

"Children, I have called this meetin' to inform you of some changes that'll be takin' place in our household and in the way we're conductin' business. I won't make it too long as supper is ready." He snickered, trying not to be heavy and overbearing. He repositioned himself in his winged-back chair. The children squirmed in their seats.

"As y'all know, Sam has been helpin' Patrick deliver firewood throughout the county this winter. He has expressed to me his desire to join him full time. I agreed until the end of April, while Joshua is still with us. Then Sam will return and finish out the harvest year and train a new employee for the next season when he leaves." Jonathan searched their faces, mouths gaped at the news. He locked eyes with Sam. "Are we in agreement, son?"

Sam pressed his elbows on his knees and rubbed his hands. "Yes, Pa."

"For the rest of us, except David, we'll need to take up Sam's slack until he returns."

"What? Huh? Why Sam?" The other children questioned as Samuel turned his head.

"All right, quiet down. Save your questions for after our meetin'." Jonathan stood and paced in front of the hearth. "Y'all also know that your dear sister, Naomi, got herself in a bit of a pickle this week." He turned to Naomi, who fixed her gaze on her shoes. "She's been grounded for the remainder of the school year and will be studyin' at home. In addition to her retribution, she'll not be allowed visitors after lessons but will be given added chores instead. Your Ma will pass on many of her duties to you, Naomi, as I'll be needin' her for Sam's chores on the weekends. Understood?"

She inhaled and frowned. "Yes, Pa."

"Sarah, Ma will train you with some of the more difficult cookin' tasks." Jonathan saw his eldest daughter's eyebrows pressed together and jaw quiver. She had questions and wanted more information about Joshua leaving, but he did not want to be the one to tell her. *That's somethin' they must discuss between themselves.*

He shifted his gaze to his youngest. "And as for you, David, I want you to study hard and redeem our family's good name at school. News travels quickly in this small town, and I'm sure your sister's mishaps are headlinin' amongst your friends and their parents. Be prepared for some backlash, son." The corners of David's eyes drooped along with his frown.

"I realize this is a difficult situation for all of us. But we're Sowers, and we come from strong stock. We can get through this together. Right?"

Scattered responses replied, "Yes, Pa."

"All right, how 'bout we get some supper?"

24

David's Calling

"Hey, y'all, how 'bout a game of Annie Over?" David asked his friends at school during the lunch break on his first day back since Naomi's incident. He noticed earlier that Dirk had chosen to sit in his sister's vacant chair beside Abigail instead of sitting next to him.

The five schoolmates shuffled their feet and nudged Abigail forward. "Sorry, David. I think us girls are gonna play Graces. There are only two sets of hoops and sticks."

"I've got some readin' to do. Perhaps next time." Not making eye contact, Dirk turned his back and walked away.

"I'd play with you, but Della needs a partner." Rebecca wasn't her cheery self. She shifted her sight between him and her friends as she clenched her skirt.

David's heart fell into his stomach. He held his breath to hold back the tears but could not stop his lips from quivering. "Uh, okay. Maybe another day?"

"Well, I think we girls want to start doin' girl stuff together from now on. Sorry, David." Abigail turned on her heels as Ruby and Della followed.

Rebecca remained and reached out to hold his hand.

"Please understand. You'll always be my friend. They like to do girl things as I do. We can play after church, though."

"Yeah, all right." He pulled his hand away, hurt filling his heart. "I guess I'll catch up on some readin' too." He stood, staring as Rebecca scurried to her friends.

He turned toward the schoolhouse, gazed up at the still bell tower, took a deep breath, and walked inside to his desk to retrieve his Bible. *Lunch breaks are goin' to be long and lonely from now on.* He brushed the leather cover with his fingertips and said a prayer. *Lord Jesus, now I understand how You felt when Your disciples, Your friends, turned their backs on You for no reason. They didn't want to be caught in public bein' seen with an accused and condemned man, even though they knew You had no fault. Father, give me the strength to forgive them and continue to love them despite the hurt they are causin' me. Thank You, Jesus.*

"PA? MA? ARE YOU COMIN' WITH ME and Sarah to church this mornin'?" David asked at the morning breakfast table in mid-April.

"Wish we could, son. You know this is our busy season with the crop sproutin'. I really need your mother's help on weekends while Sam is away." Jonathan forked into a stack of flapjacks.

Mary patted David's hand. "You and Sarah go on and greet the McSwans for us. I'm sure they'll understand."

"Tell Rebecca I said 'hello' too," Naomi said between bites. "I'll be off restriction in two weeks. By the way, how are my girlfriends doin'?"

"Well, they do miss ya, sis, although I don't see much of them since you left. They kinda stay to themselves, even Dirk." Melancholy filled David's heart from the thoughts of being shunned at school and now from his parent's unavailability. "I spend most of my time readin' durin' lunch. School's not the same without you there. In fact, home's not been the same either, with Sam gone a lot and Sarah spendin' her time with Joshua. Now you, Ma, and Pa are busy with the harvest. The only thing I look forward to these days is goin' to church and studying the Bible."

"Aw, come on now, little brother. Things will get better once Sam returns and Naomi is off restriction." Sarah put her arm around David's shoulder. "Finish your breakfast and let's go to church, huh?"

DAVID SAT AT HIS SEAT'S EDGE, listening to Pastor McSwan's sermon about sharing the gospel of Jesus Christ in Jerusalem, Judea, Samaria, and even to the ends of the earth. Closing his Bible, the minister removed his spectacles and peered out at the attentive congregation.

"Folks, as most of you are aware, it's that time of year again when my family and I will be conducting gospel camp meetings at our neighboring counties in the foothills of the Sierras. We'll conclude services at this location this month and begin our mission shortly after." A hush fell upon the congregants. "The journey starts with the furthest county of Calaveras in May, Tuolumne in June, Mariposa in July, then finally Merced in August and September. I would hope to see all your smiling faces at our county's camp meetings. Church services will resume at the Snelling Courthouse again in October."

A flood of good memories from attending the camp meeting in La Grange flurry in David's mind and his heart became more anxious. *Oh Lord, if it is Your will, I'd love to help at the meetings.* A broad smile stretched across his face as he peered up at his eldest sister beside him. She, on the other hand, did not appear happy at all. Her bottom lip pouted and her eyes reddened.

"Are you all right, Sarah?"

"No, I'm not. I'm not lookin' forward to when they leave. It means bein' apart from Joshua for three months." Her voice quivered between breaths. "Doesn't it bother you not havin' to go to church for that long?"

"Well, yes. We've done it before. Besides, I spend plenty of time readin' and prayin' every day, so I won't be lackin' for spiritual food. It's the fellowship I'll miss. Don't worry, Sarah. The time'll go by quick."

"I hope you're right, David. I'd hate to go stir crazy waitin'."

"Hey, maybe Pa and Ma will let you go with the McSwans!"

"Are you kiddin' me? That's when we'll be harvestin' the wheat. They'll especially need me on the farm. About the only meetings

I'll be attendin' are the ones in our county in late August and September, after the harvest."

"Do you suppose this is the Lord testin' you both while you're apart?"

"Boy, you are a clever one, aren't you? You may be right. Well, I'll have to prove to God that I do love him. If this is Joshua's callin', then who am I to stop him? I'll wait as long as I need to." Her eyes focused directly upon Joshua as she walked to meet him at the end of the row.

With school ending in two more weeks, David hoped Pastor McSwan and his parents would agree to allow him to serve God by helping with the camp meetings. When the congregation dispersed, he approached the minister to discuss the possibility.

"Hello, Pastor. I enjoyed your message about sharin' the Gospels. I can see why you conduct camp meetings outside of Merced County." David's heart leaped as the admirable man gathered his notes from the judge's desk.

The minister paused for a moment and stared at him. "Oh, why, thank you, David. I am pleased you understood the message and the purpose of having these mission trips. That is very observant of you. Even some of the adults can't grasp this."

"Sir, is it possible for me to go along with you and your family on this mission to serve the Lord this year? I believe God is leadin' me to do this. I enjoy readin' the Bible, and I can help out in whatever way you prefer."

Pastor McSwan's eyes twinkled at his suggestion. He inhaled, rubbed his chin, closed his eyes, and paused. Opening his eyes, his face glowed. "You know, young man, I believe the Holy Spirit is telling me that He is calling you to serve our God." Placing his hand on David's shoulder, he directed him to the chairs. "First I thought, *he is too young*. However, the Holy Spirit reminded me of the prophet Samuel and King David and how they were young boys when they were called. And so, you are too. In time, He will reveal how you are to serve him. The camp meetings may be your start."

The words pouring out of Pastor's mouth were like honey, and David soaked in every drop.

"So, is this what you truly sense the Lord is asking you to do?" Pastor McSwan dropped his chin and stared deep into David's eyes.

"Ministry is not an easy path. The camp meetings are indeed a wonderful blessing, but it's a lot of work. I'd be grateful to have you come with us and help after, of course, we receive approval from your parents."

David straightened his back and planted his feet firm on the ground. "I love the Lord with my whole heart, and I want to serve Him. I envision God usin' me at the camp meetings where I'll work really hard for you."

Settling into his chair, the pastor inhaled and grinned. "Okay. I believe you, young man. Why don't we pray together? Let's make your request known to God and ask for His guidance."

The compassionate man held David's hands. "Dear Heavenly Father, I present to You Your son, David, and his desire to serve You, Lord, at the camp meetings. If this is Your will, then we ask for Your direction and that You would open the doors needed to allow this to happen. We ask this in Jesus' name."

"Amen!" David's heart pounded and goosebumps flitted on his arms.

"Well, I think you should discuss this with your parents first. If they approve, then I'll gladly invite them over to our house to talk about the plans. Do we have an agreement?"

"We do, Pastor. I'll speak to them this week. Count on us visitin' next Sunday."

"We'll plan on it." He shook David's hand and gave him a hardy pat on the back.

David joined Sarah and Joshua at the front door of the courtroom. They walked to the farm as he shared the conversation he had with Pastor McSwan.

"I sure do envy you, little brother. I wish I could go too," she said.

Joshua squeezed Sarah's hand. "We'll be back in Merced County in no time. There is so much to do for the meetings that there is barely enough time for myself anyway. Maybe you waiting for me at home is best so I can concentrate on the Lord's work."

"That's easy for you to say. You're not the one waitin'. However, you're right. I don't want to get in the way. Besides, harvest time is the same: so much to do, and too little time. Not to worry, Joshua. I'll be here for you."

"Look. We're already home. You see? Time does go by quickly," David said.

Joshua kissed Sarah's cheek and returned home.

DURING SUPPER, David's parents asked Sarah and him about church. This subject was the open door he had been waiting for.

"The sermon today truly touched my heart, Ma and Pa," he said with confidence and told them about how the message tied into the minister's announcement regarding the upcoming mission.

David put his utensils down, fixing his gaze on his father. "Pa, I asked Pastor McSwan if I could go with them to serve the Lord at the camp meetings. I truly believe God wants me to do this. Pastor loved the idea and said he would be grateful if I did. The final decision is yours to make. I hope you'll allow me to do this. May I?"

His mother shifted her gaze over to his father, who stared at the ceiling as if deep in thought. "You'll be gone for five months, David. That is a long time, and you're only ten years old. Give me and your Ma time to talk and pray about it, son, and I can give you our answer in a couple of days. Okay?"

"Thank ya, Pa."

JONATHAN AND MARY met in his office and had a lengthy discussion about David's request while he attended school.

The concerned mother paced in front of the fireplace. "David is too young to be away this long. I trust the McSwans to watch after him, but you know they'll have their hands full overseein' the details of the camp meetings. It would be too difficult to do this and keep an eye on our son, no matter how good a boy he is. One day, I know he is destined to be a preacher, so I don't wanna discourage him. This mission would be a wonderful experience for him. It must be God's will for him, but why so soon? What should we do, Jonathan?"

"Oh, Mary!" He growled and ran his fingers through his receding hairline. "There's been so much drama in our household of late. Sam is gone pannin' for gold, Sarah is in love, Naomi is grounded, and now David wants to go away to evangelize. What's next?"

He leaned back on his chair and stared out the window. He thought about the camp meeting they had attended the previous year and how wonderful the experience had been for the children. They had all accepted Jesus as their Lord and Savior at the event.

This thought led to a possible solution. "Now, here's an idea, Mary. What if we allow David to help Pastor McSwan at the camp meetin's in Merced County when they return in August? This way he can be close enough to home should he need us. Also, this will give him time to ease into the ministry and experience it first. Plus, he'll only be away for less than two months. Perhaps, in a couple of years, when he is twelve, he can go with them on the whole five-month journey. What do you think about this?"

"That is a brilliant compromise, Jonathan! Sixty days seems reasonable for his age." Mary embraced him.

WHEN DAVID RETURNED HOME FROM SCHOOL, his mother pulled him into his father's office to explain their plan. They sat across from his father at his oak desk.

"Son, first of all, your Ma and I want to tell you how pleased we are with your desire to serve the Lord at your young age. We've known all along that God has his eyes on you."

David felt warmth flush to his face as his mother reached for his hand to squeeze it.

His father leaned forward and cupped his hands on his desk. "We've decided to allow you to attend this mission."

Grinning, he straightened his back and inhaled, preparing for more good news.

"However, since this is your first time, we thought it best that you ease into it durin' the last two months when the McSwans return to our county. That way we'll be nearby, should you need us."

David slumped back into his seat and forced a smile. Although it was not the entire summer he had hoped for, he understood his parents' concern and found contentment with their decision. "So, how old do I have to be before you allow me to attend all five months, Pa?"

Jonathan relaxed his shoulders and chuckled. "Well, at the rate you're maturin', let's aim for when you turn twelve."

David leaned forward. "You promise?"

"Yes, son ... if the Lord wills it."

THE SOWERS DISCUSSED THE CAMP MEETING PLANS the following Sunday during dinner at the minister's home. Both families were pleased with the idea and grateful for God's calling in David's life. The next three months of taking on menial tasks on the farm and waiting for the McSwan's return to Merced County would test David's patience. He was packed and ready to go weeks in advance.

25

Under the Brush Arbors

"**M**erced Falls Camp Meeting ... Under the Brush Arbors." David read the flyer out loud as he chomped on the breakfast Ruth had prepared. His father had dropped him off at the McSwan's campsite on Sunday afternoon the day before. His family had plans to rejoin them at the end of the week for the three-day event. "Will we be postin' this around town, Pastor?"

"In a couple of days from now, we will. Today we are going to get our hands dirty." Daniel rummaged behind his wagon, pulled out two crosscut saws, and handed one to David. "You and I will partner to fell the small trees in this field while Joshua partners with his mother with the other saw. With two of these working, we'll clear this place in no time."

"I'm ready, Pastor. Just show me what to do." He grabbed the handles, blade bowing and twanging as he followed the goal-driven minister to the first of many small trees surrounding the wagon.

Joshua and Ruth worked alongside them on another while Rebecca stayed behind to wash dishes.

"Tomorrow we'll strip the trunks of their arbors and build several canopies around the stage," the pastor said as he pulled on his end and David pushed. The saw teeth bit into the trunk bottom, slicing back and forth, till the tree fell. Then they moved on to the next, all the while singing hymns to keep the sawing rhythm going and the work lively.

"All creatures of our God and King, lift up your voice and with us sing, alleluia, alleluia! O burning sun with golden beam, and shining moon with silver gleam, o praise him, o praise him, alleluia, alleluia, alleluia!"

After they had erected the canopies, David helped Pastor McSwan and Joshua post flyers in storefront windows, place an advertisement in the town newspaper, and visit folks in remote locations of the county. Muscles aching and tired, they returned to the campsite hoping to rest before the crowds arrived Friday in their covered wagons.

"Supper is ready, boys. Why don't you wash up and we'll serve you." Ruth stirred the stew over the campfire as Rebecca set the plates on the table near the wagon. The pastor and David sprinted to the basin while Joshua shuffled along behind them.

"I'll be right there, Ma. I've personal business to take care of at the creek first." Joshua patted his belly.

He couldn't help but notice Joshua's lack of enthusiasm for the last few days. It seemed uncharacteristic of him. Back home, he would jump for joy when he spoke of the camp meetings. Now he seemed lethargic, sputtering along as he was told, doing the bare minimum.

"Okay, son. Make it quick. You look like you can use a good meal. You're getting as thin as a rail. Are you feeling well?"

"I'm fine, Ma. Please, start without me."

The weight of the world seemed to be upon Joshua as he dragged himself away to take care of himself. His eyes were sunken and dark, his face and skin pale, and his hands trembled despite his attempts to hide them from view by stuffing them in his pant pockets.

"Don't worry, dear. He'll be all right after supper and a couple of days rest." Pastor McSwan sat at the table. The sun dipped below the horizon, and the last rays of light mingled with the glow of the campfire.

"I sure hope so. We still have two more meetings after this."

"I'll be glad to take on Josh's chores so he can recuperate," David said, imagining the fatigue they felt after conducting three months of back-breaking ministry, plus traveling.

"We may take you up on your offer," Pastor said. "Let's take it one day at a time. We'll see how he feels tomorrow."

SARAH SQUIRMED ON THE WAGON'S HARDWOOD bench as her family approached the campsite along with the droves of other wagons.

"There, over there. There they are!" She pointed to Joshua and David, who directed the caravan to form a circle around the canopies. The flurry Of activity around them kept her from jumping off and running to her beau. As they drew closer, she called out and waved her hanky. "Joshua, Joshua!"

Her heart leaped as he craned his neck, searching until their eyes met through the dust the horses and wheels stirred. Even from a distance, she sensed his gladness through his emanating smile. Yet, something about his expression seemed unfamiliar to her. She couldn't figure it out. No matter. She was with her true love again.

Her father stopped the Conestoga behind another, which had a family with five children clamoring inside with excitement. Sarah leaped off her family's wagon as fast as she could, into Joshua's arms.

David moseyed over and hugged his parents and Naomi. "Where's Sam?"

"Someone had to stay home and mind the farm and our employees," Jonathan said as he began unloading.

Joshua pulled away from Sarah's embrace, leaving one arm wrapped around her shoulder. "Welcome, everyone. I hope your travel was pleasant. After the wagons get settled, and all of you finish supper, how about our family come and join you?"

"After supper?" Mary shoved her hands on her hips. "No such thing'! I know how busy you've been. Please let me make a meal for both our families. I will not take no for an answer. Come by around five or whenever you are done."

"I think we better do as my ma says, Josh." David snickered. "Besides, I think your mother could use the break."

"All right. I'll let her know." Joshua embraced Sarah once more.

She rubbed her fingers across the ridges of his back. *Ribs ... bones.* "Joshua, you must be overworking yourself. You feel like a sack of potatoes." She pulled back and moved the bangs from his eyes.

"Well, I told you ministry is hard work. There's been little time for myself. But it's all worth it. You should've seen all the people we reached in the foothills. Miners, Chinese, and even Indians!"

"You be sure to come back to camp, and Ma and I'll put some meat back on them bones." She giggled.

"I will." He released himself from her embrace and turned to David. "Let's go." He focused his gaze on the next wave of visitors. "More wagons just arrived."

THE AMBER GLOW OF CAMPFIRES throughout the bustling encampment swallowed the reigning shadows of the night. The aroma of kettles filled with stew and meats roasting on spits lingered in the air. Bursts of laughter reverberated as friends reunited at the annual affair. Sarah was setting the table when she recognized the dim silhouettes of folks approaching their camp.

"Heard we've been invited to supper!" The McSwan family sauntered into the Sower's campsite. Joshua and Rebecca joined her. David and Naomi were at the table as Daniel and Ruth stood by her parents beside the campfire where they were cooking.

"I brought some cornbread since I already had it made." Ruth pointed to the basket in Rebecca's hand.

"Why, thank you. Love cornbread." Her mother dipped her wooden spoon in the cast iron pot and tasted a sample. "Umm … I think the chili is ready."

Her father pierced the roasting fowl with a fork. "Y'all are just in time. It looks like the chicken is done, too." He extended a firm grip to Daniel and handed him a tin plate and bowl. "Come on, Pastor, guests first. You must be exhausted and hungry."

"Thank you. We are. Your family has blessed us again by thinking of us."

"That's the least we can do for all you do for us and our communities."

Her mother ladled the chili into everyone's bowls as her father plopped a roasted chicken part on their plates. Both families sat at the table and, with joined hands, prayed for the hardy meal.

"So, Pastor, do tell us about the camp meetings in the foothills. Were they well attended?" Her mother asked.

"Indeed, they were. Joshua and I went deep into the woods this time into the Miwok villages and met with the headman and the sub-chief. They weren't very trusting toward us at first, because the Spanish missionaries fifty years earlier forced their people to accept Christianity, only to enslave them. I had to explain to them that we do not share the same intention as they, and the true gospel of Jesus Christ is to love others and to set men free from sin through their belief in Jesus' sacrifice."

"That must've been frightenin' to sit under such scrutiny," her mother said as all eyes focused on Pastor McSwan and Joshua.

"It was. We didn't know if we were going to make it out of there alive. When we first approached their village, their scouts found us, tied our hands behind our backs, then brought us to their headman. They loosed our bonds after father explained our visit." Joshua demonstrated with his wrists together behind him.

"After several hours of discussion, I offered to leave them my most precious possession, the Bible. I also promised that no harm would befall those who would attend the camp meeting. They finally agreed to send a representative if we observed one of their ceremonies called the Uzumati or Grizzly Bear Ceremony." A warm smile crossed Pastor McSwan's face.

"And then what happened?" David asked.

"Although they didn't come forward and accept Christ as many others did at the camp meeting, they did invite us to visit with them after their ceremony to further discuss our faith. So Joshua and I returned two days later after we visited with them."

Sarah's heart beat fast in her chest with excitement and fear. She clung to Joshua's waist. "So what happened at their event? Did they force you to partake in their pagan rituals?"

Joshua chuckled. "No." He rubbed her shoulders and drew her close to his side. "Actually, it was rather fascinating. They brought my father and me into their hangi, or dance house, a large room made of four wood-center posts and walls made of bark sealed with earth. The sub-chief sat us next to their shaman, or bear doctor since they considered us as holy men.

"After everyone was seated around the hardened earth floor, the ceremonies began. The first procession of Kuksu dancers were the men and women dressed in feather headdresses stomping to the beat of a foot drum." Josh chuckled again. "The drumbeat was so primitive and tribal, that it reached the most inner core of my soul. I felt my body moving and tapping to the rhythm, wanting to dance alongside them." He peered down at Sarah, who sat frozen. "But one touch of my father's hand on my shoulder brought me out of that rhythmic trance."

Pastor McSwan chortled. "Yep. If I hadn't been there, I think Joshua would've. That's how mesmerizing these pagan rituals can be. As Christians, we must remember what the Bible says and be careful for nothing; but in everything by prayer and supplication with thanksgiving let your requests be made known unto God. And the peace of God, which passeth all understanding, shall keep your hearts and minds through Christ Jesus.

"I was doing just that. Praying throughout the entire ceremony." Pastor McSwan looked toward heaven, hands clasped in prayer.

"Father reminded me to do the same." Joshua nodded. "Good thing because the next dancer was truly captivating. It was the Uzumati or bear impersonator. Grrr!" He roared with his hands lifted, imitating the clawing actions of the ferocious beast. Everyone jumped and screamed in their seats. "He was cloaked in the head and hide of a black bear, and on his fingers were curved pieces of obsidian shaped like claws. He danced and growled like he was the creature himself."

Pastor McSwan inhaled and leaned forward. "Well, the good Lord was mindful of our efforts. After the ceremony, the headman and sub-chief invited us to share a meal with them and their families. We answered their questions as the sub-chief translated."

Turning his gaze toward the heavens, he lifted his hands. "Praise be to God; they all became believers. Afterward, they danced and chanted songs, far from what we are used to. I expect that part of their culture will not change. It's in the Lord's hands now. I am just thankful they believe and that they opened the door to allow us to return and teach them more. The experience was worth our sufferings for Christ." Pastor's eyes sparkled.

"Otherwise, countless miners, Chinese, and pioneers and their families attended, ready to leave behind their riotous lifestyles and discouragement because they didn't strike it rich. Many of them were also grieving because they had recently lost loved ones to typhoid fever and cholera. The message was timely and brought them much-needed hope to recalibrate their lives." Joshua's chin lifted as he shared their accomplishments. "Father even performed an impromptu wedding ceremony for a couple who met at last year's camp meeting."

"Aw ... just as we did. What better place is there to meet your soul mate?" Sarah squeezed her beau's hand and stared deep into his topaz eyes, although dark and sunken. *My love. What are you not tellin' me?*

"Many do at these gatherings. And I am one of those blessed fellas to have found you, Sarah Sower." He placed his hand behind her head, pressed it close to his beating heart, and held her tight.

"Oh, yuck! Are you two goin' to get all mushy again?" Naomi rolled her eyes and turned. "It's so good to be able to get together again, Rebecca. Now that my restriction is over, we've got a lot of catchin' up to do. If you're done eatin', let's play dominoes before they make us go to bed."

"I'm ready." She pushed away from the table and followed Naomi to the campfire.

"Well, now that we know how much is involved in conductin' these meetin's, the rest of our family would love to serve, too, by playin' worship songs for your services at this meetin' and the remainin' ones, if you'll take us," Jonathan said.

"Oh, my." Ruth held her hand over her heart. "The good Lord continues to answer our prayers, Daniel."

"He sure does." Putting down his utensils, the pastor leaned his arms on the table. "Not only have we been blessed by David's servitude, but now the entire Sower family will be serving. We are most appreciative indeed, especially on the last leg of our journey when we are all but exhausted and tuckered out. Our daily prayer has been Philippians 4:13, 'I can do all things through Christ which strengtheneth me.' And now the Lord has sent help to share in our distress." The wrinkles on his forehead softened, and his smile stretched from ear to ear. "Yes, we will receive your offer and shall see you all and your musical instruments before each service." Jonathan slapped his knee. "We'll be there."

26

Love Lost

The Merced Falls and Forlorn Hope camp meetings concluded well, although the days sweltered, exceeding ninety degrees. Only one meeting remained, held in early September in La Grange at Branche's Ferry.

Sarah still could not sleep through the night, as she was worried about Joshua, even though he was close by, and she could share weekends with him during the camp meetings. The moments they spent together, she found him lethargic and falling asleep from exhaustion. She grew concerned for him because his weight continued to drop, and the color of his skin was pale and clammy. Although he seemed weak, he never complained but rather spoke highly of how God had been moving in the lives of the people at these events.

During the last camp meeting, on Saturday evening, Joshua collapsed in her arms. His head felt warm, and his body lay limp and in a cold sweat.

"Joshua ... Josh? Wake up. Wake up!" Sarah screamed as she held him on her lap. "Pa, Ma, come quickly!" Trembling and rocking his still body, she sobbed, unable to control herself.

Her parents dashed to her side. They spread a blanket next to them, picked him up, and laid him upon it. After her mother placed a wet towel on his temple and a cup of water to his pale lips, her father shook his body to kindle a response. All Sarah could do was hold Joshua's hand.

"Continue to try to wake him and keep this compress to his head, Mary, while I run to find Doctor Cassidy and Pastor McSwan," her father said.

The minister arrived first at the Sower's campsite, Ruth and Rebecca following close behind. "No ... no! Not Joshua, Lord!" They fell to their knees beside his comatose body.

"Son, it's mother." The hysterical mother rubbed his hands in hers. "Please wake up." She sobbed with her daughter next to her.

"All right, folks. Doctor Cassidy is here. Give him room," her father said.

The physician checked his vitals and asked questions. "I'm so sorry, Daniel and Ruth. His pulse is very faint. I fear he contracted cholera and is dehydrated in a terrible way. He may not make it. When was the last time he ate, and was he able to hold anything down?"

"This morning," Ruth said between sobs. "He's never complained to me about feeling sick even though I asked him numerous times because he seemed so frail. He would always say, 'I'm fine, Ma.'" She paused, trembling, holding her fingertips to her mouth. "Although ... he did excuse himself often to relieve himself." Her cry turned into wailing. "I knew something was wrong, but I didn't do anything about it. We've been so busy."

"Don't go blaming yourself, dear." Pastor McSwan held his wife's hand. "We all sensed it, but Joshua refused to acknowledge that he was sick. Our boy's heart was to serve the Lord even unto death."

"No, he can't die!" Rebecca gripped her brother's shirt, yanking it, as tears tumbled to his chest.

"How can this happen to him only and not to us?" Pastor McSwan asked.

"You've been doing a lot of traveling. Cholera comes from infected water or food and is not contagious." The doctor placed his fingers over Joshua's wrist. "Enough with the questions. He hasn't much time. You need to be with him."

"I've always procured a physician for the meetings but never thought I would be the one in need for my own son." The minister broke down as he gathered Joshua into his arms, and Sarah and the others knelt next to him and began to pray.

After several minutes of cooling him down with wet towels and trying to get him to drink, Joshua's eyes rolled back, and he slipped away peacefully.

"Oh, Joshua." The heartbroken teenager sobbed, holding his hand. The comfort of her father's arms around her shoulder was the strength she needed. She dug her face into his chest as sorrow expelled from a place within her soul she never knew existed. Cries from the other family members surrounded her.

"He is with the Lord now." Doctor Cassidy pulled the blanket over his face, and the groaning and wails intensified. "Pastor, Ruth ... allow me to bring his body to my clinic in town where I can prepare him for burial. I know your hands are full here."

"Might I come with you?" The grieving mother asked.

"I would like to come, too," Sarah said.

"Of course, you may."

"Daniel, is that all right with you?" Ruth's expression begged his approval.

Jonathan placed his hand on Ruth's shoulder. "Don't you worry one bit about the camp meeting, Ruth. We'll help your husband, and I'm sure others will pitch in to assist, too. You and Sarah go and be with him."

"Thank you, Jonathan and Mary." Pastor squeezed their hands and turned to his spouse. "Please, my dear, go with Doctor Cassidy and do what is necessary to get things started for Joshua's burial. I will be home by tomorrow night to assist you." He embraced his wife and daughter as the physician dismissed himself to retrieve his wagon.

"Ruth, would you mind if Sarah spends the night with you at your home? We can fetch her when we return," her mother said.

"Of course. I wouldn't have it any other way. Neither would Joshua."

THE FOUR-HOUR RIDE TO SNELLING seemed unbearable for Sarah as she and Ruth held each other in the back of the wagon where Joshua's body lay covered. His words from the previous year when his family visited the farm for the first time looped in her mind. *"Well, my father and I believe our lives are in God's hands. If it's our time to go, then we have the peace of knowing that it will be while we are doing God's work, and we will go to be with the Lord forever."*

Was this Your plan, God, to take Joshua so soon? I don't understand. We were to be married, have children, and a place of our own. He was my life. Am I supposed to just accept this and be at peace with Your decision? The questions clouded Sarah's mind, seeking justification for Joshua's death, but she could not, and perhaps would not allow God to answer as her heart began to fill with anger.

At his clinic, Doctor Cassidy laid his body on his examining table as Sarah and Ruth followed. "Ladies, please, take your time. I'll be at my desk if you need me."

"Dear, you go first." Ruth shuffled over to the small clinic's front receiving room.

Pressing her cheek to his cold, still face, Sarah whispered in his ear. "I will always love you, Joshua." The locket he gave her for Christmas dangled from her neck when she stooped over him. "You'll forever be in my heart." She ran her fingers across his face, memorizing every detail of his features. Touching his lips, she kissed him for the last time and laid her head on his chest, hoping to hear his heartbeat, but not a sound. Bitter tears puddled on his shirt until they no longer flowed.

"I guess God must've loved you more than me and wanted you with Him. It's not fair. What am I goin' to do without you?" She peeled herself away, realizing his mother needed to be with him as much as she did. "One day, we'll meet again. Don't forget me, my love." She touched his face once more, then exited the room and allowed Ruth to enter.

Sitting in the doctor's waiting room, Sarah discerned Ruth's cry and considered her excruciating pain and agonizing sorrow. Some time had passed before the grieving mother returned, her eyes red and swollen.

The grieving mother placed her arms around Sarah's shoulders. "Dear girl, there is nothing more we can do. Shall we head over to my home?" They walked to her house a few blocks away, too exhausted to speak.

Sarah would stay the night in Rebecca's room, waiting for her family to retrieve her the next evening on their return from Branche's Ferry.

The hour drew late, and she cried herself to sleep.

AFTER PLAYING "AMAZING GRACE" ON THE FIDDLE for the Sunday morning service, Jonathan assisted Pastor McSwan up the steps of the wooden stage and to the podium under the brush arbor. Holding his elbow, he could feel the grieving minister trembling. He returned to his seat and listened as the pastor closed the session, trying to encourage the congregation, as well as himself, to find peace, knowing his only son passed away doing what he loved best, serving his Lord and Savior, Jesus Christ.

"Joshua departed in the arms of those who dearly love him, and now he is in the embrace of the One who loves him the greatest ... the Heavenly Father," he said, tears streaming his cheek.

Jonathan shook his head, amazed at Pastor McSwan's ability to stand and minister to others when it was he that needed it most. *Surely, he has the comfort and peace from God that surpasses all understandin'.* His son now rested at a good place, home with the Lord, where one day they would meet again. Joshua's death and hope of eternal life magnified the pastor's message of salvation to a lost and dying world. Of all the camp meetings, this event produced the largest amount of believers, as many people came forward and accepted Jesus Christ as their Lord and Savior.

SARAH LAY NUMB from the last twenty-four hours of trauma, too weak to bear her weight. She could hear the wagons parking in front of the McSwan's home in the late afternoon, and the muffled voices of both parents inside the home. Their wails turned into praying.

"Where is my daughter?" her father asked.

"She is in Rebecca's room and hasn't come out all day," Ruth said.

"Mary, let's get our daughter. This family needs time to themselves."

"Ruth, Pastor, I will be by tomorrow to drop off a meal," her mother said. "I'll be more than happy to lend you a hand in any way you may need."

Tap, tap, tap. "Sarah, it's Pa."

She opened her mouth to speak, but no words came forth, only tears. Watching the door open, she could see her father's lean figure approaching in the curtain-drawn room. He crouched beside the bed and ran his fingers across her face, pushing her tear-soaked hair away.

"Darlin', shall we go home?" He kissed her forehead, and with his strong arms, he carried her to the wagon. David and Naomi embraced her all the way to their farm.

Upon arriving at the farmhouse, her father assisted her to her bedroom, and her mother helped her to change into her nightgown. They tucked her into bed, where she remained the next few days. She didn't emerge from her room until the day of Joshua's funeral, feeling light-headed from lack of nourishment.

JOSHUA'S MEMORIAL took place at the Snelling cemetery. A sea of dark mourning dresses and frock coats with no faces huddled around his humble wood casket. Sarah wondered how Pastor McSwan contained himself as he conducted the service. He read Psalm 23 and reflected upon his son's faithfulness to the Lord and his family as a loyal servant and only beloved son.

The mournful expression on Ruth and Rebecca's faces mirrored how she felt numb and emotionless until the end when the gravediggers lowered his casket into the ground.

Sarah's heart ached. *This is it. No longer will I see you, my love, until we meet again in heaven.* His mother broke down in tears, causing her to fall to her knees and sob on her mother's shoulders next to her. The families and friends placed flowers over his final resting place. As the crowd dispersed, the gravediggers began returning the dirt to the ground from where it came. Compilation of sadness layered itself on Sarah's chest with each passing, dirt-laden shovel pounding Joshua's casket. When the plot was filled, and the tombstone set, both families said their final farewells and somberly returned to the McSwans' home to offer their condolences.

IT WOULD BE A LONG WHILE AFTER THE FUNERAL before Sarah interacted with the McSwans. Attendance and fellowship with them at church proved too difficult for her. Nothing seemed to have meaning, even the holidays. She became angry at God for taking Joshua away from her and could not bring herself to give Him any thanks after what happened. Her family did their best to comfort her, but she did not desire to partake in church or with the Almighty.

Her father spoke to her as they sat near the hearth, staring at the flames. "Sarah, darlin', we loved Joshua too and considered him a part of our family. He loved the Lord so much that he would do anything He asked of him, knowin' there was the possibility of losin' his own life for the sake of spreadin' the Gospel. The ultimate reward he wanted was to be with the Father in the most beautiful place of all, His kingdom. This place is where those who love Jesus shall one day reside forever. God, no doubt, has plans for him in Heaven. Don't lose your faith, daughter, for you'll see him again."

"But, I need him, Papa." Her lips trembled. "How can God do this?"

"He can do this because He is the Sovereign Lord and King. He is all knowin' and has His reasons. We need to trust Him. "His Word tells us in Jeremiah 29:11-14, *For I know the thoughts that I think toward you, saith the LORD, thoughts of peace, and not of evil, to give you an expected end. Then shall ye call upon me, and ye shall go and pray unto me, and I will hearken unto you. And ye shall seek me, and find me, when ye shall search for me with all your heart. And I will be found of you, saith the LORD...*

"He knows what is best for us. One day He will reveal this to you, Sarah."

Somehow this answer still did not settle with her, for at this moment, she did not desire to know God's reason for taking Joshua so early in life. Day by day, her heart grew colder and more distant.

She would dismiss herself anytime God was mentioned. Soon she realized the family members stopped mentioning church to her, hoping time would heal her broken spirit. *How will I live my life without him?*

27

Grown-Up

After school, David planned to spend time with the McSwans. He grew closer to them as he comforted and encouraged them. He thought his presence would help fill Joshua's void, but he knew he'd never replace him.

"Pastor and Mrs. McSwan, it's me, David. I walked Rebecca home." He strutted up the porch steps and opened the front door to allow their daughter and himself in their house.

"Hello, children, come inside." Pastor McSwan came out of the kitchen with his wife and hugged them.

"Is there anythin' I can do for y'all today?" David studied their lackluster faces.

"Oh, David, you're such a gracious young man," Ruth said, placing her hand on his shoulder. "Would ya like a glass of lemonade?"

"Yes, ma'am, if it's not too much trouble." He shifted his books in his arms. "I know. May I read to you from the Bible this afternoon? That is if you aren't busy."

"Indeed. Why don't the three of you sit out on the porch while I fetch some refreshments?" Ruth returned to the kitchen.

"Well, that's a wonderful idea, Joshua." Pastor McSwan patted him on his back as they walked outside.

"Uh, Pastor. I think you meant to say, David. You called me Joshua."

Wide-eyed, Pastor McSwan covered his mouth with his hand and cringed. A tear dribbled down his cheek.

"That's all right, Pastor. It's only been two months, and I miss him terribly too." He and Rebecca placed their books on the table and sat in the white rattan chairs across from the pastor, who sat in his rocking chair.

David's heart melted as the pastor's once glowing smile now quivered. "With school and church services startin' up again, y'all have had little time to yourselves to grieve. It must be real hard, especially with Thanksgivin' and Christmas around the corner. I know I could never replace your son, and I don't intend to. I just want to help where I can."

"I'm so sorry, David." Pastor McSwan pulled a hanky from his pant pocket, wiped his eyes, and rubbed his nostrils. "Yes, yes. It would please me to hear you read some scripture." A slight grin managed to surface as he settled into the rocker.

Ruth brought the pitcher of lemonade and four glasses. After serving them, she sat in her rocking chair beside her husband.

"How 'bout I read from the book of John?" David flipped through the pages of his leather-bound Bible.

"That's perfect. Apostle John does a good job of explaining God's awesome power. I think I could use some of His strength right now." Pastor breathed in deep and tilted his head back. A soft creak came from his chair as he slowly rocked.

"In the beginning was the Word, and the Word was with God, and the Word was God. The same was in the beginning with God. All things were made by him; and without him was not any thing made that was made. In him was life; and the life was the light of men. And the light shineth in darkness; and the darkness comprehended it not..."

David read a chapter a day to the family every day after school, up through Christmas break, and they seemed to anticipate his daily visit and reading. Pastor McSwan poured himself into David, taught him the Scriptures, and answered his questions. His visits helped to get their minds back on God and comfort their hurting hearts.

"SARAH, WOULD YA LIKE TO HELP DAVID AND NAOMI decorate the tree with the cookies they made this afternoon?" Mary entered the farmhouse's quiet living room where her eldest daughter sat in a chair by the hearth, her back facing the Christmas tree. Only the ticking of the wall clock filled the room. In Mary's hands, she held a tray with an assortment of brightly colored sugar and gingerbread cookies in different holiday shapes. The youngsters followed, humming carols and giggling.

Mary had hoped that childhood memories of the festive season would lift her teenage daughter's grieving spirit. *Oh, my dear girl. What can I do to cheer you up? You choose not to receive comfort from God or us but rather wallow in your misery. I know it's been only four months, but I see no sign of improvement. Instead, you grow angrier by the day. Your eyes and tone of voice reveal your heart.*

Sarah's sunken eyes pulled away from her needlepoint and stared back at her, emotionless. No smile. No frown. Inhaling deeply, Sarah laid her stitching over the folds of her black skirt. She glanced at her young siblings as they strategized around the tree. "No. Maybe next year."

"Aw, Sarah. It's Christmas Eve." Naomi sifted through the tray in her hands and found a heart-shaped cookie with Sarah's name written on it with sugary icing. "Look, I made this one just for you." She handed it to her sister.

Mary hoped Sarah would be touched by her sister's thoughtful gesture as she peered down at the tasty ornament. But the glimmer of the heart-shaped locket on her dark blouse drew her attention, causing her hands to tremble. The cookie tumbled to the floor, breaking into several pieces.

"No, I can't. Just leave me alone!" Sarah stood, threw her needlework on the chair, and ran to her room, past her father and elder brother as they entered the living room.

"Is everythin' all right?" Her husband spun on his heels as he and Samuel cast their sights on Sarah clamoring up the stairs.

Mary gave the tray to Naomi, then stood by Jonathan. "The grievin' is far from over, dear." She wrapped her arm under her husband's.

"Come, let's do what we can to enjoy what is left of Christmas."

The family gathered around the tree, adorning it, and sharing stories of Christmases past. To Mary, the chortles and gaiety did not seem as bright as before and felt rehearsed. Soon after the reminiscing, the room quieted, clock ticking, as they decorated. A cloud, not as menacing as the one which engulfed Sarah, seemed to hover about each one of the members. Their bodies were present, but their minds were a million miles away as they placed the ornaments on the boughs.

The contrast was especially noticeable with Samuel. He faltered over every ornament as he hung them on the backside of the tree. *What could possibly be on his mind? Probably his gold pannin' adventures and haulin' freight in towns he's never been. Oh, son, if only you'd heed your father's advice. You've given us no choice but to give in to your dreams, no matter how far-fetched they may be. I guess you'll find out about life the hard way. Maybe you'll be one of the blessed ones and find that pot of gold. You're in the Lord's hands now. All we can do is pray.* The shade of darkness on his jawline where manhood was making its mark caught her attention along with his shoulders, broad and strong, and his tall, lean physique.

She shifted her gaze to Naomi on the left side of the tree. Her youngest daughter's youthful face was bright, and the ends of her lips naturally curved into a girlish grin. The cinnamon red ribbons in her hair dulled to her spicy personality. *Oh, my rambunctious daughter. You're probably thinkin' about your friends and the fun and games you'll experience when school resumes. I realize your plans are well-intentioned, just a bit naïve, that's all. Hopefully, you've learned your lesson while on restriction and will exercise more caution when choosin' your steps.*

Mary's eyes rested on David as he arranged the wooden nativity pieces under the tree. Like an angel, his face appeared relaxed and peaceful. No worry lines, just big, soft, brown eyes yearning to learn more about God and to be the apple of His eye. *David, sweet David, my youngest. You must be envisionin' how you might serve God next year. You're maturin' faster than your ten-year-old body can keep up. Oh, how I wish you could remain my little boy for a while longer.*

Jonathan interrupted her thoughts when he planted a gentle kiss on her cheek from behind, then wrapped his arms around her waist.

"Ah, Mary." He spoke low into her ear. "This year proved difficult, but I'm not goin' to allow it to rob me of celebratin' our Lord's birth. Christmas is all about Him, after all, and a time for us to forget our sorrows."

Pressing her head into her husband's chest and adoring the tin star he had made years ago, resting upon the treetop, she sighed in agreement. *My dear husband, you are my treasure beyond all things. Without you, I wouldn't experience the joys of bein' loved and becomin' a lovin', loyal wife and mother. There's no other man I would choose to live out my days with. Despite all the difficulties we've faced, between you and the Lord, the crooked path is made straight. All is well with you by my side.* "What sorrow? Only love abounds in this family." She smiled, turned to face her husband, and kissed and embraced him.

SAMUEL HELD OFF UNTIL AFTER THE 1867 NEW YEAR and his eighteenth birthday in January to tell his parents about his plans to move from home. Before he sprang this difficult news on them, he wanted the dust of emotions from Joshua's death to settle first. He had saved quite a bit of money he earned from panning and working for Patrick for this reason.

He and his parents sat in the chairs beside the fireplace in his father's office. Clutching onto the chair's arms, they seemed to be anticipating bad news. *But it's good news. I can't wait to be on my own. Isn't that what a man's supposed to do ... stand on his own two feet ... carve out a future of his own?* Samuel leaned over with his elbows upon his knees and stared down at the woven carpet, afraid to look them in their eyes. He forced himself to meet their worried gazes.

"Pa, Ma, I've decided the time has come for me to move on. Last year I worked hard and saved enough money to live in our old wall tent at Woods Creek in Jamestown. I figure I might make a livin' from prospectin' for gold. Miners taught me what to do. If this doesn't work, I can always find employment at the railroad. Plus, I will continue to help Patrick out with haulin' freight." Samuel paused to receive a response, a film of sweat gathering on his face and at the base of his neck.

His mother coughed, cleared her throat, shifted in her seat, rubbed her hands over her lap, and pressed her skirt folds. Turning his gaze to his father, Samuel watched as he fidgeted. Yet he held his composure better than his mother did as he tried to be still and steady.

"Son, ya sound like you have everythin' all figured out." His father scratched the back of his head, and his voice was deep and raspy. "I guess we can't stop you, now that you're an adult. Are you sure about gold prospectin'? From what we're told, it's not as lucrative as you may think."

"I must try, Pa. I feel it in my bones, and I'm gonna strike it rich." Samuel stood, walked over to the window, and gazed out into the fallowed fields. He recalled himself plowing alongside the Chinese employees and sowing the wheat seed. *Never again. There are other avenues to explore. A whole world is out there waitin' for me.*

His mother's whimpering broke his thoughts. Returning to her, he knelt and held her hand. "Ma, please don't cry. I won't be far, and I'll come to visit."

Her eyes locked onto his, and her smile looked forced. "Oh, Samuel. I don't think a mother is ever ready to let her children go. But I know I must so that you won't rebel against me, and you can progress into manhood. I can't have you clingin' to my skirt forever. There is only so much your Pa and I can teach you. The rest, you must find out on your own. All I ask is that you let the scriptures guide you. We were hopin' you would want to continue in the family farmin' tradition, but we realize you are your own man."

Jonathan leaned forward. "Son, if ya ever change your mind, your ma and I..." He glanced around the room and nodded toward the window. "And the farm will always be here for you."

His mother caressed his face. "Sam, you know we love you very much. We want to support you in whatever decision you make. If this is truly the path you feel God is puttin' in your heart, then who are we to stop you? Is there anythin' we can do to help?"

After considering his mother's words, Samuel, for the first time, realized that he actually did not pray about his decisions. *Too late now. I've already made up my mind to move into the gold country.* He returned to his chair and studied his parent's facial expressions.

"I appreciate all you've done for me, Ma and Pa. Please understand, I've been plannin' this for a long time. This is somethin' I must do. There are a couple of things I would like to request. I'm hopin' you'll allow me to take Fire and perhaps one of the shotguns and revolver."

Jonathan straightened himself. "Of course, you may. But we can do better than that. Would it help you if we gave you some additional money to start?"

Relieved to have his parent's blessings, Samuel stood and embraced them. "Thanks. I will repay you as soon as I can."

"No need to pay us back, son. Count this as part of your inheritance." Jonathan opened the safe behind his desk, removed a small canvas bag filled with money, and placed it in Sam's hands. "Spend it wisely."

"I will, Pa, I will." Samuel packed it amongst his belongings, and the following week he and Fire headed to Jamestown.

28

Working for the Railroad

Two Years Later

"Lay off!" The call came from Superintendent Strobridge on a late chilly Saturday afternoon in February 1869. The railroad men had completed more than 650 miles of track through the flat, barren plains of Nevada. Samuel unhitched Fire, and Central Pacific's horse, Dusty, from the handcar as his six Chinese workers secured it for the evening.

"You men have a good day off tomorrow. Get some rest." Samuel yanked on the horse's reins to walk them over to the corral.

Ah Chy moved toward Samuel and bowed. "Sir, brief moment to give you list of supplies we need." Tea-stained teeth peeked from between his thin lips. He slipped his hand into his ragged, faded dungaree pocket, pulled out a crumpled piece of paper, and gave it to his supervisor.

"Rice, dried fish, spices, green tea, herbs, Fan laundry soap. I will see to it to give the provision boss your list. He may be takin' the train back to Sacramento this week for supplies." Samuel stuffed the note into his shirt pocket. "Is this all ya need?"

"Yes, sir."

"Any of you care to join me for a shot of whiskey at the saloon?"

Six tanned faces grinned at him, chuckling and commenting to Ah Chy, their interpreter.

"Thank you for offer, but men no drink whiskey. They tired and hungry. Also, no Chinamen allowed in bar. You like to come for supper?"

Samuel recalled the first delicious and exotic meal Mr. Chung had prepared for him and Patrick Faye on their first hauling run to Chinese Camp two years earlier. *Gosh, it seems so long ago.* "Yes, I'd love to eat with you. Let me put the horses away and wash up, and I'll meet you at your campsite."

Samuel chuckled at memories flashing through his mind as he walked to the corral. Two Christmases back, he returned home because prospecting left him penniless and hungry. His father's warning words had rung daily in his head. *Are you sure about gold prospectin'? From what we're told, it's not as lucrative as you may think.* He had to borrow money from his parents that Christmas so he could venture off again to look for work. The Central Pacific Railroad had hired him in January 1868 to oversee a Chinese gang of six men, moving track material in a small, iron handcar. *Hmm … ironic.* Here he was today with the same men and worried about becoming penniless again in a few weeks after the rail work was completed.

THE CHINESE WORKERS established their own canvas lodgings alongside the rails. Tranquil compared to the white encampment. Groups of men huddled around a campfire or table, bowls to their lips, scooping the spice-laden delicacies with two sticks, laughing, chattering in Mandarin. Sam's nostrils soaked in the different aromas coming from the exotic environment. Chicken and fish roasting, fresh stir-fried vegetables, and lemongrass from the soap used to wash their clothes.

Five of his men sat playing mahjong in front of Chy's tent while one stirred the food over the campfire.

"Just in time, sir." Chy gathered the game tiles and put them aside. "Hing done cooking. Here is bowl. Please, help yourself." The men circled the fire as the cook dished out the rice and stir-fried meal and then returned to their seats.

"Um, delicious." Sam bowed his head toward the cook who returned a nod. The chatter amongst the men in their language did not bother him at all. Trust and respect deemed a fabric of their relationship.

Listening, but not understanding a word they said, Samuel reminisced about laboring with the Chinese farmhands on his father's farm. Somehow he felt more comfortable with these men, as there was less stress and rivalry working with them than with the Caucasian railroad men. It seemed so unfair to him that they worked harder than his white co-workers, received fewer pay, and had to find their own accommodations. Although strict with them, he also gained compassion toward them and made certain they obtained their entire month's wage of thirty dollars, minus the cost of comestibles. Perhaps this explained why their encampments seemed to be much more civil. They appreciated the hard work, which paid for their comforts, whereas the Irish gangs agreed on thirty-one dollars a month, including housing and food. *And they wonder why the railroads hire the Chinese instead of them.* Sam chuckled.

He finished his flavor-rich meal, stood, and stretched. *Yum ... that was just as good as my ma's home-cookin'.* A grin of contentment beam across his face. "Thank you for the wonderful supper, men, but now I must head over to the saloon. A game of poker awaits me. See y'all on Monday." Patting Ah Chy's back, he returned to the white encampment.

Heavy drinking and visiting the saloons with the other white railroad men kept Sam from falling into depression. The twenty-by-twenty-foot wall tent swelled with gambling tables, drunken men, and thick smoke. Saloon girls dressed in only their undergarments, corsets, and petticoats meandered among the gamblers. They fetched drinks from the rough-neck bartender behind the unfinished, saw-cut-pine bar in the far corner.

"Hey, Sower! Come join us for a game of poker!" Buckeye, another foreman, sat shuffling a deck of cards. Sam recalled him losing his left eye during a nitroglycerin blast. His replacement seemed more like a rotten walnut. Samuel pulled up a chair and sorted through the hand dealt him.

Soon enough, one of the saloon girls came by flaunting herself. "Anythin' I can do for ya, gorgeous?" she whispered in Samuel's ear.

"Later, Tissa, after my game. In the meantime, can you fetch me a shot of whiskey?"

After several rounds of drinks and a few hands of poker, Samuel rose from his seat to call it quits. "I'm out."

"Ah, come on, coolie lover, don't quit now," Buckeye growled.

"Hey, you better watch your mouth unless ya wanna lose the other eye too." He snarled back, feeling the alcohol in his system.

The robust railman clumsily stood from his chair and lifted his fists. "Aw, you can't hurt me, coolie boy. Come on. Show me what you got."

Samuel felt his blood boiling from the name blurted at him. "So, is that what you think of me? Well, you're right, you big tub of lard."

He turned away from the boisterous man as if to ignore him, but instead, he clenched his right fist, and with a sharp turn, he slugged him in his good eye.

The one-eyed bully tumbled to the ground and shook his head. He staggered to his feet, rubbing his face. "Where are you?" He swung his fists around him like a blind bat flapping its wings. Cards flew, and tables and chairs crashed around them. Eventually, one push led to another, and the whole room of alcohol-soaked men brawled. The saloon girls ran outside and flying bodies followed, continuing the fight in the cold night. After the fighting ceased, bruised and battered railroaders lay about the camp in a drunken stupor, unaware of what had started the brawl.

Sam's head swam in circles as he laid on the floor. He could hear the ladies sifting through the passed-out bodies, making sure the men were still breathing. Sprawled a few feet away was his old pal, Buckeye, out cold. *Ugh*…Sam groaned from the pain in his head. *What the heck were we fightin' over this time?*

"There ya are, gorgeous." Tissa's sweet voice tickled his ears. "Come on. Let me get you back to my place, an' I'll have you feelin' better in no time." She helped Samuel up and brought him to her tent where she nursed his wounds and comforted him in the way she knew how.

The next morning, Sam and the men returned to their wall tents as if nothing had ever happened. They would brave their only day off in pain and with a hangover.

HUDDLED IN MASSES AT THE REAR GUARD, April 28, 1869, the squad of eight Irish rail handlers, a few hundred white bosses, and their small army of 4,000 Chinese men wrought a mere fourteen miles away from Promontory. The Central Pacific Railroad and their rival, the Union Pacific approaching in the opposite direction, agreed to rendezvous at this location.

Samuel could almost taste the victory. The excited rail gangs' foreign chatter buzzed about him and the white bosses. The main topic of the day questioned whether or not they could meet the challenge CP Associate, Charles Crocker, made to UP President, Thomas Durant. News declared Crocker boasted that the CP men could lay down ten miles of track in twelve hours compared to the seven laid in twenty hours by the UP men.

After a hardy breakfast and several cups of strong, black tea and coffee, Sam and his men started loading their handcar after Superintendent Strobridge yelled, "Work!"

"Come on! Put your backs into it, men. Let's get at the job. We've got a race to win." Samuel commanded his gang as they passed items from one man to another onto the human powered car's sturdy wood platform. A day before, other gangs unloaded two miles of material from the steam train, *Jupiter*. A total of sixteen rail teams, including Sam's, loaded their portion of rails, a keg each of bolts and spikes, and a bundle of fishplates to be brought to the front of the line. The six men hopped on board, and the young foreman snapped the horse's reins.

"Hee-ya!" Samuel cracked the whip as the horses trotted along the side of the tracks, pulling the heavy ladened handcar toward the end where more Chinese gangs and the eight Irish rail handlers awaited them. *Click-clack*. The wheels clattered as they moved over the fishplates joining each section of steel.

"We're comin' to a downgrade. Pull the brake slowly, Ah Lim."

The brakeman tugged and the handcar came to a halt at the hilltop. Two men jumped off the car, unhitched, and mounted the horses. They rode them while keeping pace with the car as it raced down the slope at its own speed. At the bottom, the men hitched the team to the car again.

"Frontline ahead, Ah Lim," Samuel shouted as the brakeman brought the car to a stop. The handcar gang jumped off, and the pick crew climbed on to break open the kegs and cut the fastenings on the railroad material. The gangs unloaded and distributed the bolts, spikes, and fish plates amongst each other while he inched his car along the finished tracks, allowing the Irish rail handlers to unload the rails a group at a time. The Irishmen positioned the long heavy steel on the ties and moved out of the way to allow the Chinese gangs to join and spike them into place. Another gang added ballast where needed and tamped it down. The process repeated for the next section until they emptied the car.

Afterward, Samuel and his men headed back on the single track to reload at the rear guard. Viewing a loaded handcar ahead, his men jumped off their car and removed it off the rails, so the others passed without hesitation. The teams waved and cheered one another as they crossed.

"Lunch break," Superintendent Strobridge yelled at thirty past one. Sam and his men assembled with the other gangs and clapped loudly as Stanford, Crocker, and workers of the Central Pacific joined them for a hardy meal with a handful of Union Pacific officers.

Everyone extended congratulations when Crocker crowed, "Mr. Durant never had meant to show up." Chortles and guffaws arose from the sea of men. "Furthermore," he said, "I dub this meeting place *Victory,* for no doubt the Central Pacific railroad men will meet and exceed the seven-mile challenge during the second half of the day." The men applauded.

After lunch, the human working machine slowed down a fraction as they lay track on the southwest slope of Promontory Mountain, north of the Great Salt Lake in Utah. The men and horses labored, pulling the loaded handcars up the 4,297-foot ascent to Promontory Point at the mountain's southern peninsula. Also, the men used extra time, bending the rails to the landscape's curves.

"Lay off," Strobridge roared at seven o'clock in the evening. The twelve-hour day exhausted the CP men who had laid ten miles and fifty-six feet of new track.

Sam's heart leaped with pride over their accomplishments

that day. Yet the glowing lights from Promontory Point beckoned ahead, three-and-a-half miles of roadbed waiting to be finished the next day.

THE RAILROAD MEN COMPLETED ALL CENTRAL PACIFIC WORK a week later, Wednesday, the fifth of May. The eight Irishmen returned to Sacramento, partaking in an honorary parade, while Sam and the other men stayed in Promontory awaiting the celebrations after the Union Pacific finished their portion. Only two unfinished rails remained, which they planned to join with an engraved laurel tie and golden spike to the Union Pacific's final rail. However, the UP team fell behind schedule by two days because of labor disputes.

The makeshift traveling canvas town bustled with unemployed workers, mainly Chinamen awaiting possible orders. Even Sam desperately sought other employment, only to find maintenance jobs on the completed CP line.

Finally, Union Pacific accomplished their task on the ninth of May. In anticipation of this, the railroad heads staged the Union Pacific No. 119 and the Central Pacific No. 60 (better known as the *Jupiter*) locomotives face-to-face on Promontory Summit.

At noon the following day, the celebration joining the eastern and western rails commenced. Samuel climbed onto Jupiter's cowcatcher along with others, excitement filling his heart. A large crowd gathered around the two steam powered trains, trying to get a glimpse of the festivities emceed by the wealthy Sacramento banker, Edgar Mills. After the invocation by Rev. Dr. John Todd, a Sacramento newspaper publisher and editor, Dr. H. W. Harkness presented the commemoratives. He gave an engraved golden spike to the victorious Leland Stanford of Central Pacific Railroad and a silver spike with similar engraving to Thomas Durant of Union Pacific Railroad. Both men carefully drove the precious metal into the laurel tie using an inscribed hammer. Afterward, officials removed the ceremonial items so as not to be stolen, to be replaced by a pine tie and regular spikes.

Stanford went first and swung at the spike wired to the

transcontinental telegraph line for the nation to hear. But oh! He missed and hit the rail instead. Sam and the others roared with laughter. Shamed, the UP railhead handed the hammer to his CP opponent for his turn.

"Durant's looking kind of green." A voice in the crowd snickered.

"He must be hungover from all the drink he had last night at the party in Ogden." Another voice chimed in.

Swinging the maul over his head, Durant grunted, and his face contorted. *Bam!* His hammer fell on the ballast and missed the tie and spike altogether.

A roar exploded, and Sam heard a low chant growing louder. "Hung Wah ... Hung Wah."

Sam's heart swelled, glad to hear the Asian crowd majority prompting recognition for one of their own. A rare sight indeed, when anti-Chinese sentiment was running rampant amongst the white workers. He joined in. "Hung Wah, Hung Wah."

Emerging from the dense sea of scowling railroad men came the one and only Chinese foreman, humbly bowing to his comrades. Superintendent Strobridge stepped forward and handed him the hammer. With one easy heave over his small but strong body, the maul laid low and hard over the final spike, setting it deep into the pine tie with one blow. *Huzza, huzza* filled the air. The men cleared the track, allowing the two trains to creep forward and touch nose to nose, signifying the completion of the line.

At 12:47 p.m., Monday, May 10, 1869, the telegrapher, W.N. Shilling of Western Union, sent the long-awaited message, "D-O-N-E." Whoops, hollers, and pats on the back ascended from the bulging crowd.

As Ah Chy shook Sam's hand, he glanced at the barrage of unemployed men. *What am I going to do now?* The pit of his stomach turned. "Good luck to you and the men, Chy. Maybe we'll meet again somewhere along the rails."

"And to you too, sir. It was a pleasure to work with you." He bowed and went on his way.

With a heavy heart, Sam returned to his camp and packed his things. He and his horse, Fire, headed for Sacramento, hoping to take any railroad maintenance jobs he could get.

29

Grieve No More

"Sarah Sower, will you take Lad Hampton as your lawful wedded husband, to live together in the estate of matrimony? Will you love him, honor him, comfort him, and keep him in sickness and in health, forsaking all others, be true to him as long as you both shall live?" The wiry-haired Mariposa magistrate peered at her from above his notes as he adjusted his cravat under his floor-length, dark robe.

"I...I..." Sarah's snug corset sent the knot in her stomach up to her throat. Her eyelids fluttered under her bonnet's thin veil, and her knees wobbled beneath her travel skirt. Memories flooded her mind. She looked at Lad standing beside her, perspiration gathering on his forehead under his black Coachman's hat.

"Come on. You can do it, girl. Say it!" Snickers came from the couples standing in line waiting their turn to be married in the Mariposa Courthouse that warm, summer Saturday afternoon, the seventh of August, 1869.

What am I doing? Is this real? Am I really doing this? Eloping? I just came out of mourning last year...

SARAH'S THOUGHTS DRIFTED to September 1868, two years after Joshua's death. She decided to remove the locket Joshua had given her, tucked it away in a box, and hid it in her bottom dresser drawer. To finalize her grieving, she donned a bright-colored day dress and visited his gravesite one last time to let him go.

Usually, after visiting the cemetery, she would tell her parents she was going to take her horse Belle for a ride. At first, she took refuge at the fort by the creek where she and Joshua first kissed. There she felt close to him and spent hours in solitude. But soon, that time of reflection turned into resentment toward God. She remembered slamming the wooden crate seats against the fort's walls, shaking her fists at heaven, and yelling, "I hate You! Why did You take Joshua from me?" Eventually, her pent-up anger destroyed the love she once had for Joshua.

She recalled her decision to change her life that day. Instead of riding to the fort, she desired a new start, to venture in a different direction, into town. This moment was when she discovered a place called "The Barn," a big building on Fourth Street. During the day, it served as a second-hand store, a place where she could afford to purchase some pretty dresses, of which she deprived herself while mourning — no more dark, drab clothes.

As she meandered through the aisles, a boldly printed flyer posted on one of several columns caught her attention. *Contra Dance, Saturday evenings starting at eight o'clock, seventy-five cents admission or one dollar per couple, and all-you-can-eat midnight dinner for fifty cents. Must be twenty-one years or older.*

"Can I help you with something, miss?"

The stranger's voice behind her finally broke the invisible bubble of her self-protected, silent, and grieving world.

She jerked her head and turned, eyes making contact with a young man pushing a broom. "This dance. Is it here?"

"Yep. Tonight. Once all these vendors are gone, I'll transform this place into a dance hall." He stopped sweeping and glanced around the room. "Where have you been? It's been goin' on now for the past two years."

"I...I..." Sarah felt warmth rush to her face.

"Don't you read the papers? It's been advertised in Merced County's newspaper and is a favorite meeting place for young people throughout the county."

"Oh... well... I would've been too young anyway. I...I just turned twenty-one." She lied through her teeth. Grief caused her to appear older than her sweet age of seventeen.

"You ought to come. You'll have a grand time."

"Perhaps, I shall." She curtsied and headed for home, devising an escape plan for the evening so her family wouldn't notice her disappearance.

Sarah occupied the boys' bedroom after Samuel left home. Naomi and David, who had always been close to one another, shared the same room. Once everyone fell asleep at nine o'clock, she tiptoed out of the house, fetched her horse, and rode into town to attend the contra dance. Afterward, she snuck back into the farmhouse and her room.

Slipping out at night happened for some time without anyone in the home noticing. She had sensed her parents' curiosity pique regarding her changed disposition. Yet, they didn't dare ask her, for they understood her curt response from the past, "I'm fine" as "Just let me be." So they stopped asking but rather reassured her of their love and that they'd pray for her. They even stopped inviting her to church, knowing she wasn't ready to face the McSwans yet.

Shortly after the 1869 New Year, Lad made himself known to her through a waiter who pointed him out as he stood by the Barn's bar. He was twenty-three years old and seemed like every other cowboy in town, or so she thought. Most of them were cattlemen who spent their day out on the range herding the cattle, belonging to Jackson Montana. On their days off, they frequented the saloons closest to the grazing fields. Lad had been spending time at the Barn on the weekends and staying at the Snelling Hotel and Saloon while the cattle roamed Merced Falls.

Feeling like a new woman, Sarah paraded herself like a magnet to the young men frequenting the dance hall. She knew her vivacious laugh and keen sense of humor and wit would get their attention. Having the option of any man she wanted, she had no fear of hurting a man's feelings should he not meet her satisfaction. Sarah and her lady friends enjoyed comparing the gentlemen in the hall and discussing who to accept or reject when asked to dance.

"Excuse me, ma'am. May I have this dance?" the tall cowboy said, shoulders back, left palm extended forward, and chewing tobacco.

"Why certainly. I would love to." Sarah reached out with her gloved hand as he led her to the dance floor.

Or, if Sarah decided she did not have any interest in the gentleman, her sharp tongue would answer, "Uh, no thank ya!" She'd turn the other way and begin chatting with her friends, leaving the poor fellow standing in disgrace.

Oh, I'm sure Lad must've seen my bad behavior. She grimaced at the thought.

One Saturday evening, on her way home after the dance, the hairs on the back of her neck stood as she sensed someone following her. But the night rendered no shadows lurking from behind the trees on Merced Falls Road. She kicked Belle's side through her thick-hooded cape, petticoat, and skirt, and hastened toward the farm.

That must've been Lad, curious to know where I lived or making sure I made it home safely. Whoever it was, if someone was following me, he never showed himself.

Later in their relationship, Lad informed her that he inquired about her and her family while he stayed at the Snelling Hotel.

She arrived at the Barn at her usual time of 9:45 the night the waiter informed her about Lad. As usual, she sensed all eyes turn toward her as she let her cape fall, revealing her fanciful gown and pale, soft shoulders.

Surely, Lad must've been amongst those men keeping a watchful eye on me. Hmm ... that night I wore the red-and-black ruffled dress I purchased in town. I love how that dress contrasted with my hair's ringlets and accentuated my long neckline. She let out a soft giggle. *Caught his eye, it did.*

As soon as she found her seat next to her lady friends, the waiter purposed himself at her heels. "Excuse me, ma'am. The gentleman standing at the bar over there wishes to pay for your drinks this evening." He pointed at Lad.

Her girlfriends teased her jealously. "Oh-ho. She's got herself a gentlemen suitor. Buy her a drink for a dance."

"Stop, y'all." She snapped at her friends and turned to survey the lean masculinity wearing a dark-brushed-twill longhorn shirt, brown Cassidy canvas trousers, leather Duke Vest, and Pale Rider boots. A gun belt and Colt revolver hung low on his hips. The cast of a five o'clock shadow added to his rugged facial features. And those steely cobalt eyes, which returned her gaze, made her heart skip a beat.

"Please, do tell the kind gentleman I am grateful." She smiled and nodded to the waiter then over to Lad, who leaned on one elbow propped on the bar as he gulped down a malt. He tipped his hat to her and turned around to call the bartender for another beer. She remembered thinking, *Surely he is going to come over and ask me to dance*. But he never did.

In fact, weekend after weekend for more than a month, he bought her drinks and never asked her for a dance or introduced himself. His lack of action annoyed her, and her curiosity could no longer hold her down.

"Who is this mysterious man, and why hasn't he asked me to dance?" she asked her friends.

"Honey, why don't you go over there and find out?" Sally prodded her shoulder.

"Why I think I have a good mind to do just that," she said huffing. Sarah felt obligated to at least show appreciation to this man who had been paying her way. So, she finally found the courage to walk up to Lad and thank him in her haughty manner.

The back of Lad's Coachman hat bobbed as he spoke to the bartender and drank his malt. Sarah tapped his left shoulder, and he cocked his head slowly, peering at her from the corner of his eye, not moving his position from the bar.

"Sir, I've been meaning to thank you personally for your generosity the last few Saturday evenings. Please, sir, you need to stop as I sense an obligation to repay ya somehow."

"Yes, ma'am, as you wish," Lad replied in a low, raspy tone. He didn't show any sign of emotion as he put his money down on the counter and swaggered out the door, shoulders back. He left Sarah standing there looking like the fool, just like she'd done to many men she rejected.

Fury raged to her extremities. *Who does this man think he is?* She stood justly embarrassed because this had never happened to her before and sensed everyone staring.

Turning in her ankle-high boots and heels clacking loud on the hardwood floors, she immediately followed Lad outside, screaming. "Look here! Who do you think you are treatin' me this way?" She grabbed hold of his arm to turn him around to face her.

"What way are you referrin' to, ma'am? For bein' a gentleman and buyin' your drinks or bein' a gentleman and doin' what you asked of me?" His eyes pierced hers.

Sarah's jaw dropped when she realized she had been dealt with her own game. As she got ready to slap Lad, he grasped her hand, drew her into his arms, and pressed his mouth onto her tender pink lips. At first, she squirmed in his arms and tried to push him away. But all emotions told her to let go as she swooned into his embrace.

"Now, can we start over?" Lad gazed deep into her softened eyes. "My name is Lad Hampton, and I had no intentions of you repayin' me."

"I...I...I'm Sarah." She tried to get hold of herself and find strength in her knees to stand. This warm, tingly sensation had not come upon her since the time she kissed Joshua at the fort by the creek.

"I know, Sarah Sower. Now, how about we take a seat out here in the moonlight and get acquainted with one another?" Lad loosened his arms and held the small of her back, directing her to the steps leading to the Barn.

"SARAH? I NEED YOUR ANSWER." The magistrate interrupted the pulse-racing memories.

Sarah turned to face the gorgeous groom standing next to her, reached to hold his hands, and stared into the depths of his passionate cobalt eyes. "Yes, I will."

30

The Right Direction

Knock, knock, knock.

"Sarah, are you coming down for breakfast?" Fourteen-year-old Naomi placed one hand on her sister's cold bedroom doorknob. No answer. The lowing cattle in the barn nagged at her, needing to be milked. Sarah's past two months of training after she completed grade school replayed in her mind. Wake at four in the morning, eat breakfast, milk the cows, feed the chickens, and gather the eggs. Her sister had never skipped a day of tending to the animals. The heifers wouldn't let her.

"Are you okay in there, Sarah? It's almost six o'clock. I'll gladly tend to the livestock if you aren't feeling well." She pressed her ear against the door. Not a sound. She gripped the doorknob. *What's the right thing to do? Keep knocking and wait or barge into her room.* "Sis, I'm coming in."

The knob squeaked as she turned it. Trying to be quiet should her sister not be well, Naomi cracked the door enough to slip her head through it. Her jaw dropped to find Sarah's bed made and her room vacant. An ivory-colored, unaddressed envelope lay against the brown hues of her quilt-covered pillows. She rushed inside, sat on the bed, and opened it.

Dearest Family,

You are probably wondering where I am. Not to worry. I am safe and in good hands. By the time you read this letter, I may be standing before the judge in Mariposa County getting married. Yes, I am to be Mrs. Lad Hampton. Please try to understand. He began secretly courting me six months ago. I didn't want to trouble any of you with our relationship unless I knew it would last. Not like before. We decided to elope because I couldn't bear the thought of Pastor McSwan marrying us.

We are to settle in Mariposa at Lad's small farm. He also herds cattle for Jackson Montana. I will send you posts at my earliest convenience. We hope we may be with you for a visit this winter. Now, I must meet my groom at the stagecoach. Please fetch Belle at the station. Try not to fret, Mama. I will be fine. Give my warmest love to all around.

Your daughter, Sarah
P.S. Naomi, my bedroom is now yours.

Naomi's heart stopped pounding, and her body went numb. The letter slipped through her fingers and fell to the floor.

Oh, my Lord. Elope? What have you done, Sarah? How could you do this? First, Samuel leaves. Now you. Poor Ma and Pa. We've supplied enough embarrassment for them to last a lifetime. Our family will be the laughing stock of the county. How am I goin' to tell them?

Visions of her sister saying her vows next to some roughneck cowboy with a gun to her head invaded her mind. No! She should be happy for her, but she wanted to cry. Is this the way love between a man and woman should be? So far, all she had witnessed was heartache and trouble. Marriage was supposed to be a joyous celebration. Why would Sarah be afraid to share this with her family?

The cows' painful moaning jarred Naomi out of her state of perplexity. She picked up the letter and scrambled down the stairs to the kitchen, where her parents ate breakfast and savored their morning coffee.

She burst inside and shoved the note on the table. "Sarah's gone."

Her mother put her cup down and chuckled. "Late start, dear? Well, she's probably already in the barn. Why don't you just sit down, have some toast and jam, then you can join her. You need to get used to waking up early like she does."

"No, Ma. I've been up." She scooted the letter next to her mother's cup. "Sarah ran off and is gettin' hitched in Mariposa."

"What? Married?" Her mother snatched the handwritten note as her father stood reading over her shoulder, mumbling Sarah's written words. Gasping for air, her mother managed to let out anguished wails. "Oh … oh. Jonathan."

"That foolish girl. Was she that far gone that she couldn't tell us? Where's my shotgun? I'm goin' ta—" Her father's rage-filled eyes were nearly falling out of their sockets as he stood to reach for the gun hanging above the fireplace.

"No, Jon! Don't you go doin' somethin' irrational." Mary grabbed his arm, and then broke down sobbing. "Let her go. She's an adult. She's made her choice. Heaven knows we've tried to talk to her, but she wouldn't let us in. All we can do is pray for her, just like we do for Samuel."

Breathing heavy, her father hurled himself into a chair and planted his face in his palms as her mother sat and embraced him. "Lord, where have we gone wrong?"

Her parent's anguish wrung her heart, so she situated herself on the other side of her father and linked her arm through his. As they whimpered, David pushed the kitchen door open, rubbing his eyes with his fists.

"What's goin' on in here? It's Saturday mornin', and I'm allowed to sleep in. But I can't with all this ruckus."

"Sit down, son, and we'll tell you all about it." She pulled a chair out for her young brother.

NAOMI BLEW WARM AIR INTO HER HANDS and rubbed them together. She leaned forward on her stool, rested her bonneted head on the cow's side, and reached for its udders. "Good mornin', Betsy. Sure am enjoyin' your company these days. It's been a month, and Mama is still cryin' over Sarah elopin' the way she did."

Betsy lowed and craned her neck toward Naomi, blinked her potato-brown eyes, and wagged her paintbrush tail, caressing the young girl's back.

Swish, swish. The rhythm began, and the milk splattered into the bucket.

"I do say, I miss Sarah and Samuel. Now I'm doin' both their chores. Pa says he's goin' to hire more help. No need to worry none since I'll still be the one to do the milkin'." She rubbed Betsy's side, then tugged and squeezed as she hummed the song "A Pretty Girl Milking Her Cow." Betsy mooed as the warm milk flowed.

The moments spent tending to the animals with her sister surfaced. Sarah did seem more cheerful before she left home, smiling, and even humming while she worked, even though she still spoke little and avoided long conversations at the dinner table.

Hmm, I suppose the family grew accustomed to her quiet fortitude since Joshua's death. She sure pulled the wool over our eyes. No one could've ever guessed she led another life beyond the farm. How in the world did she manage to do this? I'd hate to think what Pa and Ma might've done if they'd known about this fellow. Groundin' seems to be their solution.

Grounding. It reminded her of her mischievous dealings with the Edgar siblings. After Mr. Cavern expelled them from school, she never did hear from them. Her friends told her they moved to Merced Falls closer to the lumber mill where their father worked.

After that ordeal and watching her eldest brother and sister struggle in their lives, she hoped to learn from their mistakes and reconstruct her own life. She realized she was a tender root in the Lord back then, lacking the discernment to know evil from good. Since the Bible pointed her in the right direction, her once headstrong propensity could now be a blessing to others, rather than a curse.

She chuckled and broke the rhythm of her humming and tugging. Betsy snorted and kicked her back hoof. "Oh, sorry, girl." She resumed the proper pattern.

Naomi recalled her final days at Snelling Grade School. She excelled and finished early by one year with outstanding grades. Mr. Cavern even remarked to her parents about the change in her attitude. Freedom was something to be appreciated and not taken for granted, for the wrong decision could put her back into bondage with appropriate consequences. So, Naomi strived to keep her liberties by allowing God to direct her heart and mind to make proper choices. Daily prayer became the main facet in her life. At church, the Bible and support from the McSwans provided appropriate direction.

Naomi took over Sarah's responsibilities tending to the animals, helping her mother cook meals and maintaining the farmhouse. Rising early in the morning to tend to the cows and chickens became her favorite chore. She enjoyed riding the horses, herding the livestock, and also found pleasure in doing the practical work, such as plowing the fields with her father and their field hands.

Mooing, Betsy shook her head, clanging her bell as she pulled away.

Naomi peered down at the full bucket. "My. It seems I've exceeded our time together." She patted the cow's side. "Good girl. I best be movin' on to Daphne before she throws a fit."

THE ADDITIONAL CHORES QUICKENED NAOMI'S DAY, and soon she sat at the dinner table with her parents and David.

"Naomi. Why don't I start teachin' you to drive the wagons?" Jonathan drew his soup spoon to his mouth. "It's time you take the reins."

"Really, Pa? Can I?" Her eyes shone, and her brows nearly reached the top of her forehead.

"Yep, you sure can. Now that Samuel and Sarah are gone, I could use another driver to haul the wheat to the flour mill in Merced Falls. I believe your actions prove to me you are responsible and mature enough to handle this task."

"I'm tryin' real hard to do the right things, Pa, accordin' to God's plans, not mine." She stared at her clasped hands on the table, thinking and choosing her words wisely.

David placed his hand over hers. "She's doin' swell at church. Not only is she a hearer of the Word, but a doer."

"Pastor McSwan's teachin' on 2 Peter 1:5-10 stayed with me.

'And beside this, giving all diligence, add to your faith virtue; and to virtue knowledge; and to knowledge temperance; and to temperance patience; and to patience godliness; and to godliness brotherly kindness; and to brotherly kindness charity ... give diligence to make your calling and election sure: for if ye do these things, ye shall never fall...'" She lifted her chin and made eye contact with her mother and father. "I don't want to fall again, Ma and Pa."

ONE EARLY AUTUMN AFTERNOON following church service, Naomi chose to reconcile her relationship with the German mercantile owner, Mr. Jacobi, while her brother and parents lingered in the courthouse with the McSwans. She scurried across the street to the store.

"Hello, Mr. Jacobi. Do you remember me?" She probed his memory. Three years had passed since they last saw each other. He examined her through his spectacles.

"No. It can't be. Naomi?"

"Yes, sir. That's me!"

"My, you've grown from za last time I saw you at Snelling Courthouse." He laughed out loud.

"Yes, in more ways than one. I was just a silly little girl, with childish notions way back when. I've learned my lesson and want to apologize to you again for the trouble I caused, stealin' an' all. Is there anythin' I can do to repay you for the bad things I did? Will you forgive me?" She shuffled her boots beneath her crinoline skirt.

"Oh, Naomi, dat is vater under za bridge. I forgave you a long time ago. Besides, as you said, you vere a child back zen. Ve all made silly mistakes in our lifetime. Even I stole from a store ven I vas a little boy. In my days, Papa punished me wit za rod." The proprietor chortled as he pointed to his buttock. "He made me break my piggy bank and pay za owner myself. I learned my lesson. Maybe dat is vhy I decided to operate my own store to prove I can be a trustworthy merchant as vell as be an honest customer."

"Well, Mr. Jacobi, I would like to do this for you too. That is if you could use some help and if you can learn to trust me. I'd love to work really hard to demonstrate I can be reliable." She did her best to convince him. Since her father hired additional farmhands, she had spare time for a job.

He folded his arms as she watched him scan her from head to toe. He slowly paced back and forth behind the counter, rubbing his chin with his index finger, looking at the floor, then at the ceiling.

"Yeah, dis vould vork. I think I could use your help at za register. Vhen are you available?"

A smile stretched across her face. "I can work in the afternoons for ya and start right away!"

"Okay. How does Tuesday through Saturday from one to five o'clock vork for you?" Mr. Jacobi suggested. "It vill be part-time for now."

"That's perfect!"

"Zen are we agreed?" He extended his hand to shake hers.

"Yes, indeed." Naomi took his hand. She was excited to start working for him the following week.

31

The New Deacon

Summer 1870

The pews' fresh-cut pine scent and glossy shellac permeated the five-month new Snelling church on Green and Third Street, tickling the nostrils of fourteen-year-old David. The red brick building's recent dedication increased the congregation size to seventy-five percent capacity that summer.

David clasped his hands as he stood at the altar with Pastor McSwan. Trying to contain the spiritual joy churning in the pit of his belly, the young man shifted his weight and bit into his lower lip.

The minister opened his Bible. "David Sower, as a newly appointed deacon for our church, allow me to exhort you with 1 Timothy 4:12-16." The middle-aged minister laid his right hand on David's left shoulder. "'Let no man despise thy youth; but be thou an example of the believers, in word, in conversation, in charity, in spirit, in faith, in purity. Till I come, give attendance to reading, to exhortation, to doctrine. Neglect not the gift that is in thee, which was given thee by prophecy, with the laying on of the hands of the presbytery. Meditate upon these things; give thyself wholly to them; that thy profiting may appear to all. Take heed unto thyself, and unto the doctrine; continue in them:

for in doing this thou shalt both save thyself, and them that hear thee.'"

Pastor McSwan released his shoulder and faced the congregation. "And now, church family, let us receive our new deacon, David Sower. He has been humble and diligent in serving the Lord the past three years and is a faithful disciple in ministry." Applause reverberated and foots stomped on the shiny wood floors.

Overflowing joy swelled David's heart and soul. His eyes moistened, and his smile beamed as he turned to the cheering parishioners, searching for his parents and Naomi. There they were, faces glowing, proud of his accomplishments in the Lord. If only Sam and Sarah were here to witness this moment in his life.

God used his families' past six months of self-absorbed circumstances to guide him in the direction in which he now stood. His brother was gone, scratching at any employment he could find on the railroad. His oldest sister was now living in Mariposa with her husband and four-month-old daughter. Naomi busied herself on the farm and at work at the Mercantile, and his overwhelmed parents purchased another 1,000 acres of land and hired almost two dozen Chinese farmhands.

As they occupied themselves, he spent more time at the church, immersing himself in Bible lessons and serving where needed. The pastor even situated a desk for him outside of his office in the one-hundred-seat parish. David enjoyed greeting visitors and tending to the pastor's schedule.

From the time of Joshua's death, the heart-broken minister discontinued the camp meetings. He told David he did not want to risk his family's lives again and put them through the remembrance of that fateful night. So he concentrated on local church services, and the congregation grew. He poured himself into teaching the young deacon the Scriptures and had him fill the pulpit on occasion. Upon his sixteenth birthday and completion of grade school, the pastor planned for him to preach on a regular rotation. However, David had plans of his own. He wanted to attend seminary and bring the gospel to the many Chinese laborers who found refuge in California, starting with the farmworkers at his parents' ranch.

ONE AFTERNOON IN LATE AUGUST, a courier approached David at his desk. "I have an urgent message for Pastor McSwan."

"Yes, I'll give it to him." David took the envelope and knocked on the pastor's office door.

"Come in."

"Pastor, a telegraph from the San Francisco Methodist Church just arrived and needs your immediate attention." David handed it to the minister, who opened and read its contents.

"Oh, my. It seems this congregation is housing a Chinese family who had the misfortune of being stranded in California after the husband's brother and employer was killed on his trading ship during a fire last weekend. They are hoping we can help them locate a relative who lives in Snelling's Chinese camp."

Pastor McSwan stood and paced behind his desk, staring down at the floor. "The church is concerned with sending them to the camp because of their sixteen-year-old daughter. They fear she may be taken by the Tong society and forced into prostitution. This family worked as domestic servants aboard his brother's trading ship and cannot afford to return to China, nor do they want to because of the political upheavals taking place. They desire to seek refuge in our church until they can locate their relative."

"Where would we house them in our small building? Will the offerings be able to fund a stipend for domestic help?"

"No, no." The pastor continued to pace with his hands clutched behind him. "The tithes are enough to support my family and the mortgage payment for this property." He rubbed his chin. "I must bring their plight before the church members to see if anyone can use their services and also house them."

Visions filled David's mind of the domestic help needed at the ranch. His parents employed the majority of Chinese laborers in Snelling, and they wanted assistance with cooking meals for the farmhands and household. The small two-bedroom cabin, which his family resided in when they first purchased the property, would be perfect for employees' quarters.

"Before you do that, Pastor, let me inform my parents about their situation. I do believe we need to hire domestic help."

"Is that so, David? I know your father's wheat business is doing well. Your mother told me the other day she is stretched to her limits with all the added work."

"Yes, sir. They are growin' gray before their time. Allow me to suggest this matter to them."

"Indeed, son. Here." The minister handed David the telegram. "Take this letter with you and show it to your parents. Encourage them to pray about it and let me know their decision at their earliest convenience."

DAVID'S FATHER AND MOTHER RECEIVED THE SUGGESTION WELL, and they employed the Suen family two weeks later. His heart grew fond of the Chinese farmhands and domestic help, and his desire to share the gospel with them also increased. Speaking to the farmworkers posed a challenge for him because many of them spoke little English, and they always huddled together during their well-deserved lunch hour. He did not have the heart to disrupt them after laboring under the hot sun.

An opportunity arose with the domestic help—the father, Huang-Fu, the mother, Liang, and the daughter, Jia Li. After the first evening supper prepared by the Chinese family, David remained in the dining room, hoping to welcome the new employees and become more acquainted.

"You all speak good English." David sipped on tea with them at the table after their kitchen duties were done.

"Ah, yes. We learn while training in Nanking. Serve many Asian aristocrats and foreign guests in Shanghai. Later, my brother hire us to cook for him and crew on international trading ship. We also help translate. Poor Ah-Ling. He was rich merchant, but he die on ship while we were at market ordering supplies. Me and Liang believe anti-Chinese thugs responsible. They steal cargo and burn ship."

David realized many of the farmworkers they hired were Chinese peasants from Sze Yap in southern China. The Suens emigrated from a northern province. Listening to Huang-Fu's adventures to America intrigued him.

A few evenings later, the familiar exchange of Mandarin whispered between the workers trickled into David's ears while he and his family closed their eyes to pray for the meal. He peeked at them and noticed the inquisitive expressions upon their faces. They appeared confused, staring at each other, then at the food, then at his family, who sat quietly with eyelids shut. *Oh, perhaps they think we are unhappy with the food because we haven't touched it. This is the fourth supper they've prepared for us, and every time they've been whisperin' while we're prayin'.*

"Amen." His father ended the prayer, and they passed the platters between themselves and devoured the delectable Asian cuisine. The workers' muddled whispers resumed as they fidgeted around the room, waiting for a command. As forks are to chopsticks, the Western way of dining was something the Chinese family was not accustomed to.

Again, after supper, David lingered while his parents and sister migrated to the living room to engage in other activities before retiring for the night. "That was a lovely meal y'all prepared tonight," he remarked, hoping to stir up dialogue as they began to put away the dishes.

"I hope you like our Asian cooking, Mr. David," Huang-Fu replied.

"Oh, yes, indeed. It does my family no good to be in the food industry unless we appreciate foods of all cultures. California is a diverse state, a meltin' pot of many nationalities. In fact, God created the entire world and everythin' that is in it for good. So, why not enjoy the diversity of menus from different nations? However, the Bible tells us man cannot live by bread alone, but by every word which proceeds from the mouth of God."

A most inquisitive expression appeared upon Huang-Fu's face as his brows strained and head cocked. "Do you desire me to purchase this Word of God and cook it for your dinner? How do I do this? Will you show me? I can make anything you like."

After realizing the eager chef did not understand the allegorical spiritual principle, David held his abdomen and chortled. "Oh, ha-ha! Forgive me, Huang-Fu. Let me explain. The Word of God is referrin' to the Bible. God's book contains His words of wisdom to feed us spiritually and teach us how to live a sinless life. Not only are we to nourish our fleshly bodies with earthly food, but He tells us we must maintain our spirit with spiritual sustenance too. The way we do this is by readin', learnin', and obeyin' God's teachin's. The Bible refers to His Holy Word as the Bread of Life.

"So, ya see, Huang-Fu, eatin' and readin' the Bible every day is what we need to live a healthy physical and spiritual life," David explained with passion.

"Ah, now I understand. Methodist missionary in Nanking give me Bible, but I was only confused. He tell me Christianity similar to Confucianism, and God aim for moral righteousness. He also says Confucius different because he not offer salvation from sin as God through only son. Jesus take our punishment and die for bad things we do." He sat down next to David as his wife and daughter washed the dishes. "You help me to learn?"

"Why, gladly, Huang-Fu. Together we can read a little every evenin' after supper if you desire."

"Ah, yes. Also, you teach family?"

"Of course." The Holy Spirit residing in the young man's heart filled him with joy. "I will show you how you can speak to God, too."

"Talk to God?"

"Yes, through prayer. For example, every time my family sits down for supper, we pray first and thank Him for His provisions. Then we ask Him to bless the food and the hands which prepared it. We close our eyes, and we focus on Him alone, as father prays for all of us."

"Ah, I understand now." Huang-Fu glanced about the table as if imagining the family sitting there and praying.

"Each of us can communicate with the Lord anytime and anywhere because He is everywhere at every moment in time."

"This is most fascinating, Mr. David. When we start?"

"How about tomorrow evenin' after supper, here at the kitchen table?"

"Okay, looking forward to learning from you. I will bring wife and daughter too."

From that day onward, after David's explanation, the Suen family stood still and bowed their heads as the Sowers prayed before each meal. They met after every supper during the weekdays to read a chapter as David taught its meaning. Their knowledge grew along with their faith in God.

One evening, after a month of studying the Bible, David invited them to church. In time, they shared the Gospels with one of the farmhands, and he too began to attend. On occasion, they attended together, sitting in the back row, being careful not to mingle with the white parishioners.

It grieved the new deacon as he examined the white members struggling with their Christian beliefs to love others as themselves. The only welcome the Chinese families received from their neighbors were disgruntled stares, upturned noses, and avoidance as the white congregation made every effort not to go near them. After most of the members had dispersed, Pastor McSwan and David spent time with the Asian members, answering their questions. Their humble and tranquil nature never made mention of the distress they were experiencing from the anti-Chinese sentiment around them. The minister and the young deacon often found themselves praying for the congregation and reminding them of Colossians 3:11, *Where there is neither Greek nor Jew, circumcision nor uncircumcision, Barbarian, Scythian, bond nor free: but Christ is all, and in all.*

32

Golden Harvest

1872

David gazed out the church office window after reviewing his sermon notes. The leaves from the oak trees along Green Street were whisked about by the morning breeze like flaky winter snow that autumn morning. He was sixteen and had finished grade school a few months back. As promised, Pastor McSwan included him in a regular rotation to preach once a month. *Lord, use me this mornin' as Your vessel. Fill me with Your Holy Spirit and give me wisdom and boldness to deliver Your message to Your people. Open their eyes so they may receive Your light. I ask this in the name of Jesus, Your Son, and my Savior. Amen.*

A gentle tapping on the door broke the solitude. "Deacon, it's time."

"All right. I'll be right there." He gathered his notes, walked to the altar, and poised himself on the pulpit behind a simple oak podium. After opening in prayer, he led the people with the hymns "I Stood Outside the Gates," "I Will Follow Thee," and "Jesus-Savior-Pilot Me."

With the congregation seated, the young deacon began his sermon in the book of James verse 1:2-6. "My brethren, count it all joy when ye fall into diverse temptations; knowing this, that the trying of your faith worketh patience. But let patience have her perfect work, that ye may be perfect and entire, wanting nothing. If any of you lack wisdom, let him ask of God, that giveth to all men liberally, and upbraideth not; and it shall be given him. But let him ask in faith, nothing wavering. For he that wavereth is like a wave of the sea driven with the wind and tossed." David peered at the members.

"For years now, I watched as my parents struggled through so many trials and tribulations in their lives. My father had been wounded during the Civil War, which nearly took his life, and our farm in Kentucky was ravaged by this terrible battle. Shortly after was the six-month arduous move to California, followed by startin' a new life of farmin' in Snelling. Also, they had troubles with the four of us siblings growin' up. Most difficult of all was the loss of the ones dearest to them, either by death or by unforeseen circumstances. The last time their eldest son made contact was durin' his last visit two years ago on Christmas 1870. The oldest daughter, livin' in Mariposa, is tryin' to keep her marriage alive and raise three small children while her husband is off herdin' cattle for months on end. Their second daughter is doin' her best to assist them in the struggles of their growin' wheat business. Then there is me. Left to fend for myself most of the time, I turned to the Lord for His guidance and friendship."

He gazed down at his parents sitting in the front row. "These moments of travail and heartache can test and shake any man or woman's faith. I continue to observe them and how they patiently persevere through these situations, never losin' their trust in God to be victorious in their life and the lives of their children."

A warm and assuring smile transpired from deep within his soul. "Their belief in an almighty and all-knowin' God is givin' them the strength, patience, hope, and peace needed to endure these moments. The Lord always provided a lesson for one of us to learn through these trials and tribulations. My parents never fear durin' these times, but rather exercise self-control knowin' He uses all things for good to those who love Him." David explained boldly with passion in his voice throughout his sermon.

"This is the attitude and perspective which you, who are in Christ Jesus, should practice and hope for. God shapes you and makes you more like His Son through the difficulties you encounter in your life.

Through all their difficult circumstances, He may be teachin' you about love, patience, joy and peace, kindness, gentleness, goodness, faithfulness, and self-control. These lessons test your faith to see if you truly believe the promises in His Word through your obedience to abide by His commands. As you experience His trustworthiness to fulfill His spiritual principles, your understandin' grows deeper, and your belief becomes stronger, and the trials become much easier to bear. In place of anxiety is joy and peace, with the knowledge that the testin' has a purpose and plan for sanctification in your life. So, be patient when encounterin' difficulties, havin' peace in knowin' God will be faithful to His promises. Amen!" The deacon concluded the sermon.

Mary shuffled through her reticule and pulled out a handkerchief, wiping the tears on her cheek. His father wrapped his arms around her shoulders, loosened the cravat around his neck, and returned a warm smile and nod to David.

EARLY ONE SATURDAY MORNING after the farmhands harvested the golden wheat, Jonathan and Mary leaned back in their wingback chairs in his office. The crops grew hardy and prosperous. They sipped on their hot coffee as they stared at the tintypes of their children on the fireplace mantel. Tears surfaced as they reminisced and discussed the good and difficult times their family encountered within the last ten years.

At that moment, Jonathan remembered a particular event and its connection to their lives. "Honey, do you recall the first church service we attended with Pastor McSwan?"

"Hmm ... let me think." Mary tilted her head back against the chair. "Yes, I do, dear. We met in the Snelling courthouse."

"Do ya remember what he preached about?" Jonathan asked, aiming to make a point.

"Sort of." She furrowed her brows, set her cup on the end table, and smoothed the pleats of her skirt as she straightened herself in the chair. "I think he spoke about the parable of the sower."

"You're correct. Do you remember the message?" Jonathan

continued to probe her mind.

"I believe he used the analogy of the sower who planted seeds in different types of ground. The seeds, which fell by the wayside, had been eatin' up by birds. Seed, which was sown on stony places, grew fast but also died quickly because of the sun's scorchin' and not havin' enough soil to root themselves. Some of the grain landed amongst thorns and had been choked out. However, some were cultivated on good earth and yielded a crop of one hundred fold, some sixty, and some thirty," Mary said. "Why do you ask, darlin'?"

"Well, I realized that the Lord was usin' this parable to prepare us for what we would be experiencin' the followin' seven years of our lives with our children at that time." Jonathan beamed.

"You see, the Word of God is the seed that is shared among all the different people, or the ground referred to in the passage. The seed, or the Word, had fallen in Samuel's wayward condition, but the cares of the world, gold prospectin', took hold of him and pulled him away from the Lord."

Intrigued by Jonathan's analogy, Mary sat at the edge of her chair.

"Then, the Word fell in Sarah's stony heart. I believe she loved the Lord for the wrong reasons. She really was in love with Joshua, the pastor's son. So, she had no depth or rich enough soil in her heart to grow in God's principals. When the trial of Joshua's death came upon her, she did not have root or comfort in His teachin's, so she strayed away in her belief in the Lord."

Jonathan repositioned himself forward in his seat, sensing distress. "Simultaneously, the Word had landed in Naomi's naïve understanding, but she had been choked out by the thorns, the Edgar children, and their bad behavior. So she never gained any depth in her faith. I thank God He gave us the wisdom to provide the correct discipline, and now she is back on the right track." Jonathan took a deep sigh of relief.

"However, God's word had been cultivated in David's heart, full of rich love for the Lord who became his best friend during his lonesome circumstances. Now he has a wonderful relationship with Jesus and is developin' into an outstandin' preacher bein' used by the Almighty." The contented father relaxed in his chair, his face aglow.

"You see, my dear, God wanted to show us what the golden harvest would be in our lives. We are the ones who cast the seeds ... the Sowers!" He chuckled at his pun. "I'm gonna continue to trust Him for the complete salvation of our children because He still has many parables to apply to our lifetime." He laughed with confidence in his heart.

This wisdom brought the husband and wife much comfort, peace, and hope for their family, knowing that God's Word does not return void. They planted the seed in their children's hearts, and someone else would have to water it. Lifting their family up in prayer, they continued to look to God for His guidance and His care. They had comfort and faith that God had a plan for each of their children in His golden harvest.

About the Author

ROSANNA CEREZO SHARPS enjoys sharing God's Word to better understand and develop our relationship with the Heavenly Father, and to provide directives for life's challenges through its application. By vicariously experiencing another person's difficulties as they strive to maintain their course on the "narrow path"† to God, one can summarize his or her spiritual journey. Realizing "there is nothing new under the sun"*, she hopes to convey a picture of this process through the character's lives in her historical fiction trilogy *Golden Harvest*. The author prayerfully crafted the story, which allegorically applies to the timeless parables and other scriptural passages found in the Bible to help enlighten the pathway for God's people.

Rosanna studied Psychology at Southwestern College and theology at Calvary Chapel Bible College. She taught Bible studies for women, youth, and grade school children at several Calvary Chapel churches, including the church her husband pastored in Rio Vista, California. They have a musically gifted son whom she homeschooled. Her passion is to study God's Word and pray, to love her family, writing, fellowship with other Believers, singing worship songs, reenacting historical periods, travel and enjoying God's creation, and being creative through crafts such as crocheting, knitting, and painting. Currently, she and her husband are sole proprietors of a book and variety store in the historic town, Columbia, California, where all her attributes can be utilized by God to creatively plant the seed of His gospel to peoples around the globe.

† Matthew 7:13-14
* Ecclesiastes 1:9

The Parable of the Sower

Matthew 13:1-23 (KJV)

[1] The same day went Jesus out of the house, and sat by the sea side.

[2] And great multitudes were gathered together unto him, so that he went into a ship, and sat; and the whole multitude stood on the shore.

[3] And he spake many things unto them in parables, saying, Behold, a sower went forth to sow;

[4] And when he sowed, some seeds fell by the way side, and the fowls came and devoured them up:

[5] Some fell upon stony places, where they had not much earth: and forthwith they sprung up, because they had no deepness of earth:

[6] And when the sun was up, they were scorched; and because they had no root, they withered away.

[7] And some fell among thorns; and the thorns sprung up, and choked them:

[8] But other fell into good ground, and brought forth fruit, some an hundredfold, some sixtyfold, some thirtyfold.

[9] Who hath ears to hear, let him hear.

[10] And the disciples came, and said unto him, Why speakest thou unto them in parables?

[11] He answered and said unto them, Because it is given unto you to know the mysteries of the kingdom of heaven, but to them it is not given.

[12] For whosoever hath, to him shall be given, and he shall have more abundance: but whosoever hath not, from him shall be taken away even that he hath.

[13] Therefore speak I to them in parables: because they seeing see not; and hearing they hear not, neither do they understand.

[14] And in them is fulfilled the prophecy of Esaias, which saith, By hearing ye shall hear, and shall not understand; and seeing ye shall see, and shall not perceive:

[15] For this people's heart is waxed gross, and their ears are dull of hearing, and their eyes they have closed; lest at any time they should see with their eyes and hear with their ears, and should understand with their heart, and should be converted, and I should heal them.

¹⁶ But blessed are your eyes, for they see: and your ears, for they hear.

¹⁷ For verily I say unto you, That many prophets and righteous men have desired to see those things which ye see, and have not seen them; and to hear those things which ye hear, and have not heard them.

¹⁸ Hear ye therefore the parable of the sower.

¹⁹ When any one heareth the word of the kingdom, and understandeth it not, then cometh the wicked one, and catcheth away that which was sown in his heart. This is he which received seed by the way side.

²⁰ But he that received the seed into stony places, the same is he that heareth the word, and anon with joy receiveth it;

²¹ Yet hath he not root in himself, but dureth for a while: for when tribulation or persecution ariseth because of the word, by and by he is offended.

²² He also that received seed among the thorns is he that heareth the word; and the care of this world, and the deceitfulness of riches, choke the word, and he becometh unfruitful.

²³ But he that received seed into the good ground is he that heareth the word, and understandeth it; which also beareth fruit, and bringeth forth, some an hundredfold, some sixty, some thirty.

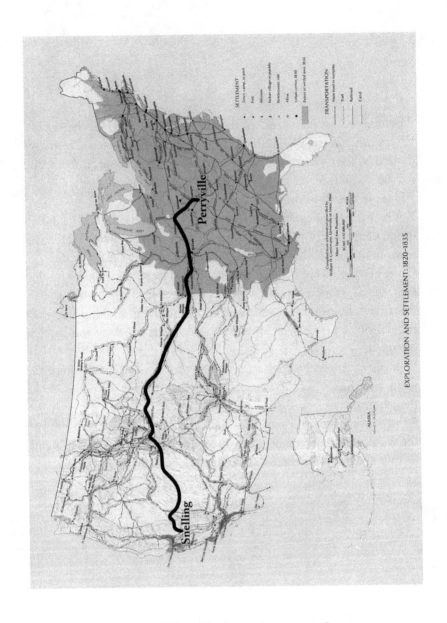

The Sower's wagon train route from
Perryville, Kentucky to Snelling, California.

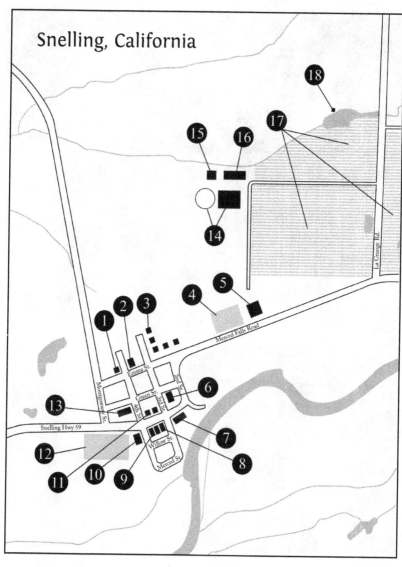

Snelling, California

1. McSwan Home *
2. Church
3. Edgar House *
4. Cemetery
5. Snelling School
6. County Courthouse
7. Jacobi's Store **
8. Snelling Saloon
9. Meat Market
10. Livery Stable
11. Dr. Cassidy's Clinic *
12. Chinese Camp
13. The Barn
14. Sower Barn *
15. Sower Cabin *
16. Sower Farmhouse *
17. Sower Wheat Field *
18. Sower Tree Fort *

*Fictitious location   **Fictitious name*

ABOVE: Snelling Courthouse, built in 1857.

OPPOSITE TOP: The Jacob's Store, built in 1858.
OPPOSITE BOTTOM: Methodist Church, built in 1871.

IOOF Dance Hall (a.k.a. The Barn).